D0497851

Salvage

Also by Robert Edric

WINTER GARDEN

A NEW ICE AGE

A LUNAR ECLIPSE

IN THE DAYS OF THE AMERICAN MUSEUM

THE BROKEN LANDS

HALLOWED GROUND

THE EARTH MADE OF GLASS

ELYSIUM

IN DESOLATE HEAVEN

THE SWORD CABINET

THE BOOK OF THE HEATHEN

PEACETIME

GATHERING THE WATER

THE KINGDOM OF ASHES

IN ZODIAC LIGHT

CRADLE SONG

SIREN SONG

SWAN SONG

Salvage

ROBERT EDRIC

Doubleday

LONDON • TORONTO • SYDNEY • AUCKLAND • JOHANNESBURG

TRANSWORLD PUBLISHERS
61–63 Uxbridge Road, London W5 5SA
A Random House Group Company
www.rbooks.co.uk

First published in Great Britain
in 2010 by Doubleday
an imprint of Transworld Publishers

A CIP catalogue record for this book
is available from the British Library.

ISBN 9780385617628

Addresses for Random House Group Ltd companies outside the UK
can be found at: www.randomhouse.co.uk
The Random House Group Ltd Reg. No. 954009

The Random House Group Ltd supports The Forest Stewardship Council
(FSC), the leading international forest-certification organization.
All our titles that are printed on Greenpeace-approved FSC-certified
paper carry the FSC logo. Our paper procurement policy can be
found at www.rbooks.co.uk/environment

Typeset in 11/15pt Caslon by
Kestrel Data, Exeter, Devon.
Printed in the UK by
CPI Mackays, Chatham, ME5 8TD.

2 4 6 8 10 9 7 5 3 1

For Kate Samano

What the wind blows away
The wind blows back again.

Cloud on Black Combe, Norman Nicholson

Part I

1

It was mid afternoon, and already the light was fading. Quinn traced the line of the narrow road as it rose ahead of him, following an excavated and straightened contour along the hillside. As he drove, he looked to the west, to where the last of the winter sun had already dropped beneath the cloud, where it shone in solid-looking columns, and where smaller, drifting clouds cast late shadows over the empty land below like the outlines of slow-moving fish beneath the opaque surface of a lake. Perhaps there *was* water in the direction he was looking – a new incursion of the sea perhaps; or an extended estuary not yet plotted on the Land Agency maps or fed into his own temperamental and outdated navigator.

He was distracted from these thoughts by the warning of a bend directly ahead of him and he slowed down. He had hoped for a more precise idea of his location, but the sign did nothing more than inform him of the approaching curve in the steep road. He slowed further and then pulled to the side of the carriageway.

Two days earlier, upon collecting the car, he had been told by the mechanic who had transferred the vehicle's codes and then added fuel credits to Quinn's account that the navigation system was faulty. 'Not working?' Quinn had asked him. The mechanic had glanced at the handset he held. 'Faulty. That's all it says,' he'd said, unconcerned, adding, 'If it had been deleted or taken out for re-programming, then it would say that.' He had then gone to the boot and taken out the ring-bound road atlas, which he'd thrown on to the seat beside Quinn. 'Most of the roads are in that,' he'd said, grinning at the old joke. 'And some of the on-board indicators don't work. Doesn't mean those functions aren't available, just that the indicators are faulty. Electronics. Not my department.' He'd held out his handset for Quinn to enter his own codes. Quinn had known better than to insist on a properly serviced vehicle; he'd already been waiting an hour for the car he was being given.

Now, sitting beside the road in what seemed to him to be the middle of nowhere, he studied the map using a torch – roads and other networks laid out in a colourful and simplified format like a giant wiring system.

A rising wind buffeted the car. It had rained earlier as he'd followed the motorway north, after which the sun had returned and the road was dry again.

The small circle of yellow light showed him where he was, or at least where he thought he was.

He had anticipated following the motorway closer to his destination, but as he'd continued north it had narrowed from eight lanes to four, and then, following a diversion around a closure, to only two lanes. As usual, the priority lane remained intact, meaning that all other traffic was restricted to single-file. In parts, the road was denied him by bollards; elsewhere by railings driven crudely into its surface. Warning signs flashed above him at his approach: some told him of further diversions and delays ahead; others tried to compensate for these uncertainties by predicting how long his journey to the various upcoming junctions might now last. But these, he knew from long experience, were equally inaccurate and frustrating, all too often replaced with yet further warnings of additional delays.

There had been little other traffic on his day-long journey: congestion before the late dawn as he'd moved away from the capital, but then a rapid decrease in traffic as the distances between the recently reconfigured exits and connector roads had lengthened. He'd been caught in queues in the Midlands and then again as he'd come to the Mid North, but after that the roads had almost emptied.

He'd been stopped an hour earlier by a workman who had signalled him off the road and into a parking bay. Sixty or seventy other motorists were already gathered there. A second man then directed him to a specific point in the otherwise vast and empty space, but could not tell him *why* he'd been stopped, saying simply and authoritatively that he and his co-workers had been instructed to clear the road ahead for the following hour. If Quinn wanted to find out what was happening, there was – as ever – a number to call, and the man recited this before Quinn could answer him.

Another of the drivers told Quinn that these things happened all the time in that part of the world. 'Military convoys,' he said. 'They like the road to themselves. You'd be going nowhere fast if you got stuck behind one.' It was forbidden to drive within 200 metres of the convoys – outriders saw to that; and to drive among the slow-moving vehicles, even by accident, was a considerably more serious offence. 'Got caught behind one three miles long last week,' the man said almost proudly.

The delay had lasted ninety minutes, during which the day had started to die. Quinn had asked others how far he was from his destination; some had little idea; some were prepared to guess; and yet others said they knew exactly where it was, but their estimates concerning the length of his remaining journey then varied from one to three hours.

He showed them the place in his atlas. Some left him to check their own navigation systems, returning with strips of map outlining his route and its timings in the smallest detail. But these too, Quinn knew, were misleading reassurances, straightening the road, offering no scale, and removing all true sense of distance and direction, and destroying completely any idea of the nature of the landscape through which the roads ahead passed. One man even suggested to Quinn that he might want to break his journey and resume the following morning. 'In the light,' he had said. The sun was falling rapidly and most of the route ahead would not be illuminated. It was as Quinn considered the wisdom of this that an announcement was made telling them they were all free to continue their journeys. They were exhorted to drive safely and then warned of the new speed limits ahead.

That had been two hours ago, and now Quinn sat by the side of the narrow, unlit road, uncertain of his way ahead, and again watching the rain as it blew against the windscreen in sudden squalls.

His destination was clearly marked on the map. Roads led in

and out of it from all directions – three major routes and twice that number of lesser connections. The motorway, though still marked, had effectively ended two pages previously, and Quinn could not now accurately locate himself on the intervening pages. He told himself he had a good idea of where he was, but that was all – an idea, a notion; wishful thinking, perhaps – something he could neither be certain of nor confirm against the other marked places. It was a rare and unsettling experience for him to be lost like this.

By now the light in the west had almost gone, reduced to a vivid orange glow along the horizon, a dividing line, soon also to be lost to him, between the land below and the sky above. There was no lake, no estuary – simply an undifferentiated expanse of terrain much the same as that which surrounded him now on the rising hillside.

In the far distance – a distance that appeared to Quinn to be beyond the divide of the briefly lit horizon – there were a few widely scattered and intermittent lights: towns perhaps; and perhaps if he looked closely enough, the lighted courses of other roads. But nothing of these clusters or their connections seemed permanent to him, flickering and dying, brightening and then fading as the greater light above them also failed.

Quinn switched off the engine and waited for several minutes in the ensuing silence. He had blankets – from long experience of countless other journeys to these distant places – and he had food and drink. He checked the car's power levels and then searched on the radio for a local news station. The autoscan ran from one end of the waveband to the other. Nothing. A few half-heard voices, whispers in the dark, the same few repeated phrases from unfixed transmitters. He took out a torch.

He switched from news to music and the screen told him

that none of the usual sound-sleeves were currently available to him. Another technical error. Meaning that the department responsible for re-licensing the sleeves had either omitted to do this or was saving money by cancelling something most employees might now provide at their own expense. Quinn pushed his card into the slot and it was immediately returned to him. His choice – though not yet made – was unavailable. No charge had been debited.

He slid his seat back and lowered the headrest. An indicator warned him that the doors were not yet locked nor the alarm set. He pressed the single button which provided these functions, cancelled the alarm and then cast what few onboard lights remained into darkness.

It was not yet five in the afternoon, but already it felt to Quinn like the middle of the night. The middle of the night in the middle of nowhere, and he was lost in both. He pointed his torch outside, watching through his own vague yellow reflection as its beam ran back and forth over the wild grass. There was now no definition whatsoever to the land around him – a falling slope below and a rising slope above; a road which curved behind him into the darkness and the day that had just passed; and the same road somewhere ahead of him, another curve, and another lost perspective and unguessable miles.

He watched the swaying grass for a moment and then lowered the torch. Twisting in his seat, he directed the light into the rear of the car, to the cases of files stacked there, facing him like a row of mute children. A dozen rolled charts lay where they had fallen from the seat to the floor.

After a while the rain eased, and only the soughing of the wind remained. In places above him, again towards the west, where all light had finally been extinguished, there were clearing patches of night sky and the stars in their scatter of constellations were already showing through. He was able to identify those outlines he knew – had known since he was a boy – and in the absence of any other identifiable features closer to him, he felt strangely reassured by this.

2

He was woken by a sudden loud banging close to his face. He had slumped in his seat and lay with his arm folded awkwardly beneath him, his shoulder hard against the door. The banging continued and he pushed himself upright. Two faces were pressed to the window, their foreheads and noses flattened by the glass. A film of condensation made them hazy. Quinn looked ahead of him and saw others standing in front of the car. He held up his hand to the men at the glass and they withdrew. He switched on the pre-ignition and lowered the window. The two men took several further paces back at this. The cold morning air stung Quinn's eyes.

He opened the door and eased out his legs, rubbing the cramp from his thighs and calves.

'We just arrived,' one of the men told him, as though Quinn

might understand this, as though he might even form some part of their reason for being there.

'I was lost,' he said. He looked around him and noticed others on the hillside above.

The two men exchanged a glance. They wore fluorescent jackets and were evidently there to undertake some kind of work.

'Then you probably still are,' one of them said. He gestured for the men on the road to join those on the higher slope.

'Lost where?' the second man asked Quinn.

Again, Quinn searched around him. He told them his destination, and upon hearing this, the two men relaxed and then laughed.

'Not as lost as you think,' the first said. 'Round that next bend and you're as high as the road goes. You can see the place beneath you. If you'd kept going, you'd have been there in two minutes.'

Quinn looked in the direction the man indicated, but saw nothing, only the same barren hillside and its incised road.

'You can't see it from *here*,' the man said. He seemed offended now, as though Quinn didn't believe him.

'He's right,' the other said. 'Two minutes.'

Quinn looked again to where he imagined he'd seen the lights of other towns and roads the previous evening, but there was nothing, only a vast expanse of near-level land surrounded by other hills, and the equally vague lines of other roads and paths.

'What's over there?' he asked the men.

Both of them looked.

'Not much.'

'What you can see.'

'I thought perhaps the town was in that direction,' Quinn said.

'Already told you – round the next bend.' The man looked past Quinn into the car, nudging his companion upon seeing the cases and charts in the rear.

'I thought I saw lights,' Quinn said, unaware of the men's new interest.

'Once, perhaps,' one of them told him. 'One or two isolated places at the bottom of the hill. They went fast enough.'

'And beyond?'

'The flooding, mostly. Or just enough of it to make life that little bit too uncomfortable to stay. Fifty years ago, you'd have seen nothing *but* lights.'

Up on the slope, others left the small group and came forward. Several of the men nodded at Quinn but no one else spoke to him. In addition to their jackets, most of these men wore chest-high waders; some of them wore helmets with Perspex visors. A stack of shovels and pick-axes lay at the roadside.

A burst of static interrupted Quinn's thoughts and one of the men beside him fished inside his jacket for the radio attached there. He silenced the static and shouted into the mouthpiece. Then he pushed the receiver to his ear, screwing up his face at what he was clearly having difficulty hearing, ducking his head out of the wind and pressing a palm to his other ear. After a minute of this he switched the radio off and refastened his jacket. The others watched him without speaking, waiting for whatever he might be about to reveal to them.

But the man said nothing.

'What?' his companion asked him eventually.

'Couldn't hear a' – and here he omitted a profanity solely in deference to Quinn – 'word. Probably just someone checking that we've arrived and that we've started work. They probably want us to—' He stopped abruptly and looked pointedly at Quinn. 'Is that why *you*'re here?' He nodded at the cases. 'Are you Ministry? Come up to join the others?'

Uncertain of precisely what he was being asked, Quinn hesitated.

'Look,' the man said, and held out his watch to him, a mixed note of anger and pleading in his voice. 'Nine. They wanted us to start at eight, but we couldn't pick up any of our stuff at the depot until then. How are we expected to start work at eight if we can't get anything out until then? *Is* that why you're here?'

'What are you supposed to be doing?' Quinn asked him. It was the safest response he could think of.

'Don't you know?'

'I think you're mistaking me for someone else,' Quinn said.

One of the men cupped a hand to his mouth and whispered to the other. Both smiled at whatever was being said.

'You're not Land?' the whisperer said.

'"Land"?'

'Land Ministry.'

Quinn shook his head.

'Your Toxic people are here working on some of the landfills. Christ knows why. Trying to make out it's all routine. It's nearly seventy years since some of them were last dug and filled. Seventy years. And now they come all this way to check if there's anything still there?'

'I'm not Land,' Quinn said. 'Is that what you're doing?'

The question surprised and further amused the men.

'He wants to know if we're digging up the landfills,' one of them called to those still waiting on the hillside, causing more laughter.

'We'd be kitted out from head to foot if we were working on the toxic stuff,' the other man told Quinn. 'Got men and women on those sites walking round like spacemen – sealed helmets, the lot, oxygen or whatever pumped into their suits. Besides, they wouldn't let us within a mile of the place. Restricted Access, three-sixty, left, right and centre.' He paused. 'So what *are* you here for?'

This time Quinn tried to avoid the question by asking the man with the radio if there was a strong signal on the hillside.

'Hardly any at all,' the man said. 'Not so bad down in the town, but nothing up here. Up here we mostly just go through the motions so that the calls get logged.' He tapped the hidden radio. 'Mostly we're just left to get on with things. They tell us what to do and, by and large, we do it. Yesterday they called us back early because of the rain – or at least that's what I thought they were doing.' He grinned at the men around him. 'Turns out they just wanted to know how we were getting on. Easy enough mistake to make on a cold, wet, miserable hillside at this time of year when you're up to your knees in muck and water.' He waited until Quinn understood what he was saying.

'And you walk to and from the town?' Quinn asked him.

'We walk. You think they'd waste fuel on this kind of work? Come far?'

Again the question caught Quinn unawares.

'I was travelling all day yesterday,' he said.

'"Travelling"?'

'Driving.'

'Pity, then, that you didn't get round the next bend.' He

turned back to his companion. 'What kind of *traveller* stops short of the last bend in the road?'

'It was dark,' Quinn said. But in their eyes this only weakened his argument. *And raining*, he wanted to add. *And windy. And I'd come three hundred miles to a place I'd hardly ever heard of before, let alone visited.*

On the hillside, the other workers started to make their way further up the sodden slope, forming a line as they went.

'What are—' Quinn started to say.

'Clearing out the drainage,' the man with the radio said. 'Don't ask. Drainage, here. What channels? You wouldn't even know they were there if they weren't marked on their precious charts.' He tapped another of his pockets.

'May I see?' Quinn asked him.

'I thought you said you weren't anything to do with it.'

'I'm not.'

After a minute, the man took a piece of folded paper from his pocket, opened it out and held it to the roof of Quinn's car. He ran a finger across it, tapping various locations.

'That's where you're going,' he said. 'And this is the road. We're here.'

It was a mostly plain sheet, not even marked with contours, only a succession of dotted lines formed into a pattern running from the top right to the bottom left.

'It doesn't show much,' Quinn said.

'How much do you need? That's the town, that's the road, this is the hill. It's more than *you* knew before you looked at it.'

Quinn conceded this. 'And the dotted lines are the drains?'

'So-called.'

'Can you find them? On the ground, I mean.'

'Some. The rest we guess at and dig out anyway.'

'To what end?'

'To get the water running to where it's supposed to run.'

'I.D.E.,' the other man said mock-seriously. 'Increased Demand Elsewhere. I.D.E. Stamped all over the permits and work-sheets. Same old lie. When did *you* last drink something clean and cold out of a tap?'

And because Quinn hesitated at this, the other man said, 'See?' and then 'Right,' and then motioned to his companion that they should join the others walking up the hillside. Some of these men had already spread out and had started digging in the knee-high grass.

'Are they working in the right place?'

The man with the chart took it from the car roof and folded it back into a small square. 'It's dotted lines on a blank sheet,' he said. 'Course they're digging in the right place.' He turned to Quinn and gave an exaggerated wink. 'You know what I'm saying, right?'

'I imagine so,' Quinn told him.

'No – I said you *know* what I'm saying, *right*?'

Quinn was surprised by the sudden hostility in the man's voice.

'I understand you perfectly.'

'See?' the man said immediately to the other. 'If *he* says we're digging in the right place, then we're digging in the right place.'

Quinn understood then that they still believed he was in some way connected to their work on the hillside, and that little of his story about being lost there had been accepted by them.

Several of the men on the slope started to sing in unison,

their voices rising until, exhausted by their digging, they one by one fell silent.

'Round the next bend?' Quinn said to the man with the radio.

The man was exasperated at being asked this again. 'If you miss the place then you're more lost than you ever imagined you could be. You should have come in on the far road. They spent a fortune elevating it. It's still clear of the water. A much better road than this one. I'm surprised no one bothered to tell you.'

'I didn't know,' Quinn said.

The man considered him for a moment and then shook his head. 'You know now,' he said, then turned and walked up the hillside to the others.

3

He reached the brow of the hill and again pulled to the side of the road. The whole of the town lay before him, half a mile ahead and surrounded by the same low hills which bordered every horizon. The place was enclosed by a recently built and almost perfectly circular ring road, and its centre marked by the only four- and five-storey buildings. Its parks and open spaces were vividly green, even at that leafless time of the year, and from where he sat, Quinn could also make out the winding course of a river as it breached the ring road and made its way through the buildings to the far side of the town, its sinuous line metallic in the morning sun. Individual roads were also evident, particularly those radiating outwards from the periphery, still illuminated by high lights along their centres.

Warehouses, large stores and industrial estates followed

the ring road for much of its circuit. Beyond these was open, empty land, deserted yards and car parks; further out still there were scattered farms, each with its own lesser network of hedges, walls and access roads. A grid of masts rose in a regular pattern across the whole place, heliographing their presence in the rising sun. Quinn switched on his phone and saw that the signal had returned.

Smoke rose from the chimneys of some of the scattered buildings, and to the far side of the town, close to the ring road, a column of much thicker and darker smoke poured from a large blaze. This rose to the height of the nearby hills, where it then levelled out and hung in a barely disturbed pall over the land below. It surprised Quinn to see such a blaze, especially so early in the day. He was surprised, too, to see the dense, hanging mass of smoke while the wind still scattered the lighter cloud above.

Immediately within the peripheral road lay a broad band of housing: crescents, circles and cul-de-sacs; thousands, perhaps tens of thousands of near-identical homes in familiar patterns. Trees grew among these, and smaller patches of green lay in a regular configuration among the dwellings.

He retrieved the atlas and aligned it to the scene before him. He learned the name of the river, several of its larger tributaries, and the names of the surrounding low peaks. A railway line was marked as 'disused', as were mines – 'disused' and 'abandoned'; Quinn wondered at the distinction, at the same time knowing that someone, somewhere, would once have made it and for a very specific reason. Another watercourse ran in a straight line through a tunnel directly beneath where he now stood. He searched around him for some indication of this – markers, perhaps, of the buried course – but could see nothing.

He saw the three major roads leaving the place, one in each direction except west, further dividing the landscape into its near-geometric segments. Looking back and forth from the reality to the map in his lap, Quinn imagined the planning processes whereby the town had come into being. Whatever its history or distant origins, everything now seemed orderly, subservient to more recent designs and needs. He felt reassured by this unconfirmed understanding; it was part of his own reason for being there.

Close to the centre of the place, this outer, converging pattern lost some of its outline clarity: buildings rose and obscured others, and roads were lost in the buildings' depths; the river ran shining into this jumbled heart, disappeared and then appeared again further on, resuming its course in the direction of the great fire. Quinn saw from the atlas that the river ran from east to west, that it rose amid the higher peaks in the east and then wound its ever-slowing way towards the sea. He turned back the pages and followed it to its estuary, childishly satisfied at having done this. Its source was harder to locate as the blue line narrowed and divided into ever thinner lines. He might as well have been looking again at the drainers' chart.

A stream ran down the hillside alongside him, channelled into a concrete culvert. He could hear the water from where he sat. Perhaps the young river had been supplanted by the road following the same course and was now diverted away from it. He guessed from everything he saw around him, and from the noise of the rushing water, that the place was a wet one. His sensored wipers swept back and forth every thirty seconds. It was no longer raining, but the air was still damp and there was moisture in the breeze.

The town sat at the centre of the page on which it appeared, and no other place even a fraction of its size existed close by; the nearest was over thirty miles away, beyond the encircling hills. And twenty miles beyond that lay the merged and seemingly endless conurbation of the Far North-East.

Individual farms were named, along with the sites of other lost, smaller places. A disused power station was marked. The cuttings and bridges of the vanished railway were also still indicated, along with all the forgotten places that had once been its lesser stations. It felt strange to Quinn, looking at a map so cluttered and confused by the past.

He was distracted from the atlas by the sound of an approaching car, and he watched as the vehicle climbed slowly towards him. Reaching him, the car slowed and then drew alongside him where he sat. The driver lowered his window and then both he and his passenger looked pointedly at Quinn. Neither of the two men spoke to him, however, and after a minute of this silent inspection they continued past him.

Quinn waited until the car was lost to sight before continuing down the slope.

A few minutes later, a flashing sign announced that he was approaching the ring road. He came to the junction and was held there as sparse traffic passed in both directions. And even when this cleared, and nothing appeared for a further minute, he was still held at the junction.

He considered turning on to this road, perhaps driving in a full circle around the town to familiarize himself with the place, but even as the thought occurred to him the signal changed and he was allowed to cross.

Immediately across the intersection, he saw a garage ahead of him and, checking his fuel gauge, he pulled on to the forecourt, where he was the only customer. He drove to the pump closest to the building, took out his fuel card and went inside.

A girl sat at the till and a youth stood close beside her. Neither of them looked up at Quinn's approach. The girl was reading a magazine and the boy was looking over her shoulder. They wore identical tunics and caps, both of which bore the logo of the fuel company. The girl, Quinn saw, had unfastened several of her buttons and the boy's eyes flicked from the pictures in the magazine to whatever else she might have been revealing to him.

'Morning,' Quinn said loudly.

The girl looked up at him and the boy took a step away from her.

'Which fuel?' Neither she nor the boy looked out of the window to see where his car stood. 'You do know that eight to twenty aren't working?'

'Functioning,' the boy corrected her.

'Functioning. Eight to twenty. That's most of the bios.' She looked at Quinn for the first time.

Quinn motioned to his car. 'Number one,' he said.

'He's right,' the boy told her.

Quinn laid his card on the narrow counter. The girl took it and slid it through the first of an array of terminals.

'Nothing,' she said.

Quinn heard the single beep and saw the flash of red light.

'It's a Ministry fuel card,' he said.

The girl blew on the card and slid it through another of her terminals. The same beep and flash.

'It's still not registering,' she said.

The boy took the card from her and studied it closely, as though expecting to identify some fault on it. Then he flicked it back and forth along the line of his fingers, annoying Quinn, but clearly hoping to impress the girl with this trick. The girl, however, refused to respond to this. She glanced at Quinn and shook her head.

'Can you try it again?' Quinn suggested. One of the machines would allow him to authorize the fuel credit.

'That's your problem, see,' the youth said, laying the card back on the counter with a slap, his fingers still moving as though he were repeating the trick. 'You've come to the wrong place. We're not Government accredited any more. We lost it.'

'Lost what?' the girl said.

'The Government account. They took it away.' To Quinn, he said, 'You can still do it on a personal card. You won't get as much, but it's do-able. Depends on how far you're going, I suppose.'

'Is there still an accredited garage in the place?' Quinn asked him.

'Course there is. Far side. I sent the others there when they arrived and wanted to—'

'So are *you* from the Ministry?' the girl asked Quinn, interrupting the boy, and appearing to be genuinely interested to know.

'Course he is,' the boy said, unhappy at having lost her attention.

'The Land people?' she said.

Quinn asked the youth where the accredited garage was, and instead of telling him the boy pointed to a map of the town taped to the wall behind him.

'Can I take one of those?' Quinn said. 'On my own card.'

The boy pulled a map from a dispensing rack and held it on the counter, firmly weighted by his hand. Only when Quinn's card was accepted did he slide the map across to him.

'I thought they'd got all the maps they needed,' he said. 'Never seen so many maps. So-called experts, lost in a place like this. You want to know anything, you should ask me. Born and raised here, hardly ever left the place. I know every street, every building.' Again this was intended to impress the girl, and again he failed.

'I'm looking for the mayor,' Quinn said.

'What mayor?' the boy said immediately.

'His name's Greer.'

'Greer? Is he the mayor? I didn't even know the dump had a mayor.'

'He's everything else,' the girl said to Quinn, 'so he might as well be mayor too.' She held his gaze and he suspected she wanted to say more to him, but that the boy's presence prevented her.

'So what is it, anyway?' the boy said. 'Mayor. What would that involve exactly?'

Quinn wasn't certain. The role, he imagined, was now wholly ceremonial and symbolic, and he knew little of whatever true or administrative powers these figureheads might still possess. All he knew for certain was that the man called Greer had been designated his First Contact in the place, the starting point for his audit. The same man, in all likelihood, to whom the Land people had also been directed upon their own earlier arrival.

'Just expensive dinners and ribbon-cutting, is it?' the girl said knowingly, smiling.

'Going to be a lot of that kind of thing round here,' the boy added absently.

'So is there a Town Hall?' Quinn asked the girl.

'Part of the Administrative Centre. A room full of old woodwork and statues.'

'*I* could give him better directions than a map,' the youth said, increasingly exasperated at his continued exclusion.

'Ignore him,' the girl said to Quinn. She leaned forward in her seat and said, her voice now mock-conspiratorial, 'He's only here because I'm a trainee.'

Hearing this, the boy said, 'Trainee Supervisor. That's me. This is on-the-job training.' He invested the phrase with a lascivious edge.

'Like I said, ignore him,' the girl repeated.

'So Mayor Greer definitely exists?' Quinn said. It was all he needed to know.

'I'm not certain about the "mayor" part,' she said. 'But Greer definitely exists. You'd be hard pressed to miss him in this place.'

'They're sorting out all the landfill sites,' the youth said. 'You know that much already.'

Quinn wondered what the remark was intended to prompt.

Then the boy said to the girl, 'He's part of it all. He's Ministry – he *must* know Greer, so why all this, eh?'

The girl considered Quinn for a moment, but remained silent.

Quinn said nothing to rebut the remark, this unfocussed accusation, choosing instead – as he always did these days – to navigate alone and unaided through all other suspicions, beliefs and considerations. He took back his card.

'Sorry about the fuel,' the girl said. 'If it was up to me . . .'

'But that's just it – it isn't, is it?' the boy said. 'You forgot to press "Transaction Completed".' He reached over her and pressed the key, leaving his arm on her shoulder for longer than was necessary. 'That's a "Cumulative Failure Factor". You only need three of those on any one session and you're back where you started.'

The girl turned to face him. Quinn waited to hear what she might say. She drew back her shoulders and again the youth's eyes tracked up and down.

'So, are you going to fail me, then?' she said, pausing, and then adding, 'Thought not.'

Quinn left them and returned to his car. In all the time he'd been there, no other vehicle had arrived on the forecourt.

He waited a moment, unfolding the map and laying it over the atlas on the seat beside him. The girl was watching him through the window. He raised a hand to her and she returned the gesture.

4

The traffic towards the centre of town was as sparse as it had been at the periphery, and Quinn passed quickly through the outer estates. Most of the housing sat with its back to the road, and with screens of high conifers protecting it further from what little noise the traffic now generated. Most of the trees were top-heavy, and with limbless lower trunks. These cast a stroboscopic pattern of light and dark across the road Quinn followed, a pattern so dark and sharp-edged that he almost expected to feel it through his tyres as he drove.

Beyond the houses, the traffic increased and was more regulated. He entered a one-way system, guided left or right every fifty metres, and delayed by further signals at each intersection. Every second signal, he saw, informed him that, whatever his eventual destination, he was now also en route for the Administrative Centre. Judging by the prominence and frequency of these markers, it seemed as though a preliminary visit to the place was almost obligatory. Perhaps it was. Wherever he travelled now, these rules and regulations disguised as courtesies were endlessly observed.

Delayed for longer than usual as a signal changed ahead of him, he lowered his window and considered the buildings on either side of the road. He was following a line of shops. Most, he saw, were empty; some were boarded up; others had metal security grilles fixed across their doors and fascia; yet others were more obviously derelict and abandoned, their doorways open, their windows broken and their interiors dark. And between the buildings were empty sites, many of which had already been cleared of rubble or whatever had once stood there and then been fenced against further trespass. Hoardings announced that some of these sites had already been acquired for development; others showed giant pictures of this coming future: new offices and malls, copses of trees, clear blue skies and golden suns.

Immediately alongside Quinn stood a deserted garage, its pumps and canopy still intact. A line of abandoned cars lay across its frontage, most of their frames rusted and blackened by fire.

He was distracted by the horn of a car behind him, and he looked in his rear-view to see the driver jabbing at the changed signal.

He crossed the junction, the following car close behind him.

At the next fork in the road, instead of continuing with the flow of traffic towards the centre, he turned to the left. Here the cars disappeared completely, and he wondered if he'd missed a No Entry sign. He followed the road for several minutes before deciding to stop and re-orientate himself.

He pulled into a vast car park and drove to its centre. The space was surrounded on three sides by the high, sheer walls of windowless buildings – warehouses, he supposed, or some kind of light industry. A notice asked him to park carefully and considerately between the lines, and to take into account the size of his vehicle when choosing an appropriate space. Quinn guessed that there were a thousand empty bays around him.

Leaving the car, he walked to the open side of the space, following a low white rail to a flight of galvanized steps.

Climbing these, he found himself above a river – the same one, in all likelihood, that he had seen from the hillside. There were no banks, only shaded, moss-covered walls rising from the water to where he stood above it. The water was dark and slow, its depth impossible to guess, though he imagined this to be no more than a few feet. To his right was a weir, over which the river flowed in a smooth brown curve, foaming and eddying where it landed. Downstream, the water was channelled even more narrowly and then lost to his sight. A succession of thick silver pipes, each with a spiked collar, crossed the water from one blank wall to another. A thick scum had formed on the water below the weir, and this and other flotsam snagged against the walls.

Leaving this vantage point, he returned to his car, pausing at the top of the short flight of stairs to see if he could identify his route out of the car park and back to the centre. Whatever happened next, he knew, had an irreversible and inevitable predictability to it. He understood that. And he understood equally well that all he was doing now – his diversion, the car park, the cold walk above the dirty river – was delaying that inevitability, delaying setting in motion the machinery he was there to set in motion, putting off his encounter with Greer, a man whom he had never met – and indeed whose existence he had known nothing of before his own assignment there had been confirmed twenty-eight days earlier.

He tapped his jacket pocket and felt the envelope which he would be obliged to immediately hand to Greer upon meeting the man. Confirmation of his – Quinn's – authority, along with the more detailed authorizations relating to all that he was now about to undertake in the town as its appointed auditor. And Greer would smile and take the envelope from him – this baton of transferred responsibility accompanied by its usual cold embrace – and he would smile and thank Quinn and offer him every assistance. A small ceremony, but a necessary one, and as vital, perhaps, as a starting pistol to a race.

He was distracted momentarily by a car entering the space below him. It looked to Quinn like a police car with an orange roof, a black stripe, and with identifying numbers stencilled across it. It approached his own car and drew up diagonally behind him, as though to prevent his departure. After a minute, two men emerged from it, went to Quinn's car and looked inside. They then searched around them and Quinn felt certain they would notice him where he stood. But they were not serious in their search and neither man saw him; they returned to their own car and left the empty space.

Quinn knew that his registration number would have been logged. Perhaps Greer already knew of his arrival in the town; perhaps that was why the police car had been sent; perhaps Greer had watched him arrive and now believed him to be lost; perhaps he was even trying to become actively involved in all those preliminary courtesies – to disarm Quinn, or to persuade him. Or perhaps simply to let him know exactly where he now was, and how far from the true source of his power and his authority he had come.

This tangle of speculation made Quinn laugh aloud, and he listened as an echo of this laughter came back to him from the high walls downriver.

This was his seventh assignment that year. He counted on his fingers and tried to remember where all the others had been. His last audit had been in the South-West, as far south and west as it was still possible to travel on major routes. And it occurred to Quinn only then that he had never before been assigned to anywhere as far north as where he now was. Much further, he guessed, and any place worthy or capable of major development would come under the jurisdiction of the Scottish Parliament and its own Audit Ministry.

Webb, Quinn's immediate superior, had assigned him to this audit, and it had struck Quinn at the time that the man had confirmed the appointment as though he were doing Quinn a great and personal favour.

Quinn and Webb had started at the Ministry at the same time. They had trained together and then worked together during the first major phase of redevelopment. Quinn had once considered the man his friend. They had socialized together, visited each other's homes; their wives and daughters had known each other. And then Quinn had lost his own wife and daughter and all this easy socializing had come to an end. Things changed. Quinn changed. A long period of enforced leave for Quinn, followed by an even longer period of stagnation. Promotion for Webb and prestigious overseas postings; no more hands in the dirt for Webb, just the power to appoint and to delegate and to watch.

Quinn was one of twelve. The Disciples. Twelve senior

auditors – always four trainees or probationers to this higher echelon; always four men and women – men like Quinn – beyond their Long Term Award Designations. Always some old wood to cut out or to allow to fall, and always some new shoots pushing up strong and vigorous into the light.

At first upon his return to work, Quinn imagined that he too might be sent overseas, perhaps to audit one of the new dependencies, of which there were an ever-growing number, and which accounted for an increasingly large part of the Ministry's work. So-called 'Holiday Postings': clean sheets, first assessments, a palm drawn cleanly and firmly across the map to smooth out all its creases.

But this was not what Webb had given him. Instead he had sent him to other places like this. Places like this, where the map was about to be screwed into a ball and then discarded like a small lost planet, and where the world was waiting to be built anew. And Quinn remembered everything about the moment when he was told about this latest destination: the arm Webb had laid across his shoulders, the tone of his voice, the shade of past intimacies, the way Webb had joked about having to look the place up on an old map. And then the way Webb had taken that very map from his drawer, positioned Quinn and himself directly over it and repeatedly jabbed at the place from above as though his finger were a falling stick of bombs dropped on to the town from a great height to strike and obliterate its centre.

5

He arrived at the Administrative Centre a few minutes later. He was stopped at the entrance by a guard who, seeing Quinn's car, stepped slowly from his kiosk, positioned himself in front of the barrier there and then held out a rigid palm to Quinn. It was a predictable routine, and one the man clearly relished. He wore a badly fitting uniform and a cap which, upon being satisfied that Quinn had stopped as directed, he took off briefly, to run his fingers over his shaved head, and then replaced. He came to Quinn, making a circling motion with his finger.

Quinn lowered his window and held up his authorization.

'Who you here to see?' the guard asked him. He took Quinn's card and studied it. It meant little or nothing to him, and imparting this to Quinn was the object of the exercise.

'Greer,' Quinn said, noticing the man's flicker of hesitation at hearing the name.

'He expecting you?'

'I wouldn't be here otherwise.' Quinn gestured for his card to be returned.

'What time?' the man said.

'Now.'

Uncertain of whether or not he was being accused of delaying Quinn, the man pointed towards a narrow archway. 'Through there, courtyard beyond. You'll get parked. Greer's straight through the main doorway. Can't miss it.'

Quinn raised his window without answering and drove through the archway.

The smaller space beyond was empty, most of its flagged floor marked with registration numbers. A second uniformed man stood at the main entrance, and Quinn wondered if the same pointless routine was to be endured again. But this second man said nothing to him, merely holding open the door as he went inside.

Quinn was surprised and impressed by the building he entered. An atrium stretched from the door to a series of radiating corridors, and rose three storeys to a conical glass roof. A circular reception desk stood at the centre of the room, from where four women sat and faced him.

Beyond, and filling most of the space there, lay a vast white model enclosed in glass: white roads, white buildings, white surrounding hills; even miniature white trees and cars lining the streets. If he'd looked any closer, Quinn felt certain he would have seen the tiny white people who already populated the place. Nearby lights shone like suns over the model, casting a few pale shadows, shades of cream and the palest grey. Only the circle of the encircling road identified the place to Quinn.

The model stood on a low platform, waist high. Any man looking down at this white town would be a god, in possession of the future.

Quinn approached the central desk and told the woman who rose to meet him why he was there.

She knew already. 'Please, take a seat, Mr Quinn,' she said the instant he finished speaking. She swiped his identity and authorization codes, nodding at everything her screens revealed to her.

'My appointment was for midday,' Quinn said. It was already several minutes past.

'I'm afraid Mr Greer is currently in conference,' the woman said. There was no note of apology in the remark.

'Oh.' Quinn looked pointedly at his watch. Procedure.

The woman, her composure intact, said, 'A few minutes, that's all. If there's anything . . .'

But she and Quinn were then distracted by the opening of a nearby door and by the raised voices of two men, who came out into the echoing space shouting at each other. The first man to emerge walked briskly across the atrium clutching a wad of paper. The second came only a few paces from the doorway and called for him to stop and to return, lowering his voice only when he saw that he was being watched by someone other than the four women.

The first man shouted that he had nothing more to say, and then warned the man in the doorway that he was going to accept no responsibility for whatever had just been discussed. Quinn heard the tempering caution in the voices of both men now that they were being observed.

The man with the papers continued to shout over his shoulder as he approached the desk. The woman who had taken Quinn's details clearly knew him, and Quinn saw her signal to him – half raising her hand in a placatory, calming gesture while simultaneously indicating Quinn beside her. The man paused at seeing this and looked at her.

'This is Mr Quinn,' she said, and then, to Quinn, 'This is Mr Stearn. Security.'

Quinn held out his hand to the man, but Stearn did not reciprocate.

'So, are you another of our high and mighty superiors come to swallow whatever *he*' – he gestured to the man still in the doorway – 'sees fit to feed to you?'

The remark caught Quinn off-guard.

'He means Mr Greer,' the woman said to Quinn, the words more mouthed than spoken.

Quinn looked across to the man. Greer had come further from the doorway, and was looking hard at Stearn, trying to overhear what he was saying to Quinn.

Quinn remained silent, waiting for Stearn's anger to subside. 'I'm here—' he began to say eventually.

'Save it,' Stearn said abruptly. 'Everybody knows why you're here. In fact, everybody here probably knows better than *you* why you're here.' The remark amused him and he laughed.

'Mr Stearn is our Chief Security Officer,' the woman said, again doing her best to placate the man.

'Police?' Quinn said. 'For the town or just this place?'

The woman waited for Stearn to answer him, but Stearn, having understood the true intent of the remark, said nothing.

Then Quinn remembered. 'You and I have a meeting scheduled for some time soon.' There had been no name attached to the appointment already made on his behalf as part of the further preliminaries to his work.

'But not until Greer's been to work on you, presumably?' Stearn said. His voice was even lower now, already making new calculations. 'In which case, I hope you're better at your job than he imagines you to be.'

Greer finally overheard this and he called to Quinn, holding out his hand, beckoning him away from Stearn and towards him.

'Perhaps . . .' the receptionist said, equally anxious that Quinn and Stearn be separated now that Greer had spoken.

'We'll talk,' Quinn said to Stearn. 'If you have anything to say to me, anything you believe might not be otherwise disclosed or revealed to me . . .' He regretted the phrasing, but he was now officially at work in the place, and it was language both Stearn and Greer would understand.

'Right,' Stearn said, clearly unconvinced of the sincerity of the offer.

Then Quinn said, 'Perhaps if Mr Greer is in agreement, you might participate now.'

It was the wrong word.

'Participate in what?' Stearn said.

'These preliminaries.'

Beyond the desk, Greer took several more paces towards them. He called again to Quinn and then gestured at the woman. At first she didn't understand him, and then she said to Quinn, 'I believe your meeting with Mr Greer was scheduled as confidential?'

She was telling him not to persist in inviting Stearn to attend.

Stearn understood this too.

'Don't worry,' he told her. 'I've had my fill of him for one day.'

'I'm sure Mr Greer might consider joint conferences once

these necessary preliminaries are concluded,' she said. More balm.

Stearn shook his head at the remark, looked from Quinn back to Greer and then continued to the entrance.

At his departure, Greer came immediately to Quinn. He took Quinn's hand in both his own and shook it firmly. The man gave off a faint, astringent odour.

'Greer,' he said. 'Chief Executive.' He motioned for the woman to return to her station.

'Not mayor?' Quinn said.

Greer paused and considered the remark before answering. 'More – what's the word . . . ?'

It was a contrived uncertainty and Quinn saw this.

'Honorarium.' Greer indicated a list of names carved in marble and mounted on the wall behind the desk. 'We had proper mayors for a few hundred years, and then all the rules changed. Different powers, different responsibilities for these changing times. I'm sure you understand all this as well as I do, Mr Quinn.'

Quinn acknowledged this.

'It was felt that "mayor" sounded a little too archaic, too out of touch with all these changes. Some said it sounded self-serving, self-aggrandizing. It was all a question of image, I suppose. Some people still like to use the title.' He spoke more confidently now, back on familiar ground. 'Sometimes I'm the mayor, sometimes merely the Chief Executive.' He sounded as though the distinction mattered only to others, was beyond his control. 'Although I am, of course, careful to maintain the distinction myself. I can show you my ceremonial robes, if you like.' He smiled at the suggestion, stepping aside as the two of them entered his office.

Once inside, he said, 'Welcome to my humble domain.' He

held up his hands and spread his fingers. 'And, please, don't think badly of Stearn – first impressions and all that. He's a capable, conscientious and committed man. And one who understands as well as any of us that a little discord – no, conflict – that a little conflict every now and again is no bad thing for the body politic.'

Quinn struggled to understand what he was being told, or, more accurately, what was being kept from him by these glib diversions.

'Quite,' he said. He looked up at the high ceiling, at the chandelier there. Marble friezes had been installed around the room, all of them salvaged from a much older building.

'I argued against the extravagance, the expense,' Greer said, but unconvincingly. 'Most of it would have been lost otherwise. I even offered to contribute towards the cost myself. I consider all this part of the town's heritage. Am I right?'

'Very impressive,' Quinn said. A succession of portraits hung between the friezes, all of them in golden frames, some of them six or eight feet high.

Greer pressed his intercom and asked for drinks to be brought in to them.

'Mr Quinn?'

'Just water,' Quinn said.

'Water,' Greer said after a pause. 'For both of us.' Another carefully maintained distance.

Quinn wondered if he'd been hoping to make the occasion a more sociable one.

Greer turned one of his screens towards Quinn, indicating a chair for him to draw to the desk. 'All your authorizations. The conditions and parameters of your work here.'

Quinn watched as the countless lines scrolled rapidly down

the screen, emerging instantaneously from a printer elsewhere in the room.

'We can get all these verified, coded and signed,' Greer said. 'Make sure we all know where we stand. You'll want copies for all the others.'

'Others?' Quinn said.

'The other people you'll need to see as part of your work, the audit. I daresay they'll want to see your authorizations, too.' A palm held to his face.

'Of course,' Quinn said.

The same woman entered the room carrying a tray with their water and glasses.

'Margaret is my Personal and Private,' Greer said. 'Anything you need or want and I'm not around . . .'

Quinn saw the sudden tightening of the woman's mouth at hearing Greer refer to her like this.

'Of course,' she said to Quinn. She took the pages from the printer and patted them into a neat pile.

'Can you see to the necessary?' Greer said to her as she left them.

'I may not need to take up as much of your valuable time as you seem to imagine,' Quinn said as Greer uncapped the bottles.

'Of course. I simply wanted you to know that you have my full cooperation in all of this. Whatever, anything and whenever.' He sipped his own drink.

The precise nature and degree of the man's involvement was already laid out in the recently printed documents, but Quinn said nothing. It was all still a show on Greer's part. He knew *why* Quinn was there, of course, what he was there to undertake and to verify, but as yet he still had no clear or reassuring idea of the true nature or process of that undertaking, of how effectively it might now proceed in Quinn's hands.

'I'm not entirely certain how these things actually get under way,' Greer prompted him.

Quinn shrugged. 'I cover the ground, consider all the basics and then proceed however I see fit,' he said, aware of how little he was revealing, that this game between them was still being played. 'A lot of it depends on where my early enquiries lead. There are seldom any real surprises. If things tally, columns add up, then I'm as happy as everyone else to make no waves. And any discrepancies, any unsound footings, any columns that refuse to tally . . . well, I do my best to put things right and steer everything in the same general direction.' *Tally.* It made him sound like a man poring over old ledgers and licking a stub of pencil. 'None of us wants these things to throw up too many surprises. I'm here to help, remember, not to hinder.' He wondered how many times he'd said this over the past twenty years, and if anyone had ever been genuinely reassured or disarmed by the remark. In other circumstances he might have made the usual small speech about the Audit Ministry – formerly Office – being the public watchdog of Government spending, there to scrutinize public-sector economy, to monitor performance, efficiency and effectiveness. But Greer, he knew, would have read the advance publicity, and this equally superficial clarification would have served no purpose.

'Meaning it's best to remain flexible?' Greer said. 'I couldn't agree more. Keep an open mind, that's the trick.'

Asking me or telling me? Quinn thought. It seemed a clumsy remark for the man to make.

Greer handed Quinn his water. He asked about his journey and was surprised when Quinn told him how he had spent the previous night. Surprised, too, to learn that Quinn had not yet gone to his motel, unpacked his belongings or started to liaise with the Ministry back in the capital.

Quinn drained his glass and looked again around the room.

'Everything's ready for you,' Greer said. 'Accounts, documents, anything relevant. Everything you asked for.'

Notice of the audit had been sent on the same day Quinn himself had been appointed to undertake it.

Greer tapped at his keyboard for a few seconds. 'You're at the Peripheral,' he said. 'Where you're staying. They hold the Government account.'

'Is it far?' Quinn asked him. He felt suddenly exhausted.

'On the ring road. A few miles. Ten minutes from here.'

'You possess a good infrastructure,' Quinn said.

'The roads? Part of why all this is about to happen to us, I suppose. They thought originally that when the flooding in the west continued for longer than anticipated, here and half a dozen other places would benefit from the overspill. And if not the west – look at what's happened to Liverpool, for Christ's sake – then that we'd get a steady influx from the North-East.'

'And they never came?'

'Not until now. If the expansion goes as planned, the first of them will be here in five years. We've been told up to three hundred thousand in total in the eight years after that. You know how these things work – everything just seems to get overtaken and changed. We got the money for the new roads almost a decade ago. There was talk – still is – of reopening the railway, and of trying to extend the motorway.' He shook his head at the idea.

'The motorway would be a good thing,' Quinn said.

'Of course it would. Not going to happen though, is it?

Not now. And certainly not with the declining traffic levels. Look at what happened to Hull. You'd hardly know the place had ever been there. A million and a quarter people. The idea then was to send them north, but most took their lives into their own hands and decided otherwise. I doubt you can walk across a patch of solid green between – where? – Doncaster and Manchester these days.'

'There was a recent report that the water in the west was starting to fall,' Quinn said, remembering something he'd read before leaving the capital.

'Too late for us,' Greer said. 'Too late for anyone.'

After that, neither man spoke for a minute.

There was a single rap on the door and Margaret came back in. She laid bound papers on Greer's desk and then left without speaking to either of them.

'Your authorizations – checked and verified,' he said to Quinn. 'I'll get them sent to whoever . . .' He left the remark unfinished. He seemed deflated, as though this long-anticipated meeting had disappointed him in ways he could never have imagined. 'Is there anything else?'

'Such as?' Quinn said.

Greer shrugged, tired now of even these small, probing pretences. 'Anything you need – local access codes, names, numbers.'

'I think I already have everything.'

'Of course. I only meant . . .'

'Though I appreciate your offer,' Quinn said.

'Will you keep me informed?'

'A great deal of what I undertake will be confidential to some degree,' Quinn said.

Greer rubbed his face. 'How could it be otherwise?' He looked again at the screen. 'Thirty days,' he said.

'It's the usual allocation for a Development or Probity Audit,' Quinn said. 'In the first instance. If I need more time, then it's a decision I have to make in the final seven days.' As far as he could remember, not a single audit – even one as important as this – had been granted an extension in the previous decade.

'It's dated two days ago,' Greer said.

'Outward travelling time.'

Greer closed his own booklet of documents and slid them into a drawer.

6

He followed the same road in the opposite direction towards his motel. The town in that quarter, north of the centre, seemed more prosperous to him, better tended, more populous and with a greater variety of housing.

Arriving at the ring road, he saw again the column of smoke which continued to rise into the winter air and form a dark cloud low over the horizon. He wondered what happened when the wind changed direction and the smoke blew or drifted back over the town centre.

He drove out on to the wider carriageway. A service station appeared ahead of him and he pulled in to this. A screen warned him that service was by automated teller only. He drew up at a pump and pushed his Ministry card into the terminal, relieved when it indicated that the card had been accepted. His transaction would be recorded and his location tracked and relayed to those responsible for monitoring this. He pressed for a receipt but this was unavailable to him. Webb liked receipts. The transaction would be logged and his mileage checked against it when he returned the car to the Ministry garage. Like most others, he had long since stopped questioning why all this might still be deemed necessary.

He waited for the pump to unlock itself and then he put the nozzle into his tank. Following his earlier encounter, he had anticipated further problems acquiring the fuel, and was relieved that the transaction had been so straightforward.

He stood and watched the distant smoke until the fuel stopped flowing and an alarm told him to re-secure the nozzle. He did this and was thanked by the machine.

Pulling to one side, he paused beneath one of the canopy lights and looked again at his map. The motel was marked only a short distance ahead of him, two miles, perhaps three. There was nothing visible along the gently undulating road, only the lights and outlines of the town stretching away from him on the far side of the carriageway. He saw how quickly the night was again falling, guessing that the sun was lost even earlier than usual here because of the height of the surrounding hills.

He restarted the engine and it faltered for a moment before running smoothly.

He yawned. He was unshaven and his eyes looked dark in the mirror. It was how he had appeared to Greer and the others. Years ago, when the work had still challenged and sustained him, and when it had provided him with all the necessary forward momentum he had believed he needed, this had formed a calculated part of his approach: appearing dishevelled, in a hurry, uncertain of the true nature of what he had come to investigate and assess. Uncertain of the place, its people and its history. Uncertain even of the veracity or otherwise of the figures and reckonings he had so far seen on his preliminary print-outs. Uncertain too of the deceits and revelations of the men and women he was there to measure and to assess.

The start of every major audit had always seemed to Quinn to consist of the same tangled ball of considerations and slow unravellings, and he had long since learned not to insist on looking for anything as simplistic or as misleading as innocence or guilt. They were all innocent men and women when he arrived. Otherwise why would they be in positions of such authority and trust? If they were wasteful, or fraudulent, or profligate, or imprudent – the usual maze of interchangeable charges – then surely they would already have been investigated and punished or removed.

Think of it as a continuum, Webb insisted on telling new appointees to the work. A kind of innocence at one end, a kind of guilt at the other. Everybody fits somewhere along the line. Some will always be more guilty than others. He later amended 'guilty' to 'duplicitous', savouring the sound of the word and all it might – or just as likely, might not – reveal. Work out who these people were and then direct your energy and resources accordingly. But neither Quinn nor his more experienced colleagues had ever accepted this, quickly learning as they undertook their own independent and varying audits what shifting and interchangeable commodities all these attributes truly were.

He drove slowly along the outer carriageway. A short convoy of identical lorries passed him, their lights filling his mirrors. He slowed even further and watched them pull away from him, reduced eventually to a chain of red lights on the rising road.

A few minutes later he saw the illuminated sign of the motel, and immediately beyond this the brightly lit compound of buildings at the end of a slip road.

He parked and walked to the reception. His back ached and his legs ached. A camera above the motel entrance swivelled towards him at his approach, registered his presence and then turned away.

At reception, a woman took his card and then repeated the details of his stay to him. He felt strangely reassured at hearing her say all this, confirming that whatever else might now happen, he was at least the right man in the right place at the right time. Another of Webb's mantras.

The woman gave him back his card and then indicated the small soft cup of the iris-recognition equipment. Quinn took this, held it to his eye and counted to three. When he put it down the woman was again concentrating on her screen. Confirmation of his identity would take at least a minute.

He stretched his arms and yawned. 'Sorry,' he said.

'You look tired,' the woman said, glancing quickly up at him, as though to lose even this instant of contact with her screen might somehow invalidate what it was about to tell her. Eventually, a succession of clicks started sounding and she looked back up, this time smiling at him. 'You've had a long journey,' she said. She seemed almost genuine, almost caring, compassionate even, and not just another key-point employee running through another unavoidable routine.

'Not really,' Quinn said, half turning to look back at the falling darkness through the automatic door.

'There,' she said eventually, almost enthusiastically.

Quinn's magnified iris appeared on her screen. A

superimposed grid of fine lines appeared and twitched in calculation for a few seconds before it, too, was fixed.

'I'm who I say I am,' Quinn said.

'You certainly are.' She began the routine of logging all the remaining codes and details – his actual name seemed the least of these – and told him of the services and amenities now available to him. She then listed the additional services he was required to pay for using his personal accreditation. She was happy to welcome him as a member of the motel.

Member? Quinn thought. *Not guest, not customer, not even client?*

'Is that what I am, then?' he said.

'Sorry.'

Whatever else he now said, she would be offended by it. She was trained well enough not to show offence, but she would be offended all the same.

'I meant am I a member of the gym?'

'For the duration of your stay,' she told him. She went on to repeat the remainder of his entitlements.

Quinn stopped listening to her.

'Do you have much luggage?'

'I can manage,' he told her.

'I meant to be secured. You have a Security Clearance listed. If anything needs to be kept secure, then you have provision. I can give you a personal clearance code now. The secure room is – ' She motioned to the door behind her.

Security was obligatory. Too many compromised investigations. The secure room was a condition of the Government contract with the motel chain. Quinn would take his files to his room, decide what he needed for immediate use and then return the remainder for safe-keeping. Precisely an hour after his arrival had been confirmed, a message would appear on the screen in his room reminding him of his need to do this. And somewhere on the screen would be Webb's name or code, confirming that the reminder had been sent.

The woman gave him the sealed sachet containing the code to his room, which Quinn opened and read. He passed it back to her and she immediately dropped it into a small shredder beneath her desk.

He assured her that he would bring down his files, and then he returned to the car and collected his belongings. It took him three short journeys to unload everything.

He was on the fourth floor, overlooking the ring road and the scattered lights of the town beyond. The room was soundproofed and overheated. The screen welcomed him and repeated most of what he'd just been told.

The bed felt soft beneath him. It was broad and low and laid out with two sets of pillows. The bedside lamps were on when he entered the room, triggered by his code being entered in the door.

He lay back and closed his eyes, opening them and pushing himself upright only on the brink of sleep.

The message warning him of his security status was already flashing and he took two of his sealed cases back down to the empty lobby.

'Access is twenty-four/seven,' the woman told him. 'And your access code can be confirmed by—'

'I know,' Quinn told her.

'Safest all round,' she said, smiling again.

Meaning you renounce all responsibility and they *seize it*, Quinn thought, meaning the Planning and Development Ministry, of which the Audit Department was a small and carefully regulated part. He had once been with Webb when the Development Minister himself had referred to one of the junior auditors as a 'functionary' and he, Quinn, had been surprised by the speed and ease – the pride, almost – with which Webb had acknowledged the derogatory title.

Quinn thanked the woman for what he'd just been told.

'It's what I'm here for,' she said.

He had stayed at countless other places, many in the same chain, where this check-in and authorization process had already been fully automated. As straightforward and as depersonalized as buying fuel. Perhaps it was coming here too, and perhaps the woman already knew that. Perhaps she already understood how superfluous to requirements she might already have become now that her every function had been reduced to these codes and confirmations. And perhaps he – Quinn – his arrival and the outcome of his work here were further parts of that same inevitable process. And perhaps the woman understood that, too.

'To get through to reception just lift your phone,' she said, the routine approaching its end.

He thanked her again and returned to his room, using the stairs this time, testing his exhaustion against the eight short flights.

He lay down on the low, wide bed, and within minutes he was asleep.

It was five o'clock, less than twenty-four hours since his arrival in the place.

7

He woke to the noise of people in the corridor outside: a succession of doors opening and closing, men and women calling to each other, laughter.

He lay fully dressed on the bed. In the room around him the lights had dimmed to a yellow glow and the curtains were now drawn, leaving only a slender gap of darkness at their centre. The window which had been open was closed and the television was muted. A message across the screen told him that if no controls were used, then at 23:30 everything would be switched to Night Mode.

He felt hungry. It was almost ten. He pushed himself upright and studied his reflection in the mirror directly ahead of him. He raised the volume on the television and the wall lights brightened simultaneously. He swung himself from the bed and went to the window. The car park below was filled with vehicles. Directly beneath him stood two rows of white vans, their Ministry markings vivid in the spotlights. He saw from their registrations that the vans had been parked in a precise and calculated sequence.

A solitary man ran the full length of the corridor, calling to someone who didn't answer. Through the walls, Quinn could hear the humming noise made by the rising and falling elevators.

He went into the wet-room and washed, standing for several minutes with his face turned to the shower.

He returned and finished emptying his case. Scanning the television channels, he watched a local news item about the fire he'd seen earlier. A woman in a bio-suit, her mask and breathing apparatus held by her side, was explaining how the toxicity of the drifting smoke was being constantly monitored. The man interviewing her ended with unconvincing reassurances that the smoke was gathering high above the locality and from there was moving far away. He made it sound like the ending of a fairy tale. The item was followed by a feature from the town's hospital, focussing on its maternity ward. A semi-circle of women and nurses held up a clutch of bundled babies for the camera, turning them as directed, and rocking them in an effort to silence their crying.

Quinn switched off the television, dressed and left his room.

A man waited by the elevator. 'Someone's holding it,' he said. He jabbed angrily at the unresponsive button.

'I'll take the stairs,' Quinn said, thinking that the man might have joined him. But instead he repeated, 'They're holding it,' sounding now as though he had been deliberately marooned there.

Quinn went down into the bar. The room was full, and men and women stood three deep waiting to be served. Tables had been pulled together. Music played. Despite the crowd, there were only two servers and the drinkers complained loudly at how long they were being kept waiting.

After ten minutes, Quinn was served and he took his drink to one of the few empty tables, by the window overlooking the motel entrance. He looked out and was surprised to see a woman only a few feet from the glass, talking on her phone. She saw him looking at her, hesitated and then nodded to him. She gesticulated as she spoke, pacing back and forth along the edge of the driveway and rubbing her exposed arms in the night air. Quinn recognized her as the woman he'd seen on the news talking about the smoke.

At the bar entrance, the man he'd left waiting for the elevator finally arrived and was greeted by a burst of laughter and applause. Someone started to sing 'Happy Birthday' to him and everyone else quickly joined in. The man raised his arms in acknowledgement, savouring the attention.

At the bar, Quinn had been told that it was too late for him to order any food. 'Exceptional circumstances,' the barman said in lieu of a proper explanation. Quinn imagined he was referring to the sudden influx of late drinkers.

He looked back outside. The woman was no longer there. He sipped his drink.

He'd brought the map of the town with him, and he was taking this from his pocket, preparing to plan his route through the days ahead, when the same woman appeared directly in front of him. She gestured to a seat and Quinn told her to take it, expecting her to join the others. But instead she sat beside him.

'I didn't mean to spy on you,' he said.

'You were probably just mesmerized by the wonderful scenery.' She held out her hand to him. 'Anna Laing.'

Quinn reciprocated. 'It's someone's birthday,' he said, indicating the crowd of others.

'One of mine,' she said. 'I can think of better places to turn forty.'

'One of yours?'

She continued looking around them as she spoke. 'I'm the chief vet. Agriculture. They call me "chief". We were late finishing today, hence all this now.'

'They're letting off steam,' Quinn said.

'Something like that. We should have been back by six. Darkness Working Practices. But the fire was still a little too . . . busy. We had to wait until the dampening chemicals did their stuff.'

'I saw you on the news,' Quinn said.

'I seem to be on every few days. Reassuring words and all that. They wanted me to walk to camera and take off my mask as I arrived. I think they even expected me to shake out my flowing tresses.'

Quinn smiled at this. 'Would that make you somehow more reassuring or believable?'

'Oh, considerably.' She shook her head, as though she possessed flowing tresses rather than short, dark hair cut sharply across her forehead and the nape of her neck. 'But you'd probably have to use your imagination.'

'Little of which the interviewer possessed?'

'It would probably have disqualified him for the job.' Then she tapped her forehead and said, 'You're the auditor.'

'That's me,' Quinn said.

'Good. Now they'll have someone else to be suspicious about.'

'It goes with the job. Mostly unfounded. I doubt if anything I turn up here will affect to the slightest degree what's coming.'

'Something else we have in common,' she said. She held her face in both her hands for a moment, yawned and then ran the balls of her palms across her eyes.

'You're tired,' Quinn said.

'I look like this all the time these days.'

A man approached them and put several colourful drinks on the table in front of Anna Laing. He told her who had sent them and she raised the glass she held to a group of nearby men.

Waiting until the man had left them, she said, 'I asked for wine.' She picked up one of the glasses. The drink it held was blue at the base, fading to yellow at its surface. 'What is it?'

'Bright,' Quinn said.

'I'm pleased you find it funny,' she said. 'Because when no one is looking you're going to have to drink half of everything that gets delivered to me.'

'Birthday equals novelty drink,' he said.

She sipped at the drink and pulled a face.

'I envy you,' she said unexpectedly.

'Oh?'

'I mean I envy the fact that you get to do everything you have to do behind closed doors, in privacy and secrecy; and the fact that you'll probably be long gone before anything untoward' – she seemed surprised at having used the word – 'comes to light.'

'Whereas you get to start and then feed the biggest, dirtiest looking fire anyone for twenty miles around has ever seen, you mean?'

'Nearer thirty miles on a bad day.'

'They all know why I'm here,' Quinn said. 'Once, an audit meant money, pure and simple – accounts, balances, funding, targets, tables, initiatives.'

She heard the lack of enthusiasm in his voice. 'And now it means whatever you want it to mean?'

'Not me, personally,' Quinn said. 'This is a so-called Strategy Audit.'

'"Democratic renewal through decentralization"?' she said.

Quinn smiled at hearing the phrase.

'No need to tell me how impressed you are,' she said.

'Next you'll be talking about "Deliverology Strategies".'

'*Do* they hide things from you?' she said unexpectedly.

'Such as?' He understood precisely what she was asking him.

'Irregularities, misappropriation, bad decisions, money being wasted, spent where it shouldn't be spent?'

Quinn considered his answer. 'I think most of my superiors stopped worrying about things like that a long time ago. My turf-hungry boss likes to look on us all as "facilitators".'

She smiled at the word.

'Exactly. The development here is a big thing. It's coming whatever I uncover. Besides, most people still think it's all about money and then hide the things I was never looking for in the first place.'

'But they still expect their own particular slates to be wiped clean?'

'Something like that. They prostrate themselves before me and receive my blessing.'

This time they both smiled.

Afterwards, neither of them spoke for a moment. Quinn picked up one of the colourful drinks and drained it. 'To fiscal absolution,' he said.

Anna Laing picked up another of the concoctions and did the same.

'It's not so bad,' he lied to her.

'Good, because there are four left.' She ran her tongue over her lips. 'Is it even alcoholic?'

'Is there still someone out there – at the fire?' Quinn asked her.

'Fires.' She nodded. 'Once they're under way we're obliged to maintain a "Watchful Presence".' She invested the phrase with a cold edge. 'To be honest, it wasn't what we'd been led to expect.'

'Here, you mean? Why, what are you burning?'

'We were told exhumed cattle and associated contaminated organic waste.' She lowered her voice. 'It turns out that some bright spark at the first outbreak had the wonderful idea of burning the carcases at the town's tyre dump. It's been there a hundred years. Our best estimate at present is twelve thousand tons of rubber.'

'And not all of it burned at previous – ?'

'From what we can tell, hardly any of it. Rubber and contaminated organics. Not a happy combination. And a situation somewhat further complicated by the better accelerants we get to play with these days. And as if that wasn't enough, not only did they choose to dispose of their foot-and-mouths out there, but then they thought they'd top up with what was left after the blue-tongue and anthrax culls. The anthrax-related material is our primary concern.'

'Active spores?'

'You sound almost knowledgeable.'

'Not really,' Quinn admitted.

'In that case . . .' She handed him another of the drinks. 'The mixture of burned and intact tyres means the site compaction is poor – stop me if all this gets too technical – and poor compaction means the spores – active or otherwise – might have gone deeper than anyone anticipated.'

'Much deeper?'

'Much.' She looked around her as she spoke.

'How long do they persist? Is that the right word?'

'One of them.'

'And so you burn the lot in the hope that the smoke will carry everything away and make it somebody else's problem? Sorry, I didn't – '

'It's as good a solution as any.' She smiled again, releasing the sudden awkwardness between them. 'On the plus side, of course, there are no cattle left to re-infect. *Nothing* left to re-infect, in fact. But the anthrax will – might – will one day find its way into another part of what we trained toxicologists happily and blithely refer to as the "Human Sphere". I don't imagine you've ever seen a photo of anyone infected with anthrax.'

'I don't think so.'

'Then you haven't. You would have remembered it, believe me.'

'Meaning you have?'

'I've seen the real thing. Three hundred children in Greece a few years ago. Another big fire and cloud of smoke. An unregulated site. Just a few locals taking things into their own hands after another developer offered them ten times more than they would ever earn in their lives off the land. A very desirable place to live these days, Greece. Once you ignore the actual cost of living there, of course. And the constant drought and the fires sent from heaven to burn away what little bit of greenery might remain.' She looked directly at Quinn as she said all this and he understood the comparisons she was making – both between there and here, and between her own work and whatever he was now there to undertake.

'You don't think the site here is likely – '

'You've seen my walk to camera,' she said. 'Don't tell me you weren't completely reassured by everything I said. Don't worry, our readings so far have been even more reassuring.'

As she finished speaking, another man approached them, this time carrying two glasses of wine.

Anna introduced the man to Quinn.

'My second,' she said.

The man smiled at her. 'I thought you might appreciate something grown up,' he said. With his back to the others in the room, he drank one of the remaining drinks and pulled a face.

Anna asked him to join them, but he declined. He told her he was going to bed, that he was expected at the site at three the following morning.

'No making toast over the flames,' she said as he left them.

When the man had gone, she said, 'He's as concerned as I am about what no one told us we'd find here.'

'You think someone knew and didn't pass the information on?'

She smiled at the suggestion and all it implied.

'Is covering the site over and leaving the deeper stuff undisturbed not a viable option?'

'A few years ago, perhaps. But not with all that's going to take place here. You've seen what's about to happen. The whole Slough of Despond for the best part of five miles in every direction is going to turn into something new, and a lot of people – locals and incomers alike – are depending on that happening.'

They fell silent again. She touched her wine glass to his, briefly resting her free hand on top of his own.

'How much longer will you be here?' he asked her.

'Two months? Not the whole team, perhaps, but some of us. Once the cappers have worked out – '

'Cappers?'

'We'll use a chemical cap to keep the anthrax-contaminated material out of harm's way. And then, just to make sure, we'll pour in a few thousand tons of concrete. It'll still be a plague pit, but it'll be a safe plague pit. You'd be surprised how many of them there are. We're burning the tyres now in the hope of achieving some degree of settlement and to give us a base level to eventually start pouring on. We'll keep a close eye on things, but, essentially, once the place is designated "reclaimed" it'll be handed over to the developers.' She looked at her watch. 'I should go,' she said.

'A three o'clock start?'

'Nearer five.'

As she began to rise from beside him, Quinn said, 'What happens if you can't make the site safe?'

She considered this for a moment. 'What, and disappoint all those tens of thousands of dispossessed people already looking forward to mowing their new lawns and building their new patios? I honestly doubt if that's an option. Much the same as you uncovering a conspiracy of financial mismanagement and telling all those same tens of thousands of people to wait where they are for a few more years while it all gets sorted out.' She stretched her arms and twisted from side to side. 'Finish the pretty drinks,' she said, and then she turned and left him.

8

The next morning he woke late. It was already nine; he had forgotten to set the alarm. A small 'm' blinked on his screen, indicating that he had messages waiting to be read. As though this lesser case were a more gentle reminder than an insistent upper-case alert. He opened these.

The first was from Webb, telling Quinn to contact him. The second was from the man called Stearn, who had apparently called the motel only a few minutes earlier, and who now wanted to see Quinn as soon as possible.

Quinn called Webb, surprised to find himself put through to the man on Webb's direct line.

'You failed to properly confirm your arrival,' Webb said brusquely, making no attempt to disguise his anger. Quinn knew that the motel codes would have alerted both the

Ministry and the Audit Department of his arrival there, and he waited without answering.

'My apologies,' he said eventually.

'All I'm asking for is a little consideration,' Webb said.

It was how the man operated; Quinn understood this and waited for him to go on.

'There were reports of delays on the motorway, closures.' Webb's tone was now almost conciliatory, his point made.

'Is there a problem?' Quinn said, already wondering about Webb's real reason for calling him so soon into his deployment.

Two years ago, Quinn and five other auditors had arrived in Manchester only to be told by Webb to return immediately to the capital. To cancel all their advance authorizations and leave no other trace of their presence there, not even to attempt to contact the Ministry until they were back inside the southern area of their operations. Quinn wondered if he was about to be told the same thing now.

'No – no problem,' Webb said. 'I just wanted to confirm personally that you'd arrived' – presumably meaning he wanted to be sure that Quinn had confirmed his authorized status in the place – 'and that things were under way.'

Things? Quinn wondered if the call was in connection with his delayed arrival or the fact that he had so far logged none of the details of his preliminary meeting with Greer, who in all likelihood would have logged those same few details immediately.

'I was delayed,' he said.

'I know. The trackers in the car.'

'I've spoken to Greer,' Quinn said. It was all he had to offer. He tried to remember how long it had been since Webb had carried out his own audits. Five years? Ten?

As he waited for Webb to reveal his true intent, he remembered the hour he had spent with Anna Laing and wondered when he would see her again.

'I heard about the excavations,' he told Webb.

Webb waited too long before answering him. 'Nothing you – we – need concern ourselves with, surely?' It was a warning rather than a simple remark. 'You know better than anyone what needs to be done; there won't be anything there you haven't seen fifty times already.' Everything the man said was either a caress or a prod.

'The size of the development seems—' Quinn began.

'What difference does that make? It's the place as it is *now* that we're interested in, not what it's going to be like in five or ten years' time.'

Quinn conceded this. He heard the rising frustration in Webb's voice.

Ever since the onset of the cycle of recurrent flooding, abandonment and resettlement, the future – those 'five or ten years' – had seldom seemed so far away, and certainly never so uncertain or unpredictable. Speculation about the 'dim and distant' future had long since become a painful and unaffordable luxury. The future now in places like this – and in all those other places abandoned or reclaimed – was, literally, tomorrow. These days, the future overtook and destroyed the careless and the heedless, the declaimers and the foot-draggers. Equally, the past itself was no longer the solid and dependable mainland it had once been. The world – or so it increasingly seemed to Quinn whenever he was forced to pause and properly consider it – had become one enormous fault line, ever-shifting and ever-threatening, and predictable only in the succession of hitherto unbelievable catastrophes it produced.

'Do what you're good at,' Webb said – another slap on the back, causing Quinn to wonder if he hadn't missed something else he'd said. 'With any luck you'll get everything you need from this Greer character.' He paused. 'You do understand, I suppose – hope – that if *I* didn't have Homeland and Internal breathing down my neck . . .' He left the rest unspoken. What he was telling Quinn was that they were all in this together, which was seldom true.

'Of course,' Quinn said. He jabbed at the muted channels on his screen. Pictures taken from a satellite showing the extent of the fires still burning the full length of the Mediterranean, their converging smoke spreading east like a windblown scarf.

'Do you need any additional or tailored authorizations?' Webb asked him.

'Not yet,' Quinn said. His existing blanket authorization and powers already far exceeded those of any individuals or institutions he was likely to come into contact with during his audit. For the next twenty-seven days, Quinn possessed complete dominion, however illusory this might later prove to be.

'I may be briefly absent from post,' Webb said unexpectedly, faltering for a moment. 'Next week for a few days. Nothing much. Certainly no longer.'

Quinn knew immediately that this was the true reason for the call. 'Oh?' he said, waiting.

'A personal matter. I'm designating John Lucas as your immediate contact. Is that OK with you?'

OK? It was like a foreign language to Webb.

Quinn trusted John Lucas, another senior auditor and a true friend, who now worked solely inside the department, more often than not seconded to one or other of the security services. Quinn and Lucas had worked together often, on cases spanning fifteen years, and Webb knew this; it was why he was using the man now.

'John Lucas is fine,' Quinn said. 'Will he have your clearances?' Meaning if his work there took an unexpected turn, would Lucas possess the powers to support him as required. Webb would sooner hand over the keys to his own home.

'Temporarily,' Webb said. 'For as long as necessary.' The same two notes of evasion and exasperation had returned.

It's either a secret or it's not, Quinn thought, but again he said nothing. Webb gave him the dates of his absence and Quinn made a note of them.

'Clearance only at Directive level,' Webb said. 'The usual restrictions will still apply.'

Of course they would.

'Of course,' Quinn said. He drew a rigid palm to his temple in salute. It was common practice for auditors working in theatre – it had been 'in field' when Quinn had started – to have as little personal contact as possible with the Ministry for the duration of the audit, and then for everything to be carefully coded before transmission. Webb liked to refer to this as 'total immersion', as though working like this produced more reliable or more credible results. And 'working in theatre' was now commonly used to refer to any investigation undertaken outside the Capital Zone; anywhere in these outer regions and barren wastes, these encircling and limitless *terrae incognitae*, these places cast endlessly in shadow and clouded over.

'Secure the screen,' Webb said then, and for a moment Quinn didn't understand him. 'I'm sending you Lucas's codes and validity checks,' Webb added.

The codes arrived, and Quinn copied, encrypted and then deleted them, confirming this to Webb.

'I have your confirmation,' Webb said unnecessarily.

Not only covering his own back, but letting me know it's covered, and possibly at my own or John Lucas's expense if anything does now go seriously wrong.

'Apparently, in addition to the exhumations, there are other Land and Ag interests in the area,' Webb said, signalling an end to this part of their conversation.

'I met some of their people,' Quinn told him.

'*They*'re the ones genuinely worried about the future of the place,' Webb said, forcing a laugh.

The Ministry of Land Use and Agriculture had become a standing joke in other Government departments. What little truly agricultural practice still remained in the country was rapidly disappearing beneath a second ocean of regulation and legislation, and the Land and Agriculture employees, fewer with each reorganization and retrenchment, were now employed largely on secondment to other agencies, most of them – as was happening here, now – in cleansing and reclamation prior to development.

Quinn heard Webb tapping at a keyboard.

'Lucas says hello,' Webb said.

'Ditto,' Quinn said. He waited while Webb continued typing, fully aware of how compromised John Lucas would now feel at having Webb as their intermediary. He would contact the man privately later.

He looked through the window to watch a succession of delivery vans draw up in the otherwise empty car park.

'You should know that there's going to be a new fuel directive announced in five days' time,' Webb said, his voice low.

'Reductions, restrictions?'

'No details as yet.' He spoke now as though Quinn had contradicted him.

'I'll bear it in mind,' Quinn said.

'Good,' Webb said. 'Right – ' It was how he invariably signalled that whatever conversation he was having was now at its end. Next he would say, 'Work to do, people to meet.' 'Work to – '

Quinn said nothing, and in that moment of silence, the connection between the two men was severed.

On his screen, the waiting-message symbol disappeared. Only Stearn's reminder remained.

Quinn swung himself from the bed.

He showered, shaved and dressed.

A short while later, he left his room and went outside, where the cold air caught him in his chest, and where frost lay outlined in the shadow of the building. A thin rime of it lay across his windscreen and he waited in his car for a few minutes while the heater and the blades cleared this. He unfolded the map of the town and held it over the steering wheel, checking his simple route back into the centre.

Ahead of him, beyond the receding line of the ring road and the curve of the land, the same black smoke rose up into the empty sky, looking to Quinn at that distance and in the clear morning air like spilled ink blossoming slowly into water.

9

Towards the town centre, at what looked to be another empty site awaiting redevelopment, Quinn pulled off the road and parked in the makeshift compound there which already contained several of Anna Laing's vans. At the far side of the site, men in protective suits moved in a line over open ground, their heads down, swinging sensors ahead of them as they went.

He approached a barrier and a guard emerged from a nearby cabin and shouted to him. The man wore no protective clothing and he stood for a moment and watched the others on the site before continuing towards Quinn.

'What are they doing?' Quinn asked him.

'And you are?'

Quinn took out his identification and held it towards the man.

'You with them?'

'I was looking for Anna Laing.' He said it in a way which suggested he didn't know her, immediately wondering why he'd done this.

'And she is?'

'I thought she might be supervising the search.' It was a guess. Now he sounded as though he knew considerably more than he did about what was happening there.

'Never heard of her,' the guard said. He was a young man. His shirt was buttoned to his thin throat, but he wore no tie. Quinn read the words 'Stearn Security' across his breast pocket.

'Do you know what they're looking for?' he asked him.

'All *I* know is that it's a routine clearance, whatever that means. Somebody probably pulled a few strings.' He grinned and then nodded up to the sky.

Quinn didn't understand him.

'It's Church land,' the guard said. He indicated a building beyond the open land. 'That's the church.'

Quinn had mistaken it for one of the town's many warehouses.

'That's the back of it. Bit more impressive round the front. They're expanding. New regulations. All new building work needs to get the land monitored and cleared. Waste of time, if you ask me.'

'Are they concerned about contamination? Here?'

The guard looked at him and shrugged.

Several of the searchers turned and started moving towards them, stopping and then turning back a few metres from the barrier. Quinn saw that Anna Laing was not among them.

'A day's secondment from one of the livestock sites,' the

guard said dismissively, explaining all Quinn needed to know.

He looked more closely at the rear of the church and saw the high metal cross rising above one side of the building.

The guard's earpiece clicked and he turned away from Quinn to talk into its stem. He said little, glancing back at Quinn and then moving further from him as he started whispering.

After a minute, he returned.

'You shouldn't be here,' he said bluntly.

It was the message he'd just been told to pass on. Cameras on high poles lined the road behind him, swivelling almost imperceptibly back and forth over the site. A more sophisticated system of small black globes decorated the high rim of the church.

'Do you work for Stearn?' Quinn asked him, already knowing.

The guard tapped his pocket in answer.

'Employed by the church or this lot?' He indicated the searchers.

The youth shrugged. 'All I know is that my name was on the rota and that this was my address. Eight hours duty box.' He nodded to the rigid plastic kiosk. 'No camera control, no site patrol, no nothing. Just eight hours of box work.'

'Is the church expanding to fill this entire site?' Quinn asked him.

Another shrug. 'Ask me – ' He was stopped by a further sudden hiss on his earpiece – another prod from someone still monitoring the cameras. 'Anyhow, you've got to leave. Absolutely no unauthorized admission.'

'It doesn't bother you that you're here with no protection

whatsoever while they're covered and filtered from head to foot?' Quinn said.

The guard looked back at the searchers, watching them closely for a moment, as though considering for the first time what Quinn was suggesting.

'You saying I should have something?'

Quinn shrugged and turned away from him.

'You want me to log you?' the youth called after him. 'For my records?' He made no attempt to follow Quinn.

Back in his car, Quinn waited for several minutes, his disappointment at not having encountered Anna Laing replaced now by his curiosity at what he had seen there.

He returned to the road and continued towards the centre, diverting briefly along the broad crescent which passed in front of the church. The building looked more like a bank or a civic institution, colonnaded for thirty metres on either side of its entrance. The whole of the high entrance was built of coloured glass set into a metal framework, a fragmentary design of bold colour with vaguely discernible figures and shapes woven into the otherwise abstract pattern. He slowed at a succession of noticeboards set into a manicured slope. Several gardeners knelt on the grass, their backs to the road.

Quinn continued driving until he regained the public road.

It was his intention to begin his work in the town at the Centre for Library and Archive Services, and to examine there whatever records the place still possessed of its more recent past. Some of these records would already have been retrieved by researchers at the Ministry, and copies would be waiting for him in his own secure files there.

He preferred to work like this – to visit the local offices and sources personally, to make himself known to the guardians of all these records – aware that whatever ripples this might cause would never be created by him sitting alone, unseen and unremarked back at his desk. And anything he wanted to know about what was happening at the church, he could learn from Anna Laing later. It would provide him with a valid reason for approaching her when he next saw her in the company of the others. *Valid*. He tried to think of a better word.

The Library and Archives building was signposted and he drew up at its entrance, activating the barrier which allowed him access to the rear of the building. Someone there had been forewarned of his arrival and of the likely records and accounts he might want to see. His authorization in the place was on an 'Every Assistance' basis. Often, someone was allocated to him for the duration of his investigation, and even the hitherto most confidential of documents were copied and coded and sent back to the Ministry in advance of his own return.

Entering the building, Quinn keyed in his codes and was led through a succession of rooms to a second-floor corridor marked 'Suites'. The woman guiding him showed him the door already bearing his own name and designation.

'We're all ready for you,' she told him. 'Two days now. Your preliminary requests are inside.' She held out her hand to him for the first time. 'I'm your searcher,' she said.

Quinn read the name on her lapel. 'M. Johnson.'

'"M"?'

She seemed uncertain what he was asking her.

'Your name,' he said.

'Mary.' She was clearly happier with the formality of initial and surname and Quinn made a note of this.

Most of what awaited him in the room – fiscal accounts mostly, from the town's various departments – had been ordered up by researchers in advance of his arrival. And if all of this material had already been waiting two days for him, then anyone with access to the Archive codes might by now have learned what those records contained. It would have served no purpose to raise this matter of security with M. Johnson, who would only have taken offence at his inferences. Besides, Quinn would remain dependent on her for whatever else he decided he needed to see in the days ahead. It was another reason why he chose to examine these otherwise freely available records at the outset of each audit, happy afterwards to leave this well-trodden common ground behind him at the earliest opportunity.

The woman opened the door and ushered him inside. A large table stood at the centre of the room. Several chairs stood precisely positioned around this, and three equally spaced lamps sat on its surface. There was no natural light in the room, and the gentle hiss of air conditioning or humidity-control filled its otherwise silent space.

'Anything you need . . .' M. Johnson said.

Quinn heard the gentle click of the door closing behind him.

Part II

10

Quinn next saw Greer five days later. On each of the previous three days there had been a message awaiting Quinn upon his return to the motel asking him to contact the man. On the third day the receptionist had reminded him of these unanswered calls – along with his as yet unreturned call to Stearn – adding that Greer himself had called in person to ascertain why Quinn was not responding. It was in these small, seemingly incidental or insignificant exchanges that Quinn gained the true measure of the man.

He finally contacted Greer's office and told one of his assistants that he was free to see Greer in half an hour's time. The woman had responded curtly by telling him that Greer himself would determine when the appointment was to be made, and for how long. Quinn hung up on her before she'd finished speaking. Greer had called him back a few minutes later, immediately apologizing for the misunderstanding.

Upon his arrival at the Administrative Centre, the woman he had spoken to left her desk in the atrium and came to Quinn in the entrance, where she too apologized to him. She then thanked him for the opportunity to be able to do this, making him even more uncomfortable at having put her in this position. The cameras high in the room were directed at the woman's back; her voice was raised. Unwilling to prolong this demeaning charade, he told her quickly that he accepted her apology and that there had indeed been a misunderstanding. He smiled at her, his eyes flicking to the cameras, hoping she understood his true intention.

The woman faltered in her short speech and smiled back at him. Quinn held out his hand to her and she took it.

'Mr Greer asked me to put you directly through to him the next time you called,' she said, the words more mouthed than spoken. She pointed to Greer's door, and as though on cue – or, as Quinn had already guessed, as though he had been watching the whole exchange on his monitors – the door opened and Greer came out to greet him. Quinn apologized again for the delay and the unanswered messages, and Greer behaved as though they were of no consequence whatsoever.

He called over Quinn's shoulder for drinks to be brought in to them, and then stood aside as Quinn entered his office.

For much of the previous four days Quinn had searched through the waiting financial records for whatever they might reveal to him. He had learned a great deal about the town itself, but very little concerning the financial footings of its imminent rebirth. Too soon, he supposed, for much of this to already be in place; and far too soon for it to have been entered into the public record. Even the advance warning of the audit had only been sent to Webb by the Ministry of Planning and Development two months prior to Quinn's arrival.

Sitting alone in the room in the Archive building he had felt himself sag at the sight of all the familiar agencies about to become involved, knowing from experience how drawn-out and convoluted the whole kaleidoscopic process was now about to become. He began to think that he had been sent too soon to make any valid assessment of the place; too soon to see how all its divergent financial commitments would be allocated and controlled; and certainly too soon to assess the fitness for purpose of the men and organizations now responsible for these burgeoning projects and budgets.

Equally frustrating to Quinn was the certain knowledge that Webb would not now postpone the audit – and thereby admit his own mistake in sending Quinn prematurely – and nor would he extend the time available to Quinn so that he might still be in the place as the development work was finally under way.

Greer indicated a seat and Quinn took it.

'You were at the new church,' Greer said.

'Meaning the guard told Stearn and Stearn told you?'

Greer dismissed the remark. 'You sound aggrieved. You spoke to the guard. You knew the site was secure. Have I offended you in some way by revealing that I know, that Stearn told me?' Greer held up his palms in an overdramatic and vaguely threatening gesture. And then he lowered his hands and smiled again just as quickly.

'Are the church architects or the builders expecting trouble with the site?' Quinn asked him.

Greer laughed. 'The security, you mean?'

Quinn had meant with the possible, but unlikely contamination of the ground.

'All our big building projects now employ somebody to keep an eye on things.'

'And by "somebody" you mean Stearn?'

Greer pursed his lips.

'Then I imagine he's going to be a very busy man in the near future,' Quinn said. 'Busy and wealthy.'

Greer shook his head at the suggestion. 'Already is. Both. Very. I even imagine—'

'Are you a major shareholder in his security concerns?' Quinn said. It was something he had learned on his first day of looking.

Greer remained unconcerned. 'Do you know of something that *prevents* me from being an investor in a perfectly legal and regulated business? Does it concern you, your work here? Do you imagine my connection to Stearn – my involvement with him – might have some bearing on your own purpose here?'

It was both a denial and a challenge, and Quinn understood this, though he was still uncertain why he had been met with this opening barrage of thinly veiled hostility following their otherwise perfunctory earlier meeting. He wondered if Greer now understood something of his own frustration, and the undeniable sense of impotence he already felt in the face of all that was about to happen there.

'I have nothing to hide,' Greer said emphatically. 'And certainly not from you. As you can imagine, a man in my position must always be seen to be above reproach and suspicion. High above. I doubt if anyone would consider my business enterprises and investments to be unworthy of me, undeserved.' It seemed a strange and unnecessary remark to make, but again Quinn let it pass.

They were interrupted briefly by the woman bringing

in their drinks, and Greer stopped talking while she was present.

'I have a simple policy,' he said when she had gone. 'If my investment goes in some way towards the betterment of this place and the people who live here, then I make it willingly, openly and gladly. *Investments*, Mr Quinn. There is always some risk.'

Betterment? Quinn almost laughed at the phrase. Next the man would be making a speech about philanthropy. He almost laughed too about the notion of risk Greer was suggesting. *He's above it all*, Quinn thought. His own tiny fiefdom suddenly given a view of its own vast, urgently needed and profitable future.

Greer poured the drinks and handed one to Quinn. 'Besides,' he went on, 'I imagine I'm a long way down your list of priorities.'

It was another probing remark and Quinn left it unanswered, further adding to the room's small tensions.

Neither man spoke for a moment. Then Greer said, 'You met Anna Laing, I understand. It's a dirty business.'

'Digging out foundations often is,' Quinn said.

'She's very good at what she does. Dependable. When she's finished, all the land will be certified clear and—'

'Ready for another of your investments?'

Greer smiled and Quinn regretted having said it.

'As it happens, yes,' Greer said. 'Mine and fifty others. You talk as though you want people to drown, families to be endlessly uprooted and shunted from one place to another. You talk as though you'd deprive them of the certainty, of the solid ground upon which to rebuild their lives, their futures.' Greer tilted his chin up as he spoke.

He's made this little speech before, Quinn thought, perhaps even to the men from Planning and Development who would have been there before him. He relaxed and started enjoying the act.

'You sound as though, through no fault of their own, people don't deserve the chance to re-establish themselves, to put down roots again, to make plans, to enjoy proper and fulfilling lives again. There will be people, families, coming here who haven't known true stability for the past decade. It's been a long time, Mr Quinn, a long time.' He meant since the first of the regular floods and policies of widespread, organized abandonment almost fifty years earlier.

'I understand that,' Quinn said. His own first development audit had taken place twenty years earlier with John Lucas as his partner. It was when the two of them had driven around another corner on another hillside and looked down at an estate of a dozen fifteen-storey tower blocks standing three feet deep in water, that he had understood – certainly as forcibly as he had ever been made to understand since – how only a relatively small degree of flooding changed everything – *everything* – about the lives of the people it affected. Three feet of water, four acres in extent, and over three thousand families – twelve thousand people – suddenly needing rehousing, struggling to stand upright again and rebuild their lives.

'Then you should embrace these things as fully and wholeheartedly as I do,' Greer said, distracting Quinn from this memory. He paused and then drove home his small advantage. 'I take it your own home is secure, safe from any current or envisaged encroachment?'

'It is,' Quinn said quickly. And even that felt like too much of a concession to the man.

'Good; I'm pleased,' Greer said.

Magnanimity, Quinn supposed, sipping his drink. Or at least that was how it would appear.

'The initial phase of development is for thirty thousand homes,' Greer said eventually. He spoke now as though he were the architect of the plan and not merely its chance and lucky recipient. 'Thirty thousand. Without investment, without vision, how do you imagine all that will come into being, to fruition? How?' He waved an arm in the air. 'I *know* you, Mr Quinn. I know your sort. I know what you see when you come here all the way from the capital. Here, a thousand places just like us. I know what you see and what you think. I know how you set your face against everything you don't want to see, and then how avidly you mark off the days to your departure back to so-called civilization.' He stopped abruptly, finally aware of having said too much.

Quinn wondered how they had come so unexpectedly on to this other path.

Greer wiped a hand across his face, shook his head and smiled. 'Forgive me,' he said. 'I forgot myself. Perhaps I thought I was at one of my council meetings. But what you must also realize, Mr Quinn, is that there has been considerable opposition to what is about to happen here, and considerable lobbying from all those other places equally anxious to be considered for development.' He drained his glass.

'And is the church being expanded to accommodate all these new arrivals?' Quinn said, allowing Greer to retreat to this safer ground.

'Church, mosque, synagogue – we'll have them all. Every denomination. It's what people want. Even people without any true or clear understanding of their own beliefs have come to crave these things, this guidance. Leisure centres, shopping malls, entertainment, everything. Thirty thousand homes, perhaps seventy or eighty thousand new inhabitants. And that's just the first phase.'

It was precisely because of this assured and overwhelming future that the past was now being so easily and readily sacrificed.

'Have Anna Laing and her team encountered anything serious?' Quinn said. 'Is the land-use certification guaranteed?'

'I'm sure you've asked her that already,' Greer said. 'I'll tell you what I tell everyone – there *are* no insurmountable problems to *be* encountered. They knew from the outset what they'd find out there. Their smoke might be a problem occasionally, but that's all.'

'Then we have a lot in common, she and I,' Quinn said.

And Greer, unable to resist, said quickly, 'You do indeed.'

Having followed so many diversions in the few minutes they had been together, Quinn began to wonder why Greer had wanted to see him in the first place.

Greer refilled their glasses. 'Has your work in our archives proved satisfactory, helpful? I spoke with your Mr Webb and I'm afraid I got the impression he was less than convinced – certainly less convinced than perhaps you yourself might be – that there was anything of real significance to be found there.'

It was a lie. Whatever his other failings, Webb would have revealed nothing about the audit to Greer, and certainly nothing that might undermine or compromise Quinn's own position.

'What did he say exactly?' Quinn said.

'No – it was just the impression I got. Tone of voice, that sort of thing, wording.'

And nor would Webb have spoken directly to Greer. Not spoken. Various lesser codes and confirmations would have been exchanged, perhaps commented upon, but that was all. Perhaps another brief and perfunctory greeting. But nothing more. Nothing that Greer might now use to his own advantage while the audit was in progress.

'I see,' Quinn said, content to leave the lie only partially exposed. And then, 'And what about the men on the hill?'

'Men on the hill? What men? What are you talking about?'

'The drain diggers. The men I encountered diverting the water off the hillside when I arrived.'

Greer laughed. 'Them? What about them? They're digging a drain, a culvert, that's all. You imagine it has anything to do with everything else that's about to happen here? It's a drain, Mr Quinn, that's all. A drain on a hillside. I'm surprised you even remembered them. Who knows – perhaps they've already dug their drain and been sent elsewhere. I believe Anna Laing employs local men on her own sites. Perhaps they've gone to work for her.' He laughed again at the thought of the men and the inconsequentiality of their work. 'You surprise me, Mr Quinn, you really do. Everything else you have to concern you, and you worry about things like that.'

Quinn looked at his watch.

'Are you leaving?'

'Unless there was something else you wanted of me.' *You contacted me, remember?*

Greer thought about this and then shook his head. 'No, nothing. Although . . .' His hesitation was contrived. 'Although I did hope you might be persuaded to perhaps make your time here a little more enjoyable. I was hoping – my wife was hoping – that you might accept an invitation to our home, that we might set aside any professional considerations, and that you would feel able to accept the invitation in the spirit in which it was extended to you.' Even Greer seemed confused by this convoluted remark.

'Against directive,' Quinn said. It wasn't.

'Oh. I imagined there might be some leeway, that you might – I don't know – initiative?'

'Sorry,' Quinn said.

'A matter of perceived compromise, I suppose.'

Quinn said nothing. He put his glass on the table, letting it fall the final inch on to the highly polished surface.

'I see,' Greer said, looking up as Quinn rose from his seat.

11

Quinn circled the town towards its northern edge and then left the road to continue even further in that direction. He drove for several miles and then drew up at the gated entrance to an estate. He had imagined his destination to be a farmhouse: a courtyard, perhaps, barns, empty cattle sheds, outbuildings, scattered disused machinery and barking dogs. But instead there was a mesh fence and hoardings. More giant boards with their visions of the coming future. He wondered who would see these, so far from the centre and on the largely empty road. They advertised country living in woodlands and pastures, overlooking lakes surrounded by lodges and small jetties; yachts with brilliantly white sails on brilliantly blue water; distant mountains considerably more mountain-shaped and appealing than the low surrounding hills which lay beyond the boards.

A swathe of long-abandoned and bladeless wind turbines stood like a coppice of bleached trunks, no doubt abandoned the day the Government withdrew its subsidy after decades of ever-hopeful and endlessly disappointing trials. Several of the stems were leaning, and some of them had already fallen completely.

Quinn left the car and walked along the high fence. An all-terrain drew up in the far distance and slowly followed a parallel track. Quinn sought out the roadside marker to ensure he had come to the right place.

He raised his arm to the driver of the all-terrain and the vehicle stopped, still too distant for Quinn to make out the writing on its door or how many people it might contain.

After a few minutes of waiting, the vehicle came towards him across the open ground. Approaching the locked gates, it drew up on a low embankment beside the newly built road there. It stopped dramatically, spraying water and gravel to within a few metres of where Quinn stood.

An overweight man carrying a shotgun climbed down from the cab, already breathless at even that small exertion.

He stood by his open door and studied Quinn, shielding his eyes. He wore dark glasses and a long coat which hung to his shins. He also wore heavy gauntlets which, Quinn realized, would make it impossible for him to hold his finger on the gun's trigger.

Quinn moved closer to the man and called out his own name.

'So?' the man shouted back. He raised the gun, though with no intention of firing it.

Quinn took out his identification and held it to the mesh.

The man laughed. 'What's that supposed to mean? You could show me fifty and each would be as pointless as the last.'

'Are you Owen?' Quinn said, his voice lower.

The man stopped at hearing this. He lowered and then raised the gun again.

'Put it down,' Quinn said, moving closer to the gate. 'If I shout an official caution we'll both get tied up in so much box-ticking that we'll wish we'd never met.' He tried to sound unconcerned, as though all this were commonplace to him. He tried to remember if anyone had approached him with a weapon before. He began to imagine the story he would tell to John Lucas.

The man called Owen lowered the gun and came towards him. After several paces he returned to his vehicle and threw the weapon inside.

'*Are* you Owen?' Quinn repeated.

'I am. You from Stearn? Is this another of his—'

'I'm not from Stearn,' Quinn said. He pushed his identification through the wire and the man took and examined it.

'No reading glasses,' Owen said. He handed the card back.

'Can I come in?' Quinn asked him.

Owen unlocked the gate and swung it open. 'Pull your car inside,' he said, and Quinn did this. Owen then secured the gate and motioned towards a distant building. 'I live over there.'

They drove to Owen's dilapidated home and Owen led Quinn inside.

It looked to Quinn as though the place might have been hurriedly abandoned a decade earlier. Every space was filled with clutter – clothes, cardboard boxes, unwashed dishes, a collection of cheap ornaments and crockery that might have once meant something to someone. Cans of food and empty bottles lined most surfaces. A sheet of hardboard nailed over the room's only window cut out most of the day's dim natural light.

'I won't ask you to excuse the place,' Owen said. He filled a kettle and put it on the stove, stoking the fire inside and then throwing in logs from a nearby mound. Another small fire burned in a grate at the far side of the room, spilling coke and ashes on to a broad hearth. The whole place looked to Quinn like a re-created museum setting from another age.

'Not too much like the posters, eh?' Owen said, and then laughed and coughed simultaneously. 'Tell me why you're here. I mean *here*.'

'I'm carrying out an audit in advance of everything that's about to happen,' Quinn said. He'd seen plans for the old farm – now estate – amid everything else he'd examined the previous day and had been intrigued by them, especially as they were one of the few tangible signs he had so far come across that anything whatsoever was either already under way or imminent in the world outside.

'Is that what it is,' Owen said dismissively. '"About to happen"? You make it sound as though there was still some uncertainty, a few minor details not quite ironed out yet.'

'It's why I'm here,' Quinn said.

'No it isn't,' Owen said immediately. He searched the floor around him, and for a moment Quinn thought the man was going to spit there.

'It's why—'

'You're here because Greer and Stearn want your nice, neat and all-empowering Ministry stamp of approval on everything. Tell me – how many more of these things have you done?'

'Twenty,' Quinn said. 'Thirty.'

'And how many have you actually stopped from going ahead? No – how many have you even properly sorted out *before* they continued on their own sweet way steamrollering over everyone?'

Quinn knew what the man was asking him – the true cause of his anger – and so he remained silent.

Owen stood without speaking for a moment and then apologized for his outburst.

'If you have any genuine complaint or grievance . . .' Quinn said.

'"Complaint"? "Grievance"?' Owen smiled at the words. 'They're like air and water to me these days.'

The man gave him a mug of tea and Quinn surreptitiously turned away the worst of its chipped rim before drinking from it.

'You're on a fool's errand, you do know that, I suppose,' Owen said, sitting opposite him, close to the stove.

'It won't be the first time.'

'But it's still not something you're going to admit to?'

Quinn shook his head.

'No milk,' Owen said, pulling a face at his own drink. 'There's probably some sugar.' He looked at the disarray around them. 'Somewhere.' He closed his eyes for a moment, screwing them tight. 'Last Ministry man we had up here – long after all the beasts had gone, this was – said he was here to investigate the unlicensed labour. There were hundreds of them up here, thousands. You know what it was like. All immigrants. Men, women, kids. Following the work. Cash in hand, usually daily. "OK, boss, OK, everything OK."' He smiled at the memory. 'This place would have died ten years sooner than it did if they hadn't turned up. They even came for the last of the culls when nobody else was prepared to do the work. No compensation, see? Not for the last few big outbreaks. Cost us more to kill and bury or burn an animal than it was ever likely to be worth.'

'Where did they all go?' Quinn asked him. 'The workers.'

Owen shrugged. 'I daresay some of them will be back when all the building work starts. Versatile, see? Ready to turn their hand to anything. Not like our lot.'

Not like you, Quinn thought.

And as though reading this thought, Owen said. 'And definitely not like me. If I'd turned *my* hand to something else then I wouldn't be up to my knees in all this now. I honestly couldn't say where they all went when the breeders lost their licences to even keep stock. We could never pronounce their real names. Most of them took on names we could get to grips with, or the names on the permits they could get hold of.' He paused. 'None of it matters now, I don't suppose. Even then it never seemed to be of any real consequence, especially towards the end. Not when all *I* needed here was just a place to sit and brood and wonder how it had all just slipped away from me. It's a long time, eight years.'

There was more self-reproach than pity in the remark, and Quinn understood this.

Owen motioned for Quinn to pull his own chair closer to the open door of the stove.

'Do you still own this place?' Quinn asked him, shuffling forward.

'The Development Corporation bought me out two years ago. The land had been on the market for six years. They gave me a fifth of what I was asking.'

'Why did you think I was from Stearn?'

Owen hesitated before answering. 'Because Stearn came

and fenced everything in and then put me on his payroll to watch over everything until the work started.'

'And because Stearn is a member of the Development Corporation?'

'And that. You'd be hard-pressed to find anyone with any so-called vested interest in the place who wasn't. Stearn even had the gall to tell me that it was where I should put *my* money.'

'Will they build what's on the posters?'

Owen laughed. 'Apparently, this is going to be part of the *executive* end of things. Plus – and I only discovered this *after* I'd accepted their offer – these hills are where they're going to put up most of the new masts. Good reception, see? According to Stearn, they'll rent on to the communication companies and earn ten times more in rentals for the masts in a year than me or my father ever made from the sheep or the cattle in two lifetimes.'

'This was a sheep farm?' Quinn said.

'Before the cows. Before the turbines. Everything up here was. It's how my father's grandfather started the place. Four generations. And now this. On my watch. There was never any money in sheep, not once *their* subsidies went. And so we changed. We took up pigs, and then they went. We tried cattle, beet and then bio fuels – don't ask – and they all went the same way. All subsidy-dependent, see? We played it safe with poultry for a few years – half a million birds we had contracts for at one time, half a million – but then that went the way of everything else with all the viruses no one ever managed to keep up with. Compensation for the cattle ended after the third blue-tongue outbreak. After that we were on our own. Nine out of ten farmers in this part of the world went out of business within two years. The last cull finished off the survivors.'

'Including yourself?'

Owen nodded once. 'There was talk of the Forestry people taking over everything, but they did tests and found the soil too sour. Too much expense involved in getting everything sorted. My father and mother died while all that was under way. I suppose you could say I just lost heart after that.'

'And so you stayed here until the Development Corporation made its offer?' The remark seemed a cruel condemnation of the man.

'Something like that. Where else was I supposed to go? At the start I tried to deal with all the individual developers myself, but the Corporation soon had everything stitched up tight. Everything went through them, still does. It seemed like a godsend at the time when the place was ear-marked for development.'

Quinn guessed he would have heard identical tales – of lives shaken loose of their moorings and cast adrift – from a hundred others. His searcher in the record office had seen him looking at the plans of the place and had told him of the countless other applications for outline development recently deposited. She asked him if he wanted to see these too and he had declined. She pulled a face on seeing the plans in front of him. 'Owen?' she said. '*Him?*' And it had been this simple, uncontainable remark that had led Quinn to the man.

'It's what killed my parents,' Owen said. 'Knowing that everything had finally slipped from their grasp after so long in the going. The cows they're digging up and burning now – some of those are ours. Six hundred head. All gone in twelve hours. We lost three thousand pigs a day during the last two culls. The pig business never recovered from the transport restrictions. Clean and healthy on the farm and in their feed lots, but when all movement was finally stopped . . .' He spoke now like a man fighting off an unstoppable landslide.

'Does Stearn check on you regularly?' Quinn asked him.

'Not as often as he'd like to. I avoid him, avoid them all as far as possible. Besides, check on what? All they're interested in now is the empty land and the fortune they're going to make from it. They've seen what's happened everywhere else – the migrations, all the homeless, all the illegal seizures and squatting and everything *that* entails. They know how vulnerable – exposed – they are in an isolated place like this. It's why Stearn put his fence up so fast. One day I was signing on the dotted line, the next I was told to dig out my gun and fill in fuel claims. I can only get that through Stearn now.'

'Protecting his own investment,' Quinn said.

'And charging the Corporation for the privilege.'

'Including your wages?'

'Such as they are. So you can well imagine how that makes *me* feel. Judas had nothing on me, Mr . . .' He'd forgotten Quinn's name.

'Quinn,' Quinn said.

'Mr Quinn. Sorry. You can imagine what *I* have to live with. Lucky I've still got this little palace to call a home. Rent-free, according to Stearn.' He looked around him as he spoke.

'Will he allow you to stay if – '

'He'll have me out at seventy-two hours' notice. It's all in my contract. And the minute that happens, the bulldozers will already be driving up to my door. You've seen the hoardings – all those lakeside lodges, meadows and pine forests; silver birches and primroses for the close-ups. Though Christ knows how they're going to get any of those to grow if the Forestry people gave the place up as a bad job.' There was more than common history now in everything Owen said; there was that geography and geology of family, too.

'Did – do – you have a family of your own?' Quinn asked him. A photograph of a woman and three young children looked down at them from the crowded mantel.

Owen glanced at it. 'She left me. Took everything that mattered. Said she saw it all coming. Last I heard, she was still in Spain. With my sons. She said the wet here was in her bones. Born and raised in the town, and then one day she'd just had enough, too much of everything. She was like the rest of them – sun, sun, sun, the answer to everything. I went once, long time ago, thinking I might even talk her into coming back with me. I was there for a fortnight and I saw her for about ten minutes. She wouldn't let me near the boys. She'd got a job, somewhere to live. She was brown, different colour hair, she'd lost weight, found herself another man, another Brit. It's like she was living the life of a completely different woman. She laughed at me and told me I never saw anything coming.' He paused and looked again at the photograph. 'I suppose she got that much right.' He turned back to Quinn. 'She only took up with the man so that she could stay there. He was already living there, had permits, everything. She even lied about my sons and told the Spanish authorities that the father was the man she was living with. I shouted a bit louder than usual about that part. You can see where it got me.'

'And so you came back here?'

'Like I said – where else was there?' He made it sound like the greatest defeat of his life. 'So,' he said loudly, slapping his palms on to his knees, 'whatever else it was you came up here hoping to find, I doubt it was this pitiful, stinking excuse for a life.'

There was nothing Quinn could say to this.

'We even had to get rid of the dogs and cats,' Owen said.

'They went with the last of the poultry. Possible carriers, see? Anything that might harbour or spread. That was what they marked on the cull certificates. Harbour and Spread precautions. You'd be surprised what they came to include by the end. Even my mother's two canaries in their cage in the kitchen.'

'It was a lot to lose,' Quinn said.

'I daresay Stearn will find a few more things for me.'

Quinn rose from his seat by the stove. He looked outside and saw again that the early winter night was already falling.

'I showed them where all the animals were buried,' Owen said. 'Over at the exhumations. They're only interested in the official sites, but there are plenty of others. No one could dispose of all those animals using only the official pits. If they want to make that land clean again, then they've got a lot more to do than they think.'

Quinn wondered if Anna Laing had been alerted to this. Another reason for talking to her when they next met. It had been three days.

'Did they listen to you?' he asked Owen.

'They're like everybody else – they make all the right noises, that's all. It's all anyone does these days. Press one to be patronized, press two to be ignored, press three to find yourself listening to your own pointless arguments going round and round inside your head.' He stopped abruptly and looked up at Quinn. 'So, like I said, whatever it was you expected to find up here . . .'

'It was good meeting you,' Quinn said, and because Owen heard the sincerity in the remark, he nodded once and said nothing.

He came to the door with Quinn. A line of white arc lights

marked the road and the fence. 'I'll take you to your car,' he said.

It was raining again, cold and sleety, and so Quinn accepted the offer and then sat with the gun between his knees as they drove.

12

Later, he waited in the bar for Anna Laing to appear. The place was almost empty at nine: a few travellers and businessmen, no families; men, mostly, sitting with their laptops talking to distant children – blurred images and voices made sharp by longing and regret.

It was almost ten before the convoy of vans and lorries appeared in the car park and went through their usual routine of queuing and parking according to their preordained routine. Anna had already explained to Quinn why they did this – something to do with the order in which they were required at the site the next day – but it had still made little sense to him. He had seen her twice since their initial encounter, but each time she had been surrounded by others and had been unable to talk to him for more than a few seconds.

On this occasion, however, she came into the bar alone while the stream of others passed through the lobby to the lifts and stairs. Some of the men still wore parts of their protective suits, and most of them carried at least one case of equipment.

Anna went to the bar and rapped for the barman, who appeared and told her angrily that he was coming anyway and that if she rapped again he would be within his rights to refuse to serve her. This response both surprised and angered her, and Quinn watched as she took a step away from the man, closed her eyes for a moment, and then returned to him smiling. She apologized and told him what she wanted. Unable to gauge either her tone or the sincerity of her apology, the man said, 'Yes, well,' and poured her a drink.

As he did this, she turned to look around the near-empty room and saw Quinn sitting by the window. She raised her hand to him and made a drinking motion, turning back to the barman and adding to her order.

She came to Quinn with the glasses. She sat opposite him, her back to the open door and the lobby beyond, and rubbed her face. A low lattice screen interwoven with plastic ivy screened them from the men still outside. She looked exhausted.

She half drained her glass and then slid it to one side.

'Bad day?' Quinn said.

'You mean it shows?' She finished her drink.

'I meant because you were so late back,' Quinn said. 'I assumed—'

'Then you probably assumed right,' she said angrily, immediately signalling her apology to him. 'Sorry, sorry.' She put her hand on his and held it for a moment. Quinn flexed his fingers beneath hers and then turned his palm until they were holding hands. He tensed against her drawing away from him, either surprised or further annoyed by the gesture. But instead she held his hand tightly for a moment. He felt her tremble and increased his own grip on her fingers.

After a full minute she looked up at him and smiled. 'Thanks for that.' She drew her hand away slowly and Quinn knew not to try and prevent her. She brushed the hair from her eyes and then put her hand back on the table close to his.

Quinn raised and then lowered his fingers, felt their heat, the returning blood after the pressure of her grip.

He suggested another drink and she looked at his empty glass and nodded. He signalled to the barman, who considered the gesture and then nodded back to him.

'He probably wants you to crawl over there on your hands and knees and ask him politely,' Anna said, her voice low.

Quinn had encountered the man often enough before. The bar was his own small domain, and in the absence of any of the motel's more senior staff, he made sure that everyone who needed him understood precisely how much they needed him.

The man brought their drinks and Quinn gave him his card, which he slid through his palm-pad and handed back in a single deft motion.

'I'm sorry,' Anna said, looking directly up at the man. 'For earlier.'

'Yes, well . . . apology accepted. Enjoy.'

'"Enjoy"' she mouthed as he returned to the bar.

'Are you going to tell me?' Quinn said after a minute of silence. 'Before everyone else arrives.'

'Tell you what?'

He waited.

'Ground toxicity levels,' she said simply. 'All over the place. The closer we get to our designated perimeter, the higher they are. Nothing whatsoever on the original environmental audit. I'm beginning to wonder if they didn't just make the whole thing up.'

'It has been known. Desperate measures for desperate times and all that.'

'We've had unprotected bodies all over the wider area before we started measuring the levels. Try telling *them* about desperate measures.'

'Sorry. And the opposite should be true – the perimeter levels?'

'It would be a better alternative.'

'Does it happen often? These days, I mean.'

She smiled. 'All the time. It's getting to be a regular occurrence.'

'What does it mean? That the original site was larger than you were led to believe? More contaminated?'

'And probably that it contains considerably *more* than we were led to believe.'

'Which is also an increasingly common occurrence?'

'We call it our "If Still In Doubt, Consult Your Doctor" clause. It's there at the bottom of every Government contract that comes our way.'

'Can you deal with it?'

She shrugged. 'We need to analyse the results of the metering and try to find out exactly what we're dealing with.'

'Is it likely to be beyond your capabilities?'

She looked up at the word. 'Why, kind sir. No – nothing is beyond my *capabilities.* It just means that when our time and money finally run out, I'll be asked to sign off on a job only half done. I'll call my superiors later and *they*'ll tell me to stick to why we're here – the anthrax.'

'In the hope that whatever else might be there will all somehow just go away?'

'Either that or turn out to be of considerably less importance than the anthrax.'

'Unimportant enough to ignore?'

She shrugged again. 'I'm probably angrier now about the fact that it's happened yet again and that I let some of my team wander around unprotected.' She emptied her second glass.

Quinn told her about his encounter with Owen and everything the man had told him about the unofficial burial pits.

'Every farmer in the country will tell you the same,' she said, unconcerned. 'Five years ago, all we ever did was look for unlicensed sites – usually either in advance of development or the rising water.'

'To clear them?'

'To mark where they were and then hope that another million or so years of being undisturbed would do our work for us.'

'And will it?'

'Possibly. If things stay put. The rising water table's still a bit of an unknown factor even after all this time. Who knows where water rising or sinking through heavily contaminated strata is going to end up. Not me. Not you. And certainly not the people a hundred miles away who might be depending on that water. Towards the end, when the final no-exception culls were implemented, and long after all the compensation had evaporated, digging a burial pit – licensed or otherwise – was like leaving out an empty skip overnight. Illicit haulage contractors and dishonest disposal workers made small fortunes. The farmers dumped everything – sick and healthy animals alike, dead and alive, notifiably diseased and otherwise. *That*'s what we're finding up on that hill.

Presumably you've seen the colourful hoardings, so you know what's in store for the place.'

Quinn nodded. 'What will you do?'

'In the time left to us?' She shrugged. 'Dig, burn, cap, clear.' She said it like a mantra. 'See how straightforward it all becomes? And who knows – perhaps whatever's down there *will* behave itself and stay exactly where it is for the next ten thousand years and then turn into somebody else's problem.'

'Fifty years would give you a head start,' Quinn said, and she laughed. He touched her hand again and she responded to him.

'Did your farmer friend tell you any more precisely where all the local unlicensed pits might be?'

'I could ask him,' Quinn suggested. 'What would you do with the information?'

She considered this. 'Get myself stuck up here for those fifty years while they were all located and cleared?' She pretended to shiver at the prospect.

Several others came into the bar, saw the two of them together and sat elsewhere.

'They don't seem too bothered,' Quinn said to her.

'They're not. Regardless of whatever God-forsaken hole *I* might get sent to next, they're all going home for a few weeks. Christmas, remember?'

The date was less than a month away.

'And your own family?' Quinn ventured, trying unsuccessfully not to appear concerned by what she might be about to reveal to him.

'Look around you,' she said, and Quinn didn't understand her. 'Imagine this – same motel, different place, lots of tinsel, flashing lights and muted carols – that'll be my Christmas.'

'I didn't mean—'

'I know,' she said quickly. She held up her ringed finger. 'We separated four, almost five years ago. My husband worked for the same people. He's a vet. He was headhunted by the Americans at the start of their selective breeding programme. He went in the first, supposedly temporary instance to help supervise the joint quarantine programme.'

'And he stayed?'

'And he stayed. It tends to happen when someone offers you six times your salary.'

'And you – '

'And I couldn't compete with that. They offered him everything. Everything he once thought he'd be offered here. He was an expert in the development of bovine vaccinations in a country that no longer had any cattle. They, on the other hand, the Americans, slaughtered and then inoculated and then set up their own regulated breeding programmes forty years sooner than anyone else saw the need to attempt it. And now everything they produce, they have a clamouring market for. When the Far East production collapsed, prices quadrupled overnight. Remember?' All of which led her further from her lost husband and everything else she was avoiding telling Quinn. 'Besides . . .' she said eventually, and he heard the whole of that unspoken history.

'Now you,' she said after a further few seconds of silence, filled only with the raised voices and laughter of the others in the room.

'Not much to tell,' Quinn began.

'I said "Now you",' she said.

'My wife died,' he said flatly.

'Oh, God, I'm sorry. Tell me to mind my own business.'

'In a car accident. A crash. Traffic incident. Five years ago. My wife and my daughter. Eve – Evie. My wife was called

Susan.' As though the passing of those two thousand days had made even the slightest difference to anything except the numbness he still occasionally felt, and which, increasingly, the harder he looked at the next two thousand days ahead of him yet to be endured, he found himself encouraging.

Anna put her hand back on to his and held it there, stroking the backs of his fingers with her thumb as though she were calming an upset child.

'Me and my big mouth,' she said when he eventually looked up at her.

'You weren't to know,' he said, wishing everything hadn't suddenly become so careful and cautious between them.

'No, but I could still employ a little tact every now and then.'

Quinn felt the watching eyes of the men and women across the room. And perhaps Anna sensed them too, for she made her stroking motion across his hand more evident.

A larger party than usual entered the bar, several of whom called to her.

'They'll want you to join them,' Quinn said.

'Not after today. They think I already knew all there was to know about what we "found". Our fuel allocation has been increased. It doesn't usually happen.'

'Everyone knows everything in this place,' Quinn said absently. He rubbed his thumb and forefinger together. 'Everything's connected. The country ran out of options and the luxury of choice a long time ago.'

'That's the same thing – more or less – that my waving-goodbye husband told me,' Anna said. 'That where he was – the States – he still had options, choice, *real* choice – that he was sick and tired of endorsing someone else's wrong or greedy decisions.'

Which was what he had then accused her of doing?

'Don't even think it,' she said to him.

'Why?' Quinn said. 'Because *I*'ve still got those honest and meaningful choices to make?'

'Perhaps not, but perhaps *you* still get to see what might happen if you didn't do what you did.' It was an imprecise suggestion and she signalled this with a flick of her hand.

'And perhaps I'd be happy to half-believe you and then half-convince myself that you were right – that what I did still—' He stopped abruptly and laughed. 'I was going to say still made a difference. Remember that? Making a Difference? The age of self-belief, free will and self-determination?'

She looked at her watch. 'I should go and make some calls, send off today's stats. People will be waiting.' She looked around her.

'Will you be told what to do?' Quinn asked her.

'They'll tell me exactly what I expect them to tell me. I daresay the word "initiative" will get thrown into the conversation a few times to make me feel a bit better about it all. They'll all do their level best sitting in their clean and tidy offices *not* to make it sound like another millstone round my neck. Relax; they hear this kind of bad news from somewhere or other every day. Last month it was the Severn Corridor and South Wales valleys. After which, I'll get a short, friendly lecture on "priorities". Perhaps they'll even send someone up to see me to ensure there are no misunderstandings. Bigger bonuses at Christmas. Perhaps I'll buy another yacht or Caribbean island. Are there many left?'

Quinn knew she was getting ready to leave him, and when she finally rose from her seat, he stood up with her.

'It was good to be able to talk to you,' she said awkwardly, knowing that everything she now said to him would be overheard by others.

'You, too,' Quinn said, similarly regretting this sudden and clumsy formality.

She looked around her as though searching for a coat or a laptop.

'Good luck,' Quinn said to her.

'Luck? Oh, right. Yes.'

He watched her go, wanting to follow her, but kept in his seat by all those half-watching others. He felt suddenly and briefly drunk, but knew this was impossible. He waited where he sat for a further twenty minutes before he too left the room.

13

'Auditor.'

Quinn shielded his eyes against the low sun and searched for whoever had called to him. The man called again, and Quinn turned to the side of the building against which he was parked. He had been on his way to the Administrative Accounts building when he had stopped to take a call.

A further shout and Quinn finally recognized Stearn. The man was coming towards him where he sat, followed by two of his employees. The men walked a few paces behind Stearn, holding their own conversation. Approaching Quinn's car, Stearn held up his hand and the two men fell silent.

'Shall we go back?' one of them asked him.

Stearn shook his head without turning. 'You'll wait where you are until I tell you otherwise.'

Stearn then came forward alone and leaned over Quinn, his hands resting on the roof of his car. He wore an earpiece and microphone.

'Off,' Stearn said as he looked inside the car, at the files on the back seat and the open laptop beside Quinn. The 'off' was an instruction to his earpiece.

Quinn, knowing that the laptop revealed nothing Stearn might be able to decipher and understand, made no attempt to close it. A tiny red light flashed on Stearn's ear lobe like a jewel catching the sun.

'Latest model,' Stearn said. 'Nothing but the best at Stearn Security.'

Quinn remained silent.

'I have to ask you why you're parked here. This is a restricted zone, private property.'

Quinn looked at the open space around him. Another patch of emptiness and loss waiting to be turned into something new.

'And presumably made secure by Stearn Security for the Development Corporation.'

'Got it in one,' Stearn said. He motioned to the insignia mounted high on the side of a nearby building. 'I don't know what level of security you put up with where you come from, Mr Quinn, but here we like to see things done properly. You might like to say we take our security seriously here.' Everything he said continued to sound like a slogan.

Quinn finally closed the laptop.

'Can we help you?' Stearn said. 'Perhaps you're lost.'

'Not really,' Quinn said. 'Hard to get lost in such a small and well-ordered place as this.'

'Small?' Stearn sounded as though he had been personally

insulted by the remark, then quickly regained his composure. 'No – you're right. It is small. Small enough – '

'For everybody to know everybody else's business?' Quinn said.

Stearn stepped back from the car and looked around him.

'Are you going to ask me to leave?' Quinn said. '*Am* I trespassing?'

'That would be for a judge to decide.'

'Seriously?' Quinn said.

Stearn shook his head. 'Fixed penalty. Awarded by me, collected by me.' Then he grinned and looked back at the two guards. 'Oh, sorry, you're above all that, aren't you?'

'You sound disappointed,' Quinn said.

One of the guards said something to the other which caused both men to laugh.

'I'm training them,' Stearn said disparagingly, beckoning the two men closer. 'You'll know one of them.'

Quinn looked harder at the men, recognizing the guard who had kept him away from the site at the rear of the church. 'The church,' he said, confirming that what had happened, been said or filmed there had already been fully related to Stearn.

'"Church"?' Stearn said, smiling. 'Oh, I think they're going to call it something a lot grander than that when they finally get round to their big reopening. Cathedral at the very least, the last I heard. Minster, perhaps.'

'A lot of new worshippers on their way, presumably,' Quinn said.

'Is that what you'd call them – worshippers?'

One of the guards turned away from them and started talking into his own microphone, making a small performance of turning one way and then another in an effort to improve the reception, and then raising his voice when this remained poor.

Stearn frowned at everything he heard and saw.

'Nothing but the best,' Quinn said.

Stearn shouted to the man to lower his voice, not to let everyone within a mile's radius in on their business.

'It's Pollard,' the man shouted back to Stearn. 'He's trying to contact you. He wants to talk to you.'

'Take a message,' Stearn said.

'I already said that. He called me an employee. He wants you.'

'Perhaps you should answer,' Quinn said, his face straight, goading Stearn even further.

'What, just because *he* says so?' He attracted the guard's attention and then drew a finger across his throat. The guard immediately switched off his receiver.

'Another satisfied customer?' Quinn said.

'He gets what he needs. You might say the Reverend Pollard has ideas above his station.'

'Reverend?'

'Reverend, priest, pastor, whatever he calls himself. You might also say that my contract there, on the church site, is more of a PR exercise than anything else.'

However dismissive and unconcerned Stearn now affected to be, Quinn guessed that he would return Pollard's call as soon as he had driven away.

'You're not a believer yourself?' Quinn said to him.

'My wife,' Stearn said, unable to conceal his true feelings. 'All her family. Every Sunday. I attend with her, but I can't pretend it's the biggest thrill of the week.'

Meaning it might have been for her? And meaning, perhaps, that she had persuaded him to offer a cut-price rate for security at the church site, which was why Stearn now employed his trainees there?

'I called you,' Stearn said, interrupting Quinn's thoughts and reminding him of the calls he had not yet returned.

'I know. What do you want?'

Stearn shrugged. 'Just to let you know that your codes were registered, that your clearances had been designated and that your trackers were operative through our own relays.'

It was more usual for Quinn to be notified of all this only when something *wasn't* available to him or functioning properly. It had been common practice for the past twenty years for security registration to be undertaken by local firms under licence from the National Police Authority. Most low and intermediate clearances were undertaken by these firms with the Government's blessing. Stearn's remark made Quinn wonder whether or not the National Police still functioned in the town or if, as in many places since the flooding and infrastructure breakdowns, they were only now a notional umbrella under which firms like Stearn's wielded the true power. There were many sparsely populated places which had no national cover whatsoever, and which were now wholly dependent on private contractors for what little enforcement and security they still received.

'So you'll know where I am,' Quinn said. 'I feel safer already.'

'You think I've got nothing better to do than sit watching you drive around all day? That's what I employ these idiots for.'

Quinn resisted the urge to tell him that he seemed well enough appraised of his movements so far.

'I employ three hundred people here,' Stearn said. 'Three hundred. That makes me the biggest employer after Greer. And everything *he* pays out he gets directly from the Exchequer.'

Quinn waited for him to go on – perhaps to reveal more than his envy of Greer; more than his disdain for the man's unearned and almost accidental status and power in the place.

But instead Stearn lowered his voice and said, 'I suppose you and Greer will be good friends by now.'

'Not really,' Quinn said. 'However, Greer – as Chief Executive – and I will need to meet on a regular basis. All part of the procedure.'

'I don't doubt it,' Stearn said.

'Is this a warning?' Quinn said bluntly. 'Are you trying to tell me something about the man? Is there something I need to know?'

'Such as?' And again Stearn took several steps back from the car, aware of perhaps having said too much.

'Because if there is – '

'There's nothing,' Stearn insisted.

But by then Quinn understood that the man's deliberately vague and non-committal remarks had served his purpose. In addition to which, they had also revealed to Quinn a great deal more about the relationship between the two men. He remembered their argument on the day of his arrival.

'I suppose he's had a few things to say about me,' Stearn said, waiting.

'Such as?' Quinn said. 'Besides, I think you overestimate my powers, my authority here.' No one would know better than Stearn the true nature and precise extent of that authority.

Whatever Stearn had hoped to achieve by approaching him like this – and Quinn was convinced that the encounter was not as coincidental as Stearn had tried to suggest – he had learned little.

Stearn slapped his palms on the roof of Quinn's car and said, 'Right, I'll leave you to it, Mr Quinn.'

'"Auditor" works,' Quinn said, reminding Stearn of his original provocation.

'I can't be expected to remember everybody's name,' Stearn said, making no attempt to sound convincing.

'Of course you can't.'

Stearn walked back to the two guards, passed them without speaking and then continued to the building from which all three of them had appeared.

The guard Quinn recognized came to him.

'You pissed him off,' he said, almost admiringly.

'It wasn't my intention,' Quinn said.

'Nearly as pissed off as Pollard sounded when Stearn didn't ask him how high he was expected to jump.'

'Perhaps it was important business?' Quinn said.

'What, him? Nah. Everything's urgent where he's concerned. First thing he'll have done when Stearn didn't mop his brow was call Stearn's wife and tell *her* how unhappy he was. She's as much into all this Second Coming crap as he is.'

'Second Coming?'

'Not what it sounds. It's just how Pollard's going round referring to the new church.'

'It sounds a little over the top for what's essentially a re-opening,' Quinn said.

'I know. The man's a fucking laughing stock. If you ask me – ' His earpiece crackled and he stood upright and held a finger to it. He turned and looked up at the camera high on the wall.

Stearn, Quinn guessed.

'I've got to go,' the man said, and he ran with the other guard to the same building into which Stearn had already disappeared.

14

At midday, Quinn left the accounts he'd been examining and walked the short distance through the town centre to the offices of the local newspaper. The editor had contacted him upon his arrival and then left a repeat message daily at the motel. The same company owned the local newspaper, television and radio stations.

He arrived at the building and pushed at its locked door. People inside turned to glance at him, but no one came to open the door. He knocked. A man sitting at a nearby screen pushed himself closer to the door in his wheeled chair. He indicated the lock and then tapped his ear to let Quinn know that he couldn't be heard.

Quinn knocked again, louder, more persistently, until others in the room also stopped what they were doing and looked at him. The man in the chair left it, signalled angrily to Quinn and then came to the door. He unlocked it and opened it slightly.

'You need the code,' he said abruptly.

Quinn held up his identification, but it meant little to the man.

'So?' he said. 'Look, we're all busy.'

'I'm here to see your editorial manager.'

'Fisher?' the man said suspiciously. 'He's not here.'

'I have an appointment with him in thirty seconds,' Quinn said. 'I'm not talking to you through a door.'

'I still can't let you in,' the man said. 'Regulations. Security.'

'Then find someone who can.' Quinn looked pointedly at his watch. 'I'll wait here for another thirty seconds and then you,' he looked hard at the man's lapel badge, 'Mr Philips, will be responsible for the consequences.'

The man, Philips, looked suddenly anxious. He looked again at Quinn's card. 'You're the auditor?'

'Well done,' Quinn said. This officiousness was uncharacteristic of him. But he couldn't deny, watching Philips's uncertain glances at the men and women behind him – more of whom were showing an interest in him now that he had been identified – that he didn't increasingly take some small satisfaction in it.

Philips left him briefly and then returned with another, older man.

'And you're here why?' this other man asked Quinn.

'To tell your editor that – '

'Editorial Manager,' the second man corrected him. 'Editors went out with the real news stories.' He and Philips shared a knowing smile. The man wore no identification.

'To tell whoever that I will no longer be seeing him, and that he, you and Philips here will be hearing from my superiors.'

Neither of the two men responded to this, uncertain of the threat's validity.

'I told him Fisher wasn't here,' Philips said.

Fisher. It was the name of the man who had interviewed Anna Laing for the television report.

'He isn't,' the second man said. 'He went back up to the burn. Some new problem or other. For tonight's news.'

Quinn waited to be told more, but it was all the man was prepared to reveal.

'You're lying,' Quinn said.

Philips laughed.

'Go and see for yourself,' the second man said, his own confidence returning and convincing Quinn that they were telling him the truth.

'You could leave a message for him,' Philips suggested.

'What sort of problem?' Quinn asked the second man.

'None of—'

'And give me your name.'

'I'm Taylor,' the man said boldly. 'Fisher's second. What used to be called his right-hand man. How quaint it's all starting to sound.'

'And the problem at the burn?'

Taylor paused before answering him. 'No idea. The truth is, everyone here is getting sick and tired of the smoke, of how long everything's taking. We just want you all to do what you've got to do, pack up and get back to where you belong.'

'Open the door,' Quinn told him.

Taylor tapped in a code and the door swung fully open.

The cold air from outside followed Quinn into the overheated room.

'Close it,' Taylor told Philips, but Quinn held out his hand.

'I'm not stopping,' he said. 'I just want a look around.' He went to a wall of framed front pages, mounted like awards, all of them proclaiming the town's coming changes, its ascendancy. He moved slowly along this.

Others turned briefly from their screens to watch him; some complained loudly that the door had been left open. Quinn saw Taylor signal to people to return to their work.

'It all *looks* good,' Quinn said to him.

'It's what people want to read,' Taylor said flatly. 'You can't begin to imagine how much bad news there's been over the past ten years.' He smiled coldly. 'We might even have to reduce our advertorial if things carry on the way they're going.'

Beside him, Philips nodded enthusiastically.

'He doesn't know the difference,' Taylor said to Quinn.

'About what?' Philips said, but neither man answered him.

'You still want me to tell Fisher you were here?' Taylor said.

'I'll reschedule,' Quinn said and left the room, walking quickly out of view of everyone inside.

Turning a corner, he saw a bar opposite him, and unwilling to return to his accounts, he went into it, passing first through an arcade of flashing and warbling machines.

He bought a drink and then picked up a newspaper lying on a nearby table. Another of those same interchangeable, self-congratulatory headlines waiting to be framed. He sat at the table and read what little the paper contained. Most of the pages were filled with advertising and with paid-for features masquerading as independently written accounts. It always surprised him, wherever he now went, that these local papers survived and that they even increased in number and circulation. Another instance, he supposed, of the centre no longer holding.

On the wall above him, a muted screen showed its silent news and he looked up to see the pieces of a crashed airliner, Japanese hieroglyphics scrolling over the images, the stroboscopic lights of circling helicopters, men dressed in white walking in and out of trees, the camera repeatedly returning to where a fire still burned. A woman was carried towards the camera by four rescuers. The word 'Survivor' flashed up on the screen in a succession of languages.

'It happened months ago.'

Quinn contained his surprise at hearing the voice so close, and his first thought was that either Taylor or Philips had followed him into the bar.

'What?' He shielded his eyes against the flickering screen. The nearby game machines cast their own kaleidoscopic patterns around the dimly lit room.

'The crash. Japan. It happened months ago. The last survivor just died. Three out of seven hundred. Then two, then one, then none.'

'I see,' Quinn said. He turned back to the newspaper, hoping the man would get the hint and leave him alone.

But instead the man stood his drink beside Quinn's, letting some of it slop from the rim of the glass on to the paper.

'No loss,' he said. He pushed back a seat and sat opposite Quinn.

'I was reading,' Quinn said.

'Not that, you weren't. There's nothing in it, and what little there is amounts to no more than a pack of back-slapping lies.'

'Oh?' Quinn said, immediately regretting this and all it suggested by way of encouragement to the man.

'And if you want to know *how* I know it's all that, it's

because I worked for the thing for fifteen years.' He held out his hand and Quinn took it. Something else to regret? Another redundant, disgruntled journalist?

'My name's Winston, Adam.'

'I don't have much time,' Quinn said.

'You're the auditor. I saw you come out of the Records Office. I was trying to get in, but apparently I have no authority whatsoever to be there, let alone to start delving into their precious secrets. Don't have much time for what? Your time's your own. Much like mine these days. And then you went to see Fisher. What happened there? You say lots of nice things about the place and then Fisher says lots of nice things about the Government and all the vital and interesting work you're involved in here? Another little daisy chain of connivance and—'

'Fisher wasn't there,' Quinn said, unwilling to prolong the man's tirade. He could smell the drink on Winston's breath. 'I spoke to no one. To a man called Taylor.'

Winston seemed to sag where he sat at hearing this. He raised and then lowered his glass without drinking from it. 'That little bastard,' he said.

It was difficult in the poor light, but Quinn guessed him to be in his mid sixties, long retired perhaps, empty years, still dwelling on past glories and certainties.

He mumbled something which Quinn did not catch.

'Sorry?'

'I said they're selling this place down the river, and now that you're finally here and doing what you're doing – all their bidding – you're as big a part of it as they are.'

'Part of what?' Quinn said.

More predictable conspiracies born of grievance. Quinn relaxed.

'I could show you things that would make you change your mind about everything you and the burners are smoothing out and hiding away up here,' Winston said. He leaned even closer to Quinn, glancing over his shoulder and lowering his voice to prevent himself from being heard in the empty room.

Quinn indulged him, copying the gesture. He wondered if the man was already drunk or merely on his regular way there. The stale odour of his clothes mixed with his breath. He wore a shirt and tie, and both collar and cuffs were dirty and frayed. Perhaps all he really wanted from Quinn was another drink. An appetite fed by strangers. Quinn tried to remember where he'd heard the phrase.

'What things?' Quinn said, more amused now than intrigued.

'Eh?'

'About this place. Things to make me change my mind.'

'He's in the Board's pocket,' Winston said.

'Who is?'

Quinn guessed what was coming.

'Who do you think? Fisher. In it as tight as the rest of them.' Winston recited a list of names, counting them on his opening fists, a practised recital, a source of pride. And of course the names included Greer, Stearn, Pollard, Fisher and half a dozen others Quinn had yet to encounter. Most of the names, he knew, would be somewhere in his files.

'Go on,' he said.

'"Good News Fisher" they call him,' Winston said, his own amusement curdling quickly to contempt.

'I told you,' Quinn said. 'He wasn't there.'

'I know he wasn't. He was back up at that anthrax site. Must have been something interesting to get him off his scrawny arse and out into the cold air.'

And just as the earlier reference to the exhumation site had caught Quinn's attention, so Winston's remark did the same now.

'Do you know what it might be?' Quinn said, drinking as he spoke to disguise his interest.

'Up at the burn? One setback after another. Ten days, they said to begin with. They've been digging and burning for over twice that already, and still with no end in sight.'

The discovery of the wider contamination.

'Besides,' Winston went on, again lowering his voice, 'they haven't found half of what they're going to find.'

'Meaning?'

But this time Winston shook his head.

'Perhaps I'm not the one you should be talking to,' Quinn said.

And hearing his dismissive tone, Winston said, 'Oh, and who do you suggest? Greer? Fisher? They're the last people who'd want to listen to what I've got to say.'

Meaning they'd heard it all too many times already.

'Everybody in this place is turning a blind eye to the past,' Winston went on. 'Seeing only what they want to see, sleep-walking into the future. What is it they used to say? "Keep your eye on the future – it's the only one we've got." What a joke.'

Maudlin melodrama, Quinn thought. He'd heard enough. A moment earlier, he'd been about to suggest buying them both another drink to encourage the man's revelations, but now he wanted only to be rid of him, to finish his own drink and to return to his work. Perhaps the next step was for Winston to become angry at yet another rebuttal and then to leave of his own accord. It was surely a familiar pattern by now. And besides, what part did any of this play in his own work there?

He tried to convince himself that he had only indulged the man this far because of the tenuous connection to Anna Laing.

But instead of leaving him, Winston remained where he sat. He breathed deeply for a moment, the thick and liquid rasping of his lungs clearly audible, and then he reached into his pocket. He took out a large envelope and laid it on the newspaper.

Quinn made no attempt to pick this up, wondering how many others it had been laid before in circumstances like this. The envelope was as worn and grubby as the man's shirt.

'Go on,' Winston said. 'Look.'

'Whatever it is, what do you think *I* can do?' Quinn said.

Winston smiled. 'It's only a photograph,' he said. 'And fifty years old at that. Ancient history as far as this place is concerned, practically the Stone Age.'

'Have you shown it to Fisher?' Quinn said.

'Of course I have. I told him he could have it for free. Splash it all across the front of his rag.' The expression amused him and he laughed, catching his breath and then coughing to clear his throat.

Quinn picked up the envelope and tapped out the single photo it held. Winston started breathing more easily and watched him closely.

The picture landed face-down and Quinn picked it up, angling it to the light above him. Winston continued watching him intently.

It was a picture of a flood. A plane of water above which there rose only rooftops and pylons.

'There must have been millions like it over the past fifty, seventy-five years,' Quinn said. He looked again at the back of the picture to see if he had missed anything there. Some places now even held Flood Festivals to commemorate their own early inundations.

'Not like that one,' Winston said.

'Where's it supposed to be?' Quinn said.

Winston leaned back in his seat, grinning again. 'Where do you want it to be? Or, perhaps more importantly, where *don't* you want it to be?' He looked up at the ceiling above him.

And in that same instant, Quinn turned the photo back to face him and looked again at the outline of the rooftops rising out of the still, deep water like upturned boats calmly adrift on its surface.

15

He finally left the bar an hour later, still uncertain of what Winston had spent that time trying to convince him of, and equally uncertain of his own motives in having encouraged him in these insistent revelations. Everything still bore the hallmark of a grudge born of the man's enforced and impoverished retirement; everything was someone else's fault; conspiracy was everywhere; vested interests were always ranged against the common man and the common good, whatever these vague and malleable notions might now be called upon to represent.

There had been a dozen further pictures held in reserve by Winston, none of them showing Quinn anything the first hadn't already revealed to him. And however emphatically Winston had made his points about the flooding, all of it had happened long ago and had not – as far as Quinn knew – happened since.

He called the Record Office and told them to secure his work there, that he would not be returning until the following day.

He drove instead back to where the new church was being built, surprised to see the number of lorries and other vehicles which now surrounded the site. Approaching closer on foot, he was equally surprised to see that the tape barrier and solitary guard he'd encountered only a few days earlier had been replaced with yet another high mesh fence topped with wire and with one of Stearn's more permanent-looking cabins. There was also considerably more activity there than previously, and he guessed that over a hundred men were now working at the site.

He went to the fence and was immediately approached by another of Stearn's men.

'I was hoping to see Pollard,' Quinn said.

'The *Reverend* Pollard's busy,' the guard said.

'Meaning what?'

'Meaning he's busy. He's—'

'No – I was referring to your emphasis, your reprimand.'

'My what?'

'Your correction. I know what he *calls* himself.' Quinn had already checked. The 'Reverend' was self-styled. Pollard had enrolled eight years earlier at the 'Forty Day and Forty Night' Ministry School in Surrey. 'Somewhere in the Home Counties desert, presumably,' Quinn had said to John Lucas, who had found this out for him.

The remark made the guard even more wary of Quinn. 'You should show a bit of respect,' he said.

'Like you do?'

The man pulled a crucifix from beneath his collar and held it out to Quinn in a dramatic gesture, almost as though he expected Quinn to flinch or turn away at the sight of it.

'You're right,' Quinn said. 'I apologize. Man of the cloth, and all that.' He watched the guard closely. 'Can I see him? It all looks very busy over there.'

The guard turned to look at the centre of the site. 'They're pouring the foundations.' He gestured to a line of tankers, their massive chutes and hoses already low in the excavated ground. 'That's why no one's allowed near. Fumes and everything.'

Quinn looked more closely at the distant figures. To one side stood a group of men in suits and clean yellow hats. 'Others are in there,' he pointed out.

'Some of them are from the Development Ministry. Here by appointment. Big day, this, apparently.'

'I'd still like to talk to Pollard. Call whoever you have to. Call Stearn himself, if you like.'

The man smiled at this. 'Stearn is over there with them. Development Corporation.'

'Then I'll see them together. Two birds, one stone.'

'What's that supposed to mean?'

'Just make your call,' Quinn said. 'Who knows – perhaps the *Reverend* would actually like to see me?'

The guard turned away from Quinn and made a call. Turning back, he said, 'Stearn is coming. Stay where you are.'

Quinn saw that the man's confidence had returned now that he was acting under instruction.

'Why the big fence?' he asked again.

'I already told you that.'

'I'll ask Stearn, then,' Quinn said.

'He'll tell you the same.'

'Because he was the one who told *you* what to say in the first place?'

The guard laughed at him. 'No, but he's told us all about you sticking your fucking nose in where it's not wanted.'

'Oh? Surely, that would be sticking my fucking nose in where I have every right and authorization to do so?'

'There's only *you* believes that,' the man said, still smiling. 'I don't know what it is you think you're looking for, but whatever it is, you're looking for it a long way from home . . . auditor.'

The word was made to sound like 'Inquisitor'.

'And you're somewhere you've never left in your entire life,' Quinn countered, guessing.

'I've been to – ' But wherever he'd been about to mention had been too close to add any weight to his argument.

'See?' Quinn said. 'I think that just about makes us equal.' It was an uncertain seal on a worthless victory.

The man simply shook his head. 'Think what you like,' he said.

Quinn felt and then resisted an urge to apologize to him for whatever he'd just achieved. He motioned over the man's shoulder to where six or seven of the figures in suits were now approaching the fence single-file along a dry and solid walkway across the building site.

Quinn recognized Stearn at the front of the line. As he came he gestured for the guard to stand back from the fence and then he approached Quinn ahead of the others.

'Are *you* going to tell me I'm not welcome here?' Quinn called to him, ensuring the others heard. 'It's a popular refrain.'

But Stearn feigned surprise and then indifference at the remark and turned and shrugged emphatically to the men following him.

At the front of this group was a short, overweight man who walked cautiously over the uneven ground, causing the others to bunch behind him. He wore a pearl-coloured suit with a waistcoat, occasionally pinching the material at his knees to keep the bottoms clear of the dirt. The yellow hat he wore was too small for him, and sat high on his head, making him look ridiculous. Approaching Stearn, he took the hat off and waved his hair free. This lay over his collar and looked to Quinn to have been both dyed and curled. He pushed it behind his ears with his finger. He cupped a hand over his chin and then smoothed the arc of his forefinger and thumb over his neck, which bulged and quivered over his collar. He wore a thin tie, the knot of which was pinned with a crucifix. Pollard.

'May I introduce the Reverend Pollard,' Stearn said as the man approached the fence. Stearn looked quickly back and forth between the two of them and Quinn noted this wary deference.

Pollard stood beside Stearn and looked at Quinn, waiting for him to speak. Quinn wondered how much Stearn had already told him. The other men, Quinn noticed, held themselves back from these two. Pollard threw his hat to one of these others and the man caught it to a round of applause.

Pollard himself clapped twice, smiling at the man; and the man, Quinn saw, almost bowed at this.

'As you can see, Mr Quinn,' Stearn said loudly, 'happy though any of us here would be to accommodate you, now is hardly a convenient time to—'

'I came to see the Reverend, not you,' Quinn said, equally loudly. 'All *you* ever do is tell me what I can and can't do, put these fences up, position guards everywhere and then sit watching it all on your endless monitors.'

Pollard, Quinn saw, smiled at each of these remarks.

'I act only in the best interests of—' Stearn began.

'And then every time someone stands up to you, you make the same tedious and predictable speech.'

Stearn looked at him hard, his face colouring.

Pollard went to him and put a hand on his shoulder, reaching up to the taller man. 'He's provoking you,' he said. 'Try to control yourself. Ask yourself why.' He looked at Quinn as he said all this, his voice low and even, and everything said through a pitying smile.

'What he says—' Stearn said.

'What he says is probably true, Matthew,' Pollard said. 'But no one else here blames you for any of this. You *do* act in everyone's best interests. Including your own.' He paused. The hand on Stearn's shoulder opened and closed, bunching the material there. 'Please, find it within yourself to forgive Mr Quinn.' His gaze still fixed on Quinn, he said, 'And you, Mr Quinn – you too, I daresay, would admit that that's what you are doing here – working in everyone's best interests. So, why don't we leave all this harmful and demeaning animosity where it belongs and start again.' He took his hand from Stearn's shoulder and swung it towards the foundations behind them. 'I'm sure you'd agree that *this* is hardly the place for all our posturing and declamations.' He turned back to Stearn. 'Matthew?'

'My apologies, Mr Quinn,' Stearn said.

'And mine to you,' Quinn said, equally coldly and insincerely.

Stearn ran a hand over where Pollard had held him.

'Now, what can I do for you, Mr Quinn?' Pollard said.

'I was hoping for a tour of your new church,' Quinn said.

'But as you can see, it is not yet built – risen. All we are doing today is reconfiguring the crypt.'

It seemed a long way from 'risen' to 'reconfiguring'.

At the centre of the site, most of the tankers had stopped pouring. Several men held conversations on their phones.

'Ah, silence at last,' Pollard said. To Quinn, he said, 'And please accept my personal apology that you were unable to enter the site. Today was an unfortunate choice for your unscheduled visit. Perhaps if you came back in two or three days' time, having made an appointment, then I could take you to our solid foundations myself. Who knows, we might even be able to walk upon them. Just as our Lord himself walked upon the water.' He looked to the others for their endorsement of this and several put their thumbs up to him. 'It's the concrete, you see,' Pollard said. 'Apparently it gives off toxic fumes as it sets. If you look closely, you'll see that those working closest to where it's being poured are wearing breathing apparatus. We had to request a dispensation to use the stuff. Proscribed. Health and Safety. Your own Environmental people were none too happy, either. The cost, you see. Always a cost. To someone or something.'

Quinn looked to Stearn for confirmation and Stearn nodded once.

'I doubt if it's any of Mr Quinn's business,' Stearn then said to Pollard.

'We had hoped to save some part of the original vaults,' Pollard said. 'But all the engineers' and architects' reports warned us against this. Just as I'd hoped to save the original steeple or some part of the fabric of the first church. Victorian. Almost two hundred years old. We're already looking forward to celebrating our bicentenary as part of all the forthcoming development. After a design by Scott, I believe. You've heard of Scott?'

Quinn nodded.

'Responsible for a great many of your own city's fine buildings; some stations at a time when the network covered the whole land – country.' He continued to smile at everything he said, the distinction made.

Whatever little might actually remain of the original church had been long since hidden by later renovations and cladding.

'Perhaps we might even find a few photos of the early church,' Pollard went on. 'A display, perhaps. In the foyer of the new building. A reaching out of the hands of faith and friendship from the past to the present and then onward into the future. It will be a great building, the new church, a beacon for both our old and all our coming worshippers.' Even Pollard seemed surprised by how easily his explanation had lapsed into this easy sermonizing, and he drew the words into an even tighter smile and fell silent.

Quinn wondered about the reference to old photographs.

'A lot of people collect that kind of stuff – old photos, that sort of thing,' Stearn said. He touched his ear lobe and Quinn saw the same small red light there.

'Then I shall definitely look into it,' Pollard said, unaware of Stearn's true inference to Quinn and all the remark revealed.

Without warning to any of them, Quinn then grabbed the mesh in front of him and shook it. The whole panel trembled and the guard ran forward to hold it.

'Not a wise thing to do,' Stearn said, amused by the gesture. 'Some of our perimeters are live. Besides, if it does fall, it'll fall on you.'

'If it *falls*?' Pollard said.

'It won't,' Stearn said confidently.

Several others also showed concern at what Quinn had just done.

'My apologies,' Quinn said to Pollard. 'It just seems very uncivilized, talking like this. You might all just as well be animals in a zoo.'

'Get used to it,' Stearn said.

'Ah, now there was a thing – zoos,' Pollard said quickly. 'My father once took me to a zoo. Not a thing with cages, though. A park, a reserve. Are there any of them left?' He looked to the others. 'Are there any animal reserves still in existence?' he called to them. The men shared glances and shrugs. 'Perhaps it might be something for our own Development Corporation to consider. In fact . . .' He paused for effect.

'What?' Stearn prompted him.

Pollard spoke directly to Quinn. 'At our last Corporation meeting we received a proposal from the Independent Restraint and Rehabilitation people to consider incorporating a new facility in our extended plans.'

'A prison,' Stearn said.

'Perhaps we could locate one at the centre of the animal reserve.' Pollard finally grinned at this. 'Something of an incentive, perhaps, for the inmates to stay where they are?'

Stearn shook his head at the impossible suggestion.

'People will need to fill their leisure time somehow,' Pollard said, still grinning. 'And let us not turn away from the reality of the situation – there's precious little else here to keep them entertained.'

'They'll have the church,' Quinn said.

'Sustenance rather than entertainment, Mr Quinn.'

Quinn remained uncertain how serious Pollard had been about his suggestion – about the reserve, at least, if not the prison. Who had truly cared about the final dozen or so pandas still alive in the same year when a hundred million cattle had been slaughtered? There were still rare-species breeding programmes elsewhere in Europe – in the East – but none in the United Kingdom. He wondered if everything Pollard now said was intended to divert his interest from the church. He wondered, too, and not for the first time since his arrival, about the interconnectedness of all these men, about their growing authority and merging responsibilities.

Pollard tucked further loose strands of hair behind his ears with the same practised motion.

'If it was up to me,' he said, returning to Quinn's original demand, 'then I should be only too happy to give you a tour of everything that is finally starting to happen. But some of my colleagues here' – he motioned to both the nearby and the distant men – 'are from the Executive. And, as I'm sure you of all people can appreciate, Mr Quinn, my hands are somewhat tied by their own directives and conditions. Even the house of God, you see, must abide by *their* rules.' He laughed at the remark.

By 'Executive' he was referring to the small body of senior executive officers from the ministries of Health, Security, Development and Enforcement, and Quinn looked more closely at the distant men to see if there was anyone he might recognize. He knew better than to get involved with them, and then wondered if they were already aware of his own presence in the place via Webb.

'In fact you may already be familiar with some of them,' Pollard said. Another warning. He recited a short list of names, but Quinn recognized none of them. The Executive was known for the rapidity of its expansion and the equally swift turnover of its lesser members. It was unlikely that any of those at the head of the body would have come this far north at this time of the year. Quinn tried to remember how far away the nearest airport was.

'You seem surprised to see them here,' Pollard said. 'Perhaps you'd like me to call some of them over to join our conversation. I assumed, of course, that they were already well appraised of your own vital work among us.'

Quinn could neither confirm nor deny this, and Pollard and Stearn shared a glance to seal their small victory.

Pollard looked at his watch. 'I don't wish to appear rude or abrupt, Mr Quinn, but . . .'

'You're wasting our time,' Stearn said bluntly. 'We should get back to them – the Executive. Perhaps you want us to pass on your regards?'

Quinn refused to be drawn by the remark.

Sensing this sudden return of tension between the two men, Pollard said, 'I'm sure Mr Quinn understands the true nature of our purpose here.'

Neither Quinn nor Stearn understood him.

'Our church. The necessity of such a place in this particularly blighted part of the Lord's Kingdom.' He clasped his hands as he spoke. 'I'm sure that none of us – none of us here and none of these outsiders come to shine their lights on us – would ever find it in their hearts to deny the importance – the *need* – of what is being set in motion here today.'

And again, neither Quinn nor Stearn fully understood the convoluted remark.

Pollard looked at Stearn, clearly expecting his support, but Stearn looked away from him and then started a separate conversation with the guard through the mesh.

'I think you've upset him,' Quinn said to Pollard. 'I think he's one of your heathens still awaiting conversion.'

'Then you're wrong,' Pollard said. He paused for a moment, a finger to his lips. 'Tell me, Mr Quinn, are you a church-goer – a believer – yourself?'

The question caught Quinn by surprise. 'I was,' he said. 'Some time ago.' But never by need or conviction.

'I see,' Pollard said. 'Then deny it as loudly and as vehemently as you like, but the seeds of uncertain doubt and desire remain within you.'

Quinn wanted to laugh at the contradictory remark. 'You don't know the first thing about what I want and what I doubt,' he said.

Pollard smiled at the denial.

Neither man spoke for a moment. Stearn returned to them.

'Perhaps you might one day return and visit us when our church is finally built,' Pollard said eventually.

'I doubt it,' Quinn said.

'You doubt a great deal, it seems to me.'

Behind them, the tankers restarted their engines and resumed pouring concrete. Men with rakes and shovels moved around the foundations, pushing and scooping the liquid into place, making the noise of waves on a shingle coast.

Pollard turned away from Quinn and walked carefully back over the same uneven ground, placing his feet as though he were following the exact footsteps of his outward journey.

He joined the others and they continued in a group back to the tankers.

Stearn remained where he stood.

'Pollard's going to click his fingers when he sees you're not following him,' Quinn said. 'Straying sheep and all that.' He pretended to think. 'Or perhaps you're the one strayed sheep he's happy to leave wandering out here in the wilderness.'

Stearn shook his head at the remark and whatever it might imply, and then he too turned and left him.

At the foundations, several tankers left the site and were immediately replaced by others. Their chutes and hoses were lowered and the noise resumed.

16

Two more days passed before Quinn next saw Anna Laing. He looked out for her in the bar each evening, but for the first time since his arrival, neither she nor any of her staff appeared there. The vans and lorries continued to come and go, sometimes earlier, sometimes later than usual, but the days now ended in periods of unnatural emptiness and silence.

Quinn sat at his window overlooking the vehicles and watched for her. It occurred to him – especially after all she'd told him about the problems she'd encountered, and what he himself had heard over the previous few days – that she might even have been recalled to the capital.

On the third day he went directly, and for the first time, to her room. He waited until the others had returned and dispersed, checking that the corridor was empty before leaving the stairwell. He waited at her door and listened for voices, but heard only the noise of the television.

He knocked, suddenly uncertain of his reasons for being there, of what he would say to her after so long an absence. A further minute passed, and then Anna asked who was there. He stood back from the eye-piece and smiled, knowing how ridiculous his distorted face would look. 'It's me,' he said. 'Quinn.'

He presented his profile and then face. The door clicked open and she told him to come in.

She looked anxious, perhaps suspicious of his unexpected appearance.

'You didn't need to add the name bit,' she said, finally smiling. 'I would probably have remembered.'

It was almost ten. Only an hour had passed since she and the others had returned. She looked exhausted. It had grown dark at four. It was still not yet freezing cold – not as cold as early December had once been – but it had rained intermittently for the past few hours and there had been no sun whatsoever to mark the day's rapid passing.

Entering her room, identical to his own, Quinn wanted to tell her that no one had seen him arrive. But he wondered what this might suggest to her about his motives for being there, and so he said nothing.

She switched off the screen at which she had been working and motioned to the bottle of whisky beside the bed. She went into her shower room and returned with a glass for him, tearing off its seal and then throwing this over her shoulder. One of her cases lay open on the bed, her clothes scattered around it.

'If it's inconvenient . . .' Quinn said.

'Everything's inconvenient,' she told him. She smiled again

and poured him a drink. She sat on the bed and Quinn sat on the room's solitary chair, facing her.

'New problems?'

'What else is there?'

'I meant at the site. Other than the ones you were telling me about.'

She sipped from her glass. 'Has someone been talking?'

The remark made Quinn cautious. 'It's just that Fisher decided you were considerably more newsworthy than my own semi-human-interest story, that's all.'

She watched him for a moment before responding.

'A few days ago? He was back up there. I think the natives are getting restless. We have our own press officer. However, I doubt if we'll get anything but a glowing report from Fisher. Necessary evils and all that. In all likelihood, he'll just repeat what we tell him to say and then pretend he came up with it all himself. You know how these things work.'

Her tone kept Quinn guessing.

'But there *are* problems?' he said.

She pushed her case to one side and swung her legs on to the bed. 'We've got rising groundwater levels at both sites,' she said. 'Exhumation and burning.'

'Surely not *that* unexpected?' He was almost relieved by the revelation.

'A *lot* of rising groundwater. It's causing problems with both the digging and the burning.'

'Is there no—'

'No what? No contingency plan? No way of pumping it out and then of stopping it from coming back in?'

Quinn nodded, unwilling to provoke her further.

'I'm sorry,' she said. 'No – no contingency plan. But you're right – we get this all the time. We can usually find a way around it, or somehow manage to ignore it all until we've finished.'

'Can't you pump it out?'

'Not fast enough. We've tried. They're both much deeper pits than usual. They told us ten metres; it's beginning to look more like twenty. Plus we have no fixed or guaranteed boundaries, no parameters. I went to see your farmer friend to find out more about what he'd already told you. He thought that deep in our exhumation site we'd come across remains of the very first cull – contaminated biomass over a century old.'

'Meaning the water's also contaminated?'

She pursed her lips.

'Meaning it is – and probably a lot worse than anyone here wants to admit to?' Quinn said.

'"Anyone" including me?' she said. It was only half a question. She refilled his glass and then her own 'I doubt if anyone – us, them, anyone – wants to look too long or too hard at this one.'

'What normally happens?'

'With groundwater flooding? It's usually containable or of little lasting consequence.'

'So the problem often just goes away?'

'So the problem often just goes away. You'd be surprised how many problems of that kind I come across these days. Sometimes, if the water isn't contaminated we can simply drop in a pump, bring the water to the surface and let it go on its way with a cheery wave.'

'And here?'

'Too contaminated. And it's land that's being made ready for imminent development, remember? Both sites are High Priority. Once they're cleared, sealed and capped, we have to be able to sign them over with certain guarantees. And to do that as things stand, we'd have to pump the holes dry – a near-impossibility anyway – and then tanker the water away to somewhere it could be treated. And that means a long way away. From here, I'd guess we're looking at the Bristol Channel. It would take us for ever to get the necessary permits.'

'To say nothing of the cost?'

'Or the legal wrangling involved to determine who might actually be *responsible* for all that extra expense.'

'By "treated" do you mean just flushing it away into the sea?'

She laughed at this. 'When did you last eat fresh fish?'

Quinn pretended to think. And then he genuinely failed to remember. 'Ten years?' he said, unexpectedly saddened by the realization.

'At least. And even then perhaps "fresh" might have undergone another of its wonderful metamorphoses.'

'Probably,' he said.

'Greer's already been on to my superiors,' Anna said. 'He's not a happy man.'

'Because this might scupper his great golden vision of the future? We all know how unlikely that is.'

'Why? Because after decades of slowly circling the open plughole, *we*'re the ones finally pushing the plug back in for them.' She sat with her head bowed for a moment, and when she raised it, she looked directly at him and said, 'I've been recalled.'

Quinn was unable to conceal his sudden alarm at hearing this. 'To the capital?' he said. He held the glass close to his mouth.

'A meeting with the Ministry geologists. To work out the

best way forward. Or – as usually happens – to be told I can't be encountering what I say I'm encountering. And *they*'ll have the maps to prove it.'

'On the grounds that a lot of other things might change, but not the geology?'

'It's a good argument to fall back on. All *I* ever have to counter it is to keep banging on about our capabilities.'

'Perhaps this time they'll recognize that more needs to be done – here, I mean, with everything that's dependent on the land being made ready.'

She shrugged. 'If there was any real likelihood – and they do enjoy using that particular word – if there was any real likelihood of the problem moving beyond us, beyond our capabilities to deal with it, then that problem will be redesignated, redefined, whatever.'

They both considered for a moment what she was suggesting.

'Surely the geologists must have known that the water was likely to be there?' he said. 'Especially after everything that's happened in the past seventy years.'

'Why? Because it's everywhere else? We excavated below their recommended levels, remember?'

'And if you'd stopped digging at ten metres?'

'Half a problem?'

'And there's no possibility of just leaving the deeper stuff where it is?'

She contained her anger at the question. 'We could try capping and sealing it, but it would remain one more unticked box when we came to sign over the supposedly cleared sites. Greer's already made himself perfectly clear on that particular point. As far as he's concerned – as far as they're *all* concerned – it would have been better all round if we'd never come here in the first place and just let them get on with the money-making, empire-building part of it all.'

Quinn shook his head at this. 'He knows that if that had happened, then the problem would one day have been his.'

'Not if everything had stayed undisturbed until he was finally buried in it.'

They both laughed.

'Or until Stearn or one of the others deposed him,' Quinn said. 'And until then—'

'And until then, I'm still the one who uncovered – some might say "created" – the situation we all now find ourselves in.' She put down her glass and pressed her face into her cupped hands.

'How long will you be gone?' Quinn asked her, bracing himself against being told that her removal from the place might be permanent.

'As long as it takes for them to point out to me the full extent and consequences of my responsibilities and failings?'

'But they will send you back?'

She looked directly at him, holding his gaze. 'I'll be back. It's poisoned-chalice time. Who else do you think is going to pick it up?'

'Perhaps one of the geologists . . .'

'The closest *they* ever get is their maps. Beautiful things. You see all that mud and dirt and sludge up at the sites? Well, on their maps it's all vivid yellows and blues, a variety of pinks and ochres. It might be the real world to them . . .'

'I'm pleased,' Quinn said. 'About you being sent back.'

She looked at him again. 'I know you are,' she said.

'Is there no one to whom you can appeal? For more time, money, operatives?'

'Everything was fixed a year ago, longer. Besides, when did anyone ever come out into the real world to mop *your* brow or hold *your* hand? We're God's lonely men, you and me.'

Quinn acknowledged both the reference and the deeper truth of what she was saying and they touched glasses. It seemed to him another of their cautious intimacies.

'How long will you be gone?'

'Five days, six.'

'Can't they do anything over a protected link?' He meant a video conference, for which the motel would have the facilities and necessary security.

'They could. But I suspect I'm going to be told what to do in somewhat unprotected language and in a manner that even a protected link wouldn't quite do justice.'

'It doesn't seem fair,' Quinn said uselessly.

'It's not,' she said. 'It's another reason why people like us exist. It's why we do what we do. We're cut-off points, you and me. We're *their* dirty hands. I'm surprised you haven't—' She stopped abruptly, aware that she had said too much, that she might be forcing him to deny whatever she went on to reveal to him.

But she was right and Quinn understood her perfectly.

She held out her hand to him and then pulled him to sit beside her on the bed. She added more drink to both their glasses.

'The others . . .' she said, uncertain how to continue.

'On your team?'

'They're worried that they're now going to be stuck here longer than any of them expected.'

'Which is what will happen if you have to drain and clear the sites properly?'

She nodded. 'The fires are already being compromised. Smoke is always somebody else's problem. Contaminated groundwater, on the other hand . . .'

A thought occurred to Quinn. 'But what will it matter – anthrax, foot and mouth, whatever – if there is never going to be any livestock kept on the land ever again?'

'Foot and mouth we could live with – *they* could live with, Greer, the Development Corporation, all those shiny, glassy-eyed young couples sucking up their unending mortgages – but anthrax is something completely different. I imagine one of the ways they'll try and resolve the problem – here, and everywhere in the future as more "here"s need to be found and developed – is by approaching the Executive and seeing if it can't be conveniently removed from their Hazard Designation list. Removed or given a lesser designation.'

'Is that likely?'

She considered this and shook her head. 'Like I already said, you've never seen what happens to someone who contracts anthrax. Besides, none of that can happen in the time still available to us. The signing-off is sixty days away.'

'And Greer – '

'And Greer is proving to be particularly intractable on that particular point.'

'Only because it strengthens his own hand,' Quinn said.

'I doubt he needs it. Whatever's been set in motion here by those higher powers – and, let's face it, to them Greer's just one name among many on a piece of headed notepaper – will be seen to its conclusion by those same people. Imagine if Greer had wielded the same lucky power in Cambridgeshire, or Lincoln, Suffolk or Essex.'

She pushed herself upright and looked at the darkness outside, at the lights of the distant ring road.

Quinn felt her leg against his. She sat close to him and slid her arm through his own.

'When do you go?' he said, looking at the same distant lights.

'First thing in the morning.'

He wished he'd come to see her sooner, when he'd first started to wonder at her absence.

'No – first light. It sounds better.' She pressed the back of her hand to her brow in a theatrical gesture. 'I go at first light.' She laughed at the remark, her first genuine laughter in the hour he'd been with her. 'Ignore me,' she said, 'I'm probably drunk. I've got my route and my fuel authorizations, everything's ready.'

'Except you,' Quinn said.

She held his arm. 'Except me.'

It had been part of his intention – excuse – in going to see her to tell her everything he'd learned from Winston in the bar, but after all she'd just told him, he saw how unwelcome – inconsequential, even – all these cold and second-hand recollections would now seem to her. More dark fairy tales; another morass of tangled undergrowth and soft, uncertain ground.

'Will you get to see anyone, family, while you're there?' he asked her.

Anna considered this and then again drained her glass – almost as though to clear any thought of this from her mind.

'Unlikely,' she said, and as she spoke, unable and unwilling to say more, she let herself fall back on to the bed and her scattered, unpacked clothes. And because her arm was still through Quinn's, he was pulled back with her, spilling what remained of his own drink over his chest.

He turned to look at her and she did the same to him, their

faces close. She kissed him – first on his chin, and then on his lips, and Quinn responded to her, his free hand against her cheek.

When she finally drew back an inch, her eyes looking directly into his, she said, 'You taste of whisky.'

'It's a trick I've perfected,' he said.

'To get all the objects of your desire drunk and in thrall to your charms?'

'Has it worked yet again?' he said. He kissed her lightly on the side of her nose and she closed her eyes.

'It's a good trick,' she whispered to him. She pulled her arm from beneath him and held it to his wet chest.

'You ought to finish packing and then get a good night's sleep,' he whispered to her.

'I know what I *ought* to do,' she said. Her finger touched his lips and she put her palm firmly over his mouth.

17

The next morning, Quinn returned to the drain diggers on the hillside above the southern edge of the town.

Earlier, he had gone out with Anna to her car, and had then waited with her as the windscreen was cleared of its thin ice, both of them – or so Quinn had hoped – putting off their separation until the last possible moment. Afterwards, he had returned to his own room, but had then been unable to sleep again.

He had expected to find the same few men on the hillside, digging the same shallow runnels on the same broad slope, but as he rose and turned the corner, leaving all sight of the town behind him, he was surprised to find a barrier across the road close to the bend, forcing him to brake hard, slewing sideways on to the same gravel patch where he had spent the night in his car.

Yet another of Stearn's employees stood with his palm held rigidly out until Quinn's car stopped moving, its engine stalled at his sudden braking.

Quinn climbed out and stood with his hands on his knees for a moment. Only then did the man leave the barrier and come to him.

'That would have been entirely your fault. The visibility-stroke-speed-stroke-braking-ratio was properly calculated prior to the barrier being erected. You were driving too fast for your braking speed.'

'And your barrier was too close to the bend,' Quinn said angrily. 'I only saw it once I was round it.' He looked at his hands and saw that they were shaking.

'Whole point,' the man said. 'Speed, braking distance, visibility.' He looked down the hillside. 'Lucky you had your wits about you, otherwise you might have been down there by now and I'd have been alerting the emergencies to get you blue-lighted out.' He spoke as though he regretted not being able to do this.

'Only after you'd called Stearn with the bad news,' Quinn said. He breathed deeply; his right leg felt numb, cramped.

'Naturally,' the man said. He paced the skid marks across the wet road and into the gravel, turning on his heel and retracing his steps in a second, confirmatory calculation.

The road, Quinn saw, was now running with water, streaming across the hillside and filling the cambered edges of the tarmac in the direction of the town.

'*That*'s what made braking difficult,' he said, wondering

why he was bothering to prolong the unwinnable argument.

'Then *you* should have been showing more due care and attention.' The man pronounced the words as emphatically as all the others.

'The equation changes in wet weather,' Quinn said, repeating uncertainly something he might have learned thirty years ago.

'What?'

Quinn walked around his car, waiting for his aching muscles to relax.

'Stay away from the tyre marks,' the guard said threateningly, as though believing Quinn might be about to try and somehow erase these.

Quinn walked back to the edge of the slope and looked down, seeing his own near-missed path down through the rough grass and exposed, stony soil.

'You all right?' A different voice.

Quinn turned and saw the man who had woken him after his night on the hillside.

'He was going too fast,' the guard shouted.

'When I want your worthless opinion, I'll ask for it.' The drainer put his hand on Quinn's shoulder.

'I'm fine,' Quinn told him.

'See?' the guard said.

The drainer ignored this. 'I'm Wade,' he told Quinn. 'Wade by name, Wade by nature.'

Quinn didn't understand him for a moment.

'I thought I'd say it before you did,' Wade said.

'It would never have occurred to me,' Quinn said.

'It would have . . . eventually,' Wade said.

Quinn was surprised to see the man still working on the same part of the hillside and told him so.

'You'd be even more surprised if you saw how many of us there are up here now.'

'More diggers – drainers?'

'Even had a few of Greer's tame engineers up here.'

'Problems?' Quinn said. He held out his arm and saw that his hand had stopped shaking.

'They want the run-off *redirected.* In my opinion, they're asking for trouble. Water finds its own way. You'd think it was something they'd have learned by now.' He beckoned for Quinn to follow him a short distance, which Quinn did. They walked further around the curve in the road and Wade pointed out the men higher on the hillside. Where previously there had been only a dozen or so others, there were now closer to fifty men, all of them clearly visible in their jackets and helmets.

Several small mechanical diggers stood in a line facing uphill from the road.

Anxious that Quinn had wandered even further from the barrier, the guard followed the two men and called for Quinn to go back to him.

'Ignore him,' Wade said. 'His father works for me.'

Up on the hill, the men dug and scraped in the same sodden grass. There seemed to be little order to their work, but Quinn guessed that the rise of the slope distorted any pattern there might be to their task and hid this from him.

Water ran at his feet, perhaps an inch deep over the surface of the road.

'Where's it going?' he asked Wade.

Wade shrugged, seemingly unconcerned. 'Not really for me to say. You'd have to ask the clever engineers that one.'

'But you know?'

Wade acknowledged this. 'I know it seldom flows uphill

or along the hardest line. It's water. I'm arthritic up to my thighs. I've learned one or two things about it in my time.' He nodded almost imperceptibly in the direction of the unseen town, sitting in its bowl of hills.

The Slough of Despond, Quinn remembered Anna saying.

'And where do Greer's engineers *want* it to go?'

Wade smiled again. 'Their plans have got it flowing away over the col here – ' He indicated the gap through which the road ran east into the world beyond.

The water at their feet, Quinn guessed, flowed in the opposite direction. Either way, it would soon join all the other water flowing into the vast and ever-widening estuaries to both the east and the west.

Wade stamped his feet in the water in which they stood. 'It's as much as we can do now to keep the road even passable, let alone dry. I never seem to be out of the stuff these days.'

'So I see,' Quinn said.

'Which is more than *they* do,' Wade said, meaning the engineers.

'Do you think you're wasting your time, digging up here?' Quinn asked him.

'They tell us what to do, and then they pay us for doing what we're told. There might be lots of *talk* of coming work, but as far as I'm concerned, there's precious little sign of it yet. Especially for old men like me.'

Quinn guessed him to be in his early sixties.

'It's an easy enough equation to follow,' Wade added.

As easy as the line the water now followed.

Quinn looked again along the road. 'Why is there no traffic stopped on this side of the barrier?'

'They put another up on the far side of the gap. Everything's being sent the long way round.'

It was the road Quinn had arrived along, and it would be his route out of the place, his way home. Others remained available to him, but this was the shortest route, the most direct, the one he had planned to take upon completing his work there.

'Do you know how long for?' he asked Wade.

'Long as it takes, I suppose.'

A surge of water swept over their feet and both men stood to one side and watched it pass.

'New channels,' Wade said absently. He looked from side to side over the hillside above him, making calculations. 'They wanted us to use the diggers before we knew where the water would start running. If they come back to check our progress, they'll insist on it. But until then . . .'

The water on the road eased off as quickly as it had come and the flow slackened.

Wade spat into it and watched as the glob of phlegm was carried away from them into the grass.

'Do you know a man called Winston?' Quinn asked him.

Wade made a circling motion at his temple. '*That* Winston? Doom and Gloom Winston?'

'He showed me – '

'I can well imagine what he showed you. He was sacked from the paper for wanting to investigate stories concerning the fraudulent dealings of the Development Corporation.'

'What sort of stories?'

'Stuff about the pressures they brought to bear on everybody who resisted their compulsory purchase orders, that kind of story.'

'He showed me photos of the whole town under water.'

'Fifty years ago – longer. Nothing unique in that.'

'It was still—'

'Whatever else it was, it was still fifty years ago. It's old news, best forgotten.' He made it clear by his tone that he was unhappy discussing the man and his familiar revelations – though whether out of some other, older attachment to him, or because he better understood the true nature of the contagion Winston might now be trying to spread, Quinn was uncertain.

The harshness of these rebuttals made Quinn cautious. 'I'm sorry if I – ' he began.

'I've got sixty men up on that hill. Guaranteed work for a month. A month minimum, judging by what the engineers weren't telling us. And if we do what's necessary – what's being asked of us – up there, then there'll be another contract and then another after that. That's how these things work. Short-term contract after short-term contract. One day it's ten men, the next a hundred. Do you imagine this place is going to get any *less* busy over the next ten years? And do you imagine there won't be tens of thousands of incomers all clamouring for that same work and forcing the prices down even further?'

Quinn shook his head at what Wade was telling him.

Then Wade fell silent for a moment and looked back up to the diggers on the hillside. 'And soon it'll be winter proper,' he said, as though a thousand other complaints and concerns were included in the simple remark.

'Will it snow?' Quinn asked him. The last time he'd seen snow in the capital had been eight years ago. A single fall in the middle of one night. He and his wife had stood in their small garden, their faces raised to it, their eyes closed, hearing their neighbours enjoying the same rare and simple pleasure on either side of them. It had fallen for less than an hour, and then it had stopped. And an hour after that it had started to thaw.

'Probably,' Wade said, looking up into the sky. 'Not yet, though. In the New Year. Most likely to the north and the west, and then only on the tops. The last time we needed ploughs in the town was five years ago. What concerns me more is that the ground never freezes these days. Not like it used to. It's why we're here now – all this.' He kicked again at the water on the road. He touched Quinn's arm briefly. 'Winston's my stepbrother,' he said. 'When he lost his job . . . He should have left this place when he had the chance. You've seen him. His wife left him. He's got a grown daughter – Rebecca. She left him too for most of her childhood.'

'And you?' Quinn said.

'We meet up occasionally. Though it usually ends badly. Did he tell you that Greer offered him a job in his press office? Thought not. Did he tell you that Fisher has taken out an injunction to keep him away from the office window he smashed the day he was thrown out? No? Nothing about that other injunction his wife took out? Anything about the welfare officers telling him he wasn't able to see his daughter until she came of age and could make up her own mind about it all?'

Quinn shook his head at each of the questions, hearing Wade's buried affection for the man in everything he said.

'It's all one big conspiracy to Winston,' Wade said. 'To be honest with you, I don't know what he's got left to lose.'

'He told me—'

'*Whatever* he told you, he told you because you were probably the only person in the place who didn't already know who he was or what he'd become. You listened to him, that's all – probably even showed some interest, and it's more than anyone else here is prepared to go on doing.'

Everywhere you looked in the place, Quinn thought, *that same creeping blight.*

'I didn't know any of that,' he admitted.

'How could you?'

'Does his wife still live here?'

Wade shook his head. 'Took advantage of one of the early relocation schemes. The girl went with her and then came back when she was older.'

'To live with her father?'

Wade nodded once. It was the only flaw in his argument against the man. That, and the photographs of the same water flowing over their feet.

'How's your own work going?' Wade asked him, and for a moment Quinn considered the consequences of his answer.

Wade saw this. 'Forget it,' he said. 'I only asked.'

Quinn apologized to him. 'It's just that when people ask me that particular question they usually have their own agendas.'

'Own *what*?' Wade understood him perfectly. This was his way of releasing the sudden tension between them. 'Greer, you mean? Stearn?'

'And others.'

'I can imagine.' Wade waited.

'I met Pollard,' Quinn said.

'Our very own self-righteous and self-appointed reverend?' Wade spat again into the water, this time pointedly ignoring where it ran and causing both of them to smile. 'We had a proper vicar once. Several, in fact. They prayed with us and then they prayed *for* us. When things changed, people drifted away. Pollard arrived, worked out what people wanted to hear, and then he told it to them. He treats his flock like the chosen few, always pointing out to them the abundant horrors everywhere else in the world.'

'Horrors?'

'He terrifies them with tales of whatever they're ignorant of. Two generations ago, people from here travelled the world. Now you'd be hard pressed to find anyone who'd spent a week away anywhere. Abroad? Forget it. Even before all the flight and travel restrictions. No – Pollard has got them all exactly where he wants them. Added to which, he's got the advantage of making them pay for the privilege of listening to all his easy-read Bible sermonizing.'

'They pay?'

'All very voluntary, all very private.' Wade tapped his nose.

'I take it you're not a religious man yourself,' Quinn said.

'Not as such.' Wade again looked around him, and then up at the low cloud and distant peaks, already lost. 'This, all this. It's enough for me.'

Coming from anyone else, the remark would not have convinced Quinn; but coming from this man, who dug into the sludge and clay of sodden hillsides, he understood and believed and accepted it. He looked along the hidden horizon, where darker shadows in the cloud suggested coming rain.

'You should go back to your car,' Wade said. He indicated the guard, who was now returning to them, talking into his mouthpiece as he came. 'He got brave. Somebody's told him he has every right to tell you to turn around and leave. He'll probably even be able to quote the relevant by-law at you.'

Both Quinn and Wade turned to face the approaching man.

'What?' Wade said to him. 'What?'

'He's got to leave, to turn back.'

'We know. He's going. What else?'

'He's got to do it now,' the man said. 'He should have done it immediately. When I first told him.'

'Why? Because your word's law now, is it?'

'Actually . . .' the man began, clearing his throat and raising his chin slightly.

'Don't,' Wade said. 'One more smug, supercilious word from you and I'll get your father to come down here and listen to it all.'

The guard looked up at the hillside and stopped talking.

Wade and Quinn continued past him to Quinn's car.

As Quinn turned it on the gravel, Wade slapped the roof and then stood aside to watch him go.

Quinn looked at the man in his rear-view mirror, and as though Wade could see him doing this, he raised his hand and held it there until Quinn rounded the downhill curve and both the man and the hillside were lost to view.

18

He spent the rest of the day back amid the Administrative accounts, reading more of the files that had been selected and prepared for him to scrutinize; brought to him where he sat, and then later taken away from him, checked against another list – one presumably compiled and now being equally closely scrutinized by Greer or one of his Finance officers – and then returned to the cabinets, shelves and drives from which they had been taken: out of the darkness into the light, and then from the light back into the darkness again.

It was routine work. Financial projections, budgets, spend, underspend, overspend, and much of it only half-revealed in a reassuringly – to Quinn at least – familiar tangle of equations, projections and mirror-like double-entry sleights of hand. Tens of billions, billions, hundreds of millions, tens of millions and millions washing back and forth like the tides of a great, ever-changing and yet ultimately predictable ocean.

By late afternoon, and with no good reason to either continue or to return to the motel, Quinn left the building and walked for an hour in the streets.

Leaving the immediate centre behind him, he arrived at a district more derelict than most, and where the streets were deserted. Buildings stood without their roofs; almost every window and door was either missing or covered with sheets of metal and wire mesh. The place was mostly in darkness, with only a few vivid lights shining down from those buildings still inhabited or in use.

He was about to turn back when a car drew up alongside him and stopped. At first he imagined it to be another of Stearn's interventions. His uncertain wanderings – trespass? – would certainly not have gone unnoticed. But as he prepared to identify and then account for himself, the passenger door opened and Winston climbed unsteadily out. He looked at Quinn briefly but seemed not to recognize him. He carried a bottle, which he held to his stomach as he steadied himself against the car. There were few other vehicles along the street.

Quinn spoke to him and Winston looked at him hard, an eventual double-take of recognition finally crossing his face. Then he leaned forward and vomited at his feet. The liquid splashed in a wide circle and Quinn stepped back to avoid it.

At the far side of the car, the driver's door opened and a girl climbed out. She stood in the darkness for a moment and then came to where Winston stood, now wiping his mouth on his sleeve. She looked at Quinn briefly and then started berating Winston. She tried to take the bottle from him, but he struck her on the shoulder and she backed away from him. She swore at him, the same few words over and over. And hearing her speak, Quinn thought he recognized her, too, though he couldn't place her; perhaps she worked at the motel, cleaning, serving.

'Is he all right?' he asked her.

She looked at him again, but said nothing.

'I know him,' he said. 'Winston, right?'

'Everybody knows him,' she said, investing each word with its own particular edge.

'I spoke to him. He showed me his pictures, told me about—'

But before he could finish, Winston vomited again, causing both Quinn and the girl to move even further away from him. This time the vomit was less liquid and a string of viscous saliva hung from Winston's chin to his hand.

'He's disgusting,' the girl said. She waited for Winston to wipe himself again before returning to him. This time when she held him he made no attempt to push her away. 'He's my father,' she told Quinn. 'This is what he does. If when you say you spoke to him you got more than a dozen words that made any sense, then you can consider yourself lucky.'

She took a key from her pocket, motioning for Quinn to hold Winston while she unlocked the door of a nearby house. Before she'd approached it, Quinn had imagined the building to be abandoned.

He helped Winston inside as the girl went ahead of them along a narrow hallway into a small room. Inside, the house was little warmer than the street had been. The girl switched on a portable gas heater which added more smell than warmth to the room. A damp odour of rot and decay filled the hallway.

'It's condemned,' she said. 'He's got two more months and then it's coming down. They all are, middle of February.'

It was then that Quinn recognized her as the girl who had been unable to serve him at the petrol station. He told her he remembered her, but the news was of little consequence to her.

'Do you live here with him?' he asked her.

'Sometimes.'

'I met his step-brother this morning,' Quinn said.

'So you'll probably know all there is to know about him, then.'

'Probably,' Quinn admitted.

'Help him into that chair. I'm Rebecca.'

The daughter who had been taken away from him, and who had then returned.

Quinn took Winston's arm and lowered him into the armchair facing the heater.

Rebecca crouched in front of her father, her sleeves held to the flames. Steam rose from her cuffs.

'Apparently, Rebecca was his grandmother's name,' she said. 'I never knew her.'

'You left with your mother and then came back,' Quinn said, wishing this sounded more friendly and disarming than it did.

She looked at him for a moment. 'Biggest mistake of my life,' she said.

Quinn wondered how old she was. Nineteen, twenty?

'I went when I was thirteen,' she said. 'Courts. Stayed away eight years and then came back. I've been here two years now. If it wasn't for what's happened to him . . .' The rest remained unspoken. 'Watch him,' she said, and then she left, returning a few minutes later with a tray of three mugs. She gave one to

Quinn and put another on the arm of Winston's chair, uselessly warning him against knocking it off.

'Why doesn't he leave?' Quinn asked her, sipping the bitter liquid. 'Has he never considered – '

'He was offered a new apartment. All this is being demolished as part of the redevelopment. The railway station used to stand at the back of these houses. The line of the track's still there. It's where they want to build the new station – interchange – and they'll use the original route for the trains.'

Quinn heard the slight but rising enthusiasm in her voice. He had seen the gently curving line on maps of the place, another severed connection.

'There used to be a tunnel,' she said. 'Still is. About a mile away. Three miles long. They've already cleared it. You can walk from one end to the other.'

'Where will it run to?'

She shrugged. 'Who cares? Anywhere. At least it would be going somewhere.' She spoke now as though he'd contested what she'd just told him.

Even she, it seemed to Quinn, understood how far in the future all this lay.

'Where did you go with your mother?' he asked her.

'Wade told you that, did he? The Midlands. She had family there. Or thought she did. By the time we got there and started knocking on doors, she found that most of them had gone.'

'Relocated?'

'Just gone.'

'Why did you come back?' It was the biggest question of her young life, and Quinn understood this.

'Where else would I go? I had no points, no priority. I left the Midlands on the same day the Thames barrier failed for the final time. Even if I *had* been on anybody's list, I was suddenly a long way further down it after that happened. And then there was all this talk of what was going to happen here. I deserved *something*.'

They weren't even winds of chance and circumstance, let alone fortune. Not even that. And perhaps she understood this a lot better than he did.

'It's why *you*'re here,' she said, challenging him.

'It is,' he said, uncertain of what more she might hope to learn from him, knowing only that any honest answer he gave her would only disappoint her further.

But she didn't press him on this, perhaps preferring the security of her own half-believed dreams and expectations.

'What happened to the apartments?' Quinn asked her.

'What do you think happened? He refused to move and then he started making trouble for everyone involved, saying everything was wrong, that all their plans would come to nothing, that he was being cheated, denied what was rightfully his. He worked at the paper and then they sacked him for some of the things he wanted to write about.'

'I heard. Was any of it actually published?'

She laughed at the suggestion. 'Too many people keeping an eye on that kind of thing. Especially when everything *was* finally given the go-ahead.'

'Protecting their interests,' Quinn said, wishing he hadn't. *People like me*, he thought.

'What else did Wade tell you?'

Quinn tried to remember. 'Not much.'

Beside them, Winston slumped sideways in his chair and started mumbling to himself.

'I've just spent an hour looking for him,' Rebecca said. 'One of his cronies said they'd seen him in the street.'

Quinn wondered about the nature of the responsibility she now felt for the man.

'Perhaps you could leave and take him with you,' he suggested.

She responded to this as though he'd just said the cruellest thing imaginable to her. She held her mug in both hands, and for a moment Quinn thought she might be about to throw it at him. But she quickly controlled herself, content merely to look at him and to cause him to turn away from her.

'And perhaps *you* could arrange all that for us,' she said eventually. 'A nice little house in the countryside? Somewhere dry and sunny, preferably. Perhaps a village with a green and a little shop, a church and a pub for Winston here. A wooden bench would be nice, somewhere for him to sit until opening time, a nice view over a river, fields, a ruined castle perhaps, swallows flying overhead. Perhaps you could even arrange for the same clear blue skies and little white fluffy clouds the Development people like so much. You know – the same ones that are going to miraculously appear over this place at the same time as all their fabulous new buildings rise up into the sky.' She ran out of breath and stopped talking.

Beside her, Winston, alerted by her raised voice, said, 'What? Little clouds?' He looked from side to side, his eyes barely open.

'Up in the sky,' Rebecca said to him.

And just as Quinn had heard Wade's affection for the man in everything he'd said, so he now understood the strength of the connection between the girl and her father.

'I'll have a word with Greer,' Quinn told her, causing her to smile. 'Do the swallows still come this far north?'

She didn't know, but she accepted the remark for the apology it was intended to be.

'They offered him every chance they were legally obliged to offer him,' she said. 'But most of those opportunities involved him finding a bit of money. Besides . . .'

'He wasn't considered shiny enough for one of their new apartments?'

'Something like that. Me neither, in all likelihood. Young professionals, people with skills, entrepreneurs, media, IT, creative people. There's not much in any of their brochures or downloads about people like him and me.'

'They'll always—'

'Don't say it,' she said, stopping him. 'Next time I *will* throw the coffee.'

'I was only going to say that the place will need all sorts of people if it's ever going to get off the ground and function properly afterwards.'

'Of course you were. All sorts of people, even garage card-watchers. I'm twenty-three. How long do you think it will be before everything here is what they say it's going to be – five years? Ten? Twenty?'

'It might be sooner than you think,' Quinn said, disappointing them both.

Beside them, Winston fell back in his chair and started snoring wetly. Rebecca finally took the untouched mug from the arm.

'Did you believe any of it?' she said, avoiding his eyes. 'What he told you.'

'About the floods? He showed me the pictures.'

'Everyone else wants to think he's—' She tapped her forehead.

'I can imagine,' Quinn told her.

'So it flooded. So what?'

Winston started mumbling in his sleep and they both watched him for a moment.

'I used to try and listen to what he was saying,' she said. 'Make some sense of it all.'

Quinn waited a moment and then rose and told her it was time for him to leave. She seemed genuinely disappointed by this.

'Will you talk to him again?' she asked him hesitantly.

'Of course.'

'He won't remember any of this.'

Quinn looked down at the sleeping man, pleased that he remained oblivious to the small dark history that had been woven and then just as rapidly unpicked around him.

Part III

19

Anna returned from the capital seven days later, two days later than anticipated. On the day she originally planned to return, Quinn called her, hoping to meet her before she arrived at the motel, but her secure number had been diverted. She had not returned any of his calls, and so he'd assumed she hadn't received them. When she didn't reappear on the fifth day, he stopped calling.

On the evening of that day, alone again in the bar, and with only a few of Anna's colleagues gathered in small groups around him, he had convinced himself that she was being kept away from the place and that he would never see her again.

Her recall to the capital, he decided, had been a ruse. She had returned and had been either dismissed or reallocated elsewhere, most probably the latter. Perhaps some of the men and women sitting around him now already knew this, and perhaps that was why they kept their distance from him, why no one spoke to him, why they looked away or pretended to be otherwise engaged each time he glanced in their direction.

She reappeared two days later, mid afternoon, shortly after Quinn himself had returned to the motel following yet another unrewarding morning amid the Administrative records.

He watched from behind his blinds as Anna pulled into the car park and then as she sat in her car for a further ten minutes. When she finally emerged she went to the low wall surrounding the space and sat there with her coat over her shoulders. Quinn observed her, only stepping back when she looked up to search the building's front.

After a further quarter of an hour she finally left the wall and entered the motel.

And twenty minutes after that, Quinn went down to her room and knocked, again calling to identify himself.

She shouted back to him to wait a moment and then came to the door with a towel wrapped around her and with her hair encased in the turban of another.

'I saw you get back,' Quinn said.

'Spying from on high?' The words told him a great deal.

'Waiting. I was beginning to think they weren't going to let you return.' He tried to make light of the remark, but with enough of an edge to convey his concern to her.

She kissed him and unwound the towel from her hair, sitting at the mirror to dry herself.

Quinn sat on the bed beside her.

'Was it as bad as you imagined it was going to be?'

'Worse, probably. I'm late back because there was a big interagency get-together and they wanted me – their only operative currently *in theatre*, and, oh, how my bosom swelled with pride at *that* particular introduction – to front a presentation on how fabulously well everything was going up here.'

'A presentation to potential private investors?'

'Mostly. Men in suits rubbing their hands and licking their lips.'

'Did you have anything prepared?'

'No need. It was all ready and waiting for me. All I had to do was to show them the dirt beneath my otherwise impeccably manicured nails.'

'Smiling in all the right directions and telling everyone exactly what they wanted to hear.'

'You've done it yourself,' she said.

'Before or after you'd told your superiors what was *really* happening at the exhumation site?'

'After. For all the good *that* did. Apparently, this has become a bit of a showcase. The first of a whole new era of resettlement programmes.'

Quinn considered this. 'Meaning it won't be allowed to fail, whatever happens? Meaning they'll pour as much money into it as it needs to succeed?'

'Meaning it will be *seen* to succeed, whatever the cost or the short cuts taken.' She rubbed her hair and then combed it out with her fingers. Quinn felt the spray on his face. 'It's probably no more or less than we already knew.'

'Where are they going after here?' he asked her.

'Apparently, the Scots are finally preparing to relax their own immigration policy.'

'Meaning that now they're about to lose the Clyde–Forth axis, they'll sign over the Southern Highlands?'

She shrugged and then nodded. 'That's the plan.'

'The developers will have a field day,' Quinn said. *The jackals are running out of prey*, John Lucas had once whispered to him at a similar meeting.

'That, too, is the plan. And all those private investors might first be brought here to see exactly how valuable their investment will be made to be.' She turned to face him. 'The meeting had a banner – "Positive Progress". Catchy, eh?'

'Unlike every other resettlement initiative,' Quinn said.

The latest of these, a decade earlier, moving the last of the inhabitants of East Anglia into the West Midlands, had failed when almost half of them had chosen simply to return to live as closely as possible to their no longer viable former homes, however short-lived their return proved to be. 'Viability' had become a measure, judgement, justification and clarion call for half a century.

'Another of the reasons I was late back is because they've closed off more of the old M1. Sections in the Home Counties Zone are already undermined. I had to detour to the new elevated sections. I wasn't authorized. A lot of phone calls.'

'How are they proposing to get people to move to Scotland?' Quinn asked her, knowing that even the first of these programmes was unlikely to come to fruition for at least another decade.

'Completely destroy their old homes was plan A,' Anna said. She rubbed cream into her face.

Neither of them spoke for several minutes.

And then Quinn said, 'And what do they expect you to do here? Surely, the problems of—'

'What problems?' she said, turning to face him as she said it, her meaning clear to him. 'All *they* know is that they want the place cleared *as specified*, capped and made ready. Any problems – "eventualities" being once again their preferred designation, and no longer qualified by that old standby "unforeseen" – any eventualities not identified in the original plan of work are to be either overcome or redefined in accordance with objectives. It's nothing we haven't both heard fifty times before.'

'You're still the one with the dirt beneath your nails,' Quinn said.

'Thanks for pointing that out.'

He apologized and put his hand on her arm.

'These things will be done,' she said, as though completing a sermon. 'And then you and I – the instigators of these things that will be done – shall go elsewhere and perform the same shoddy miracles there.'

'And keep our mouths shut?'

'And our dirty hands clean. Though possibly more in the hope that our enforced failings don't come to light and that we are never brought to account for them.' She turned back to the mirror. 'The first hour of the day during "Positive Progress" was a run-down – more bullet-pointed smiles and reassuring virtual re-creations – of all those Big Science things we were all once supposed to have had so much faith in.'

'Like filling the oceans with manufactured bacteria and dragging the Gulf Stream back to where it belonged?'

They both laughed at this and some of the room's lesser tensions were released.

'I met John Lucas,' she said. 'He sends his regards.'

'John? At the conference?'

'He was there to represent your lot.'

'Not Webb? It sounds like the kind of thing he actually enjoys attending.'

She shook her head. 'It was definitely John Lucas. He knew

who I was, asked if we'd run into each other. He gave me a letter to give to you.' She took this from her bag and gave it to him. 'A new address and a closed phone line. He wants you to call him. He reminded me a lot of you.' She smiled at him.

'Oh? Hard-working, decent and with his integrity and firm belief in the future and the inherent goodness of humanity still intact?'

She laughed again. 'The last of a dying breed. Besides, what belief in the future? Wait until they tell everyone still hanging on in Cambridge that they'll all soon be relocating to Dumfries. What kind of future do you think they'll consider *that* to be?'

'They'll do what people have been doing for the past fifty years and keep pushing the worst of everything ahead of them.'

'Making sure nothing's believable until it actually happens?'

'Until it's already happened, in most cases. People were still driving through six inches of water on the old motorways long after the roads had been put out of bounds by the insurers.'

'Speaking of which, you'll probably have to make alternative arrangements for your own return,' she said. 'Trying to do it once you're on the move is a nightmare. No one's happy about sending fuel accreditation or travel authorizations along unsecured channels these days.'

Quinn considered this. He tapped the envelope John Lucas had sent him on his knee.

Anna watched him do this, guessing his thoughts. 'He told me to tell you not to delay. He meant here. Thirty days and then get back to the capital. He sounded serious.'

'He never sounds serious,' Quinn said.

She watched him for a moment. 'He did this time.'

'He audited the new road system when the comprehensive tolls were introduced. He sent the Ministry of Transport a graph compiled of crushed cars showing them how many millions in taxes they were going to lose each week.'

'What happened?'

'They ignored everything he told them. The Treasury backed them up.'

'And the motorists just either disappeared or went on driving through the water anyway?'

'A year's work for nothing,' Quinn said. It was when John Lucas's own seeds of disillusion had been sowed and then stamped firmly into barren ground. 'A week after they read what he had to tell them they extended the fuel-accreditation scheme. How are people supposed to respond rationally to all their predictions and warnings when the sky falls in on them day after day after day?'

Anna unfastened the towel and revealed her back to him. And then she refastened it and sat staring at her own reflection.

'What are you going to tell everyone here?' Quinn asked her eventually.

'What a good and vital job they're all doing?' she said mechanically. 'Same old same old. Build the future by burying the past.' She reached over to her bag and lifted out a bottle. Branded whisky. 'A gift from John Lucas.'

'For me?'

'For both of us,' she said.

'At his last assessment he was flagged up to Webb as a borderline alcoholic,' Quinn said, remembering the night he and John Lucas had then spent celebrating this.

'I imagine that covers just about anyone who drinks anything these days,' Anna said.

'It does.' He took the bottle from her and unscrewed the cap, catching the sudden sharp aroma of the drink.

'No glasses,' Anna said.

'Shame.' Quinn drank from the bottle and handed it to her. She did the same, blinking and then coughing at the impact of the spirit.

'Our predecessors – Lucas's and mine – used to undertake day-long audits two hundred miles from the capital,' Quinn said. 'Early departures and late returns, four-hour audits and real lunches. And two fast, straightforward journeys there and back. They used to talk about them as though they were passing through unmapped country to places that might not even exist. *My* first probationary audit was in Sheffield. A day to get there, a day to carry out what should have been an hour-long audit, and then another day to get back. Lucas still has a bottle of green ink on his desk to remind him that he trained as an actuary before that particular department was swallowed up by the auditors.'

'Along with the scriveners and notaries, presumably.' She paused. 'He seemed serious about you not getting yourself mired in things up here.'

She stood up and Quinn rose with her and held her, feeling the knot of her towel hard in his chest.

They kissed, and Quinn knew by the way she held his arms that their embrace would go no further. She was the first to withdraw.

'Sorry,' she said.

Quinn shook his head. 'You've had a long day.'

She nodded. 'The others will be back soon, gathered around the campfire to nod and shrug sympathetically at all my lies.'

'They're not *your* lies,' he said.

'Yes they are. Lies plus complicity are still lies. Perhaps they're even something worse.' She screwed the cap on the whisky and gave it to him. 'Read your letter,' she said. She kissed him on the chin and sat back down.

20

Alone in his room, Quinn opened John Lucas's letter.

Webb, Lucas wrote, was currently undergoing a week-long interview for a position on the Executive Body of the National Development Agency. They were the men Quinn had seen at the church site, the ones who had remained standing over the foundations as Pollard and Stearn had come to him. Members of the Executive were all-seeing and all-powerful, seconded to every other governmental body and agency, and had offices inside every Government department – most notably these days in the departments of Homeland and International Security, into which much of the work previously undertaken by the National Police Force and the Armed Forces had long since disappeared. The two security services, it was now calculated, were responsible for almost half of all Government expenditure. It seemed a perfect place for Webb to be.

Quinn remembered an old adage, often repeated to him by his father, an architect: 'Build a trough and the first thing you do is attract pigs.'

John Lucas's letter was short, intended as a signal to Quinn to start to prepare for his return, and for the changes Webb's departure and replacement would now entail.

The Public Audit Commission had been one of the first bodies to have been wholly consumed and reshaped by the Development Agency, renamed the Ministry of Public and Environmental Audit.

If Webb *were* to rise into the higher echelons of the Executive, then presumably one of his own favoured employees in the Audit Department would be chosen to succeed him. And if Webb were to rise that high at such a propitious time – at the very start of this new era of resettlement – then he wouldn't tolerate even the slightest degree of risk or failure beneath him, and certainly not from the department he himself had so recently been the head of.

What Quinn also began to understand as he considered the outcome of all this, was that whatever faults or discrepancies he discovered as part of his current investigation, these would be made to disappear – flooded with newly calculated figures and restitutional-entry equations until every stormy surface was made calm again. Whatever he submitted in his report about the place would now be considered and then amended by Webb before being handed over to his own new masters.

Quinn called the number attached to the letter, but there was no answer. It was shortly before six. John Lucas would not be home for another hour or two, later if he was still pursuing his borderline-alcoholic status. The thought and the memory made Quinn smile.

Lucas finally called him back at nine, just as Quinn was preparing to go back in search of Anna.

The first thing he asked was if the network line was secured, and Quinn told him it was. It was something Lucas always did, fuelling the clouds of benign conspiracy which seemed to endlessly enclose him.

'Nice woman,' he said, meaning Anna.

'If you like all that animal-corpse-exhumation thing.'

Lucas laughed.

'Is Webb going to get the job?'

'The smart money's been piling up on him all week. It's not what you should be asking me.'

Quinn considered this. 'Meaning it's more important now to consider who might be about to replace him?'

'That "might" might come to sound a little superfluous.'

'Todd?' Quinn said.

'More smart money piling up. Plus, the greasy little bastard's been sitting in Webb's chair all week with his feet up on Webb's desk.'

'Are you certain?' Quinn said.

'Don't sound too surprised or delighted. We should all have seen this one coming.'

'I didn't even know Webb had higher ambitions,' Quinn said.

Lucas laughed at the phrase. 'It's what sets us apart – you and me, Quinn – ambition.'

'I have ambitions,' Quinn said, but with no true conviction.

'Of course you do,' Lucas said. 'But not ambition like Webb and little Todd have ambition.' He paused. 'In addition to which, I imagine your own ambitions are a little more specific and personal-fulfilment-directed at present.' Again, he meant Anna.

'"Personal-fulfilment-directed"?'

'See?' Lucas said.

Todd had been appointed as Webb's deputy only a year earlier. He had come to the Audit Ministry from Security and Intelligence and his brief had been to help oversee and implement procedures adapted from Security and Intelligence whenever any new development project was being considered. He had arrived shortly after the department had doubled in size, and when its budget had been increased five-fold – behaving, as John Lucas had pointed out to Quinn, like a groom arriving at a wedding with a fabulous dowry. No one had been in any doubt about where all this extra money was to be spent, or who would oversee that spending.

Todd was married with a young son and was fifteen years younger than either Quinn or Lucas. In all likelihood, he was already preparing to follow Webb into higher office.

'Is security becoming a bigger problem?' Quinn said.

Lucas laughed. 'On the building sites? Not that I'd noticed. Besides, we're not the ones who get to say what is or what isn't a security issue. The main thing to remember now is that everything's about to be cranked up a gear.'

'Because we're entering another new era?'

This time they laughed together. 'They're already talking about your place as a flagship project,' Lucas said.

'Anna already told me during one of our personally fulfilling encounters.'

'They're going to start abandoning as many marginals as possible. A lot of their beloved lines are being redrawn. They've lost too much time and money on holding actions. Don't tell anyone, but the last two parks are being redesignated next month.'

He meant National Parks. The last two being the Dales and the Lakes. The rest had already been effectively handed over to regional development agencies twenty or thirty years earlier, after which the land had been released for development as the flood waters elsewhere had risen and spread.

'And Scotland?' Quinn said.

'It's going to happen,' Lucas said. 'Birthright, mess of potage and all that. They're drawing up a thousand-year lease on everything south of Glasgow. The rest of them are packing up their tents and moving even further north.'

'And you think Webb will have some part to play in all of this?'

'All this momentous history? Yes. Webb and Todd alike. According to some, Webb's already participating. His appointment to the Executive is guaranteed.'

Meaning Webb knew all this before sending Quinn to this lost and failing place, and that all those others already beckoning Webb further up the ladder towards them also knew it was about to become the brightest of their visions for the future.

Quinn knew that John Lucas would be thinking these same thoughts, and the unspoken revelation hung between them for a moment.

Then Lucas said, 'He was thinking about bringing a delegation of his new friends all the way up there to see you. Show you off to them. Let them see what a safe pair of hands you are. You and wherever it is you've landed.' He knew exactly where Quinn was. There was now a kind of pleading in everything he said.

'It's nothing,' Quinn said absently. 'Nowhere.'

'And that might just be the point of it all,' Lucas said. 'Like I said, ambition, big ambitions, even bigger ambitions.'

'And afterwards?' Quinn said.

'After what? There won't be any afterwards, at least not for the likes of us. The "afterwards" for us will always be something else and somewhere else. Who knows, perhaps you'll get to join in the new Scottish adventure. Todd was talking earlier about three million new homes being needed. Seven million people. You can imagine how excited the Boy Wonder's getting about it all.'

Quinn heard footsteps and voices in the corridor outside, men and women leaving their rooms and converging. He waited for a moment, listening, wondering if Anna was among them, straining to hear her voice.

'You still there?' John Lucas said after a minute.

'*Has* Todd said anything about what *we*'ll be doing in this new phase?'

For the first time, John Lucas seemed uncertain of his answer and Quinn knew that he was trying to conceal something from him.

'What is it?'

Lucas let out a long breath before speaking. 'Todd's already wondering aloud about the value of our probity audits. He says we're living in desperate times which call for desperate measures. Welcome to the party, eh?'

'Steamrollering?'

'Something like that. I'm sure he'll come up with a fancier name for it. "Expediency" always sounds good to men like him. Let the developers bid, the planners plan and the builders build. Upwards and onwards. Nothing we haven't heard before. The mortgage economy is already non-existent in some places.'

'They'll be the places already under water,' Quinn said. It was an old joke, but Lucas acknowledged their shared history and laughed at it.

'Plus,' Lucas said loudly, interrupting Quinn's thoughts, 'most of the Scottish projects will be Green Field. Remember that? According to the new regulations, they won't *need* an audit. Besides, no one's carried out a proper Environmental for years.'

'The developers might still call for one,' Quinn countered.

'Of course they might. Unless they let it be known to the Executive beforehand that the idea of such a thing would be a great disappointment and expense to them, offensive even. Against the *spirit* of the thing. Unless they stamped their feet and threatened to withdraw from all these desperately needed projects. Unless that happened.'

'You think Webb would give them carte blanche?'

'I think Webb will do what he always does – work out where the real power lies and then make sure he's on the right side of the line. He gave us all a rousing little speech on the eve of his departure for interview, telling us all to try and look fifty years into the future as though it were tomorrow. He even sent us all a copy of it to take home with us. Fifty years into the future. Apparently, he's that kind of man now. He also wants us all to dress more smartly. We're letting the side down. What "side" would that be, do you think?'

'Even you?' Quinn said.

'I know. I'll have to buy a tie. He accused me of being obsessed with the past, said I was like a man poring over the minutiae of the title deeds when the roof had just blown off the house.'

'That's exactly what you are,' Quinn said. 'What, if anything, did he have to say about me?'

'He made a point – as these people always make their point – of saying that he didn't feel comfortable discussing or commenting on anyone who wasn't there to represent themselves in person. I've been on Courts for the past fortnight. I think it's Webb and Todd's way of giving me an unhappy glimpse of my own long, unwinding, downhill road ahead.'

Court work involved the auditors being called in person to give evidence, usually in cases concerning contested or illegally amended contracts based on audit findings. It was tedious and time-consuming work, requiring little more from the attending auditor than the swearing of an affidavit relating to the relevant records of audit. Actual involvement might have lasted only a minute or two, but the assigned auditor was then required to remain in attendance throughout the hearing. Sometimes this lasted an hour, sometimes a week. In the past the work had been delegated to juniors and probationers. To allocate a man of John Lucas's expertise and standing to the work signified a great deal – not only to Lucas himself, but to everyone who knew him.

'And before you tell me to tell Todd to find somebody else for the work,' Lucas went on, 'you might also like to consider the fact that Todd's father is the brother of the man about to lay the sword on Webb's less than noble shoulders.'

'Seriously?'

'Serious enough for Todd to already be arranging Webb's celebratory dinner. To which, incidentally, neither you nor I are invited.' He stopped talking to allow Quinn to continue to grasp the ever-growing implications of all this unexpected news.

'Anyhow,' he said eventually, 'back to our conversation about ambition.'

Quinn heard the sound of glass on glass and imagined Lucas pouring himself a drink, another drink.

'I could finally buy that Lakeland cottage I always fantasized about,' Lucas said. 'Except now it's more likely to be a twentieth-floor apartment in a block of five hundred other apartments in a development of five hundred other blocks. Not much room for the lake, I imagine.'

'Or the mountain view,' Quinn said, glancing to the window and imagining the circle of invisible hills which surrounded him where he sat. 'Do you think Webb was serious – about coming up here to show everything off to his new friends?'

'Todd certainly thinks it's on the cards. He was talking about joining the party. Something else for you to look forward to.'

'Meaning you think I ought to use it to my own advantage?' Quinn said.

'It's the world we live in,' Lucas said.

And for the first time in their conversation, Quinn heard the defeat in his friend's voice. It was beyond him to ask what Lucas himself might now do.

'Tell Anna that I send my regards,' Lucas said. 'She struck me as being one of us.' He seemed more convinced of Quinn and Anna's relationship than Quinn himself was. *Only two sorts of people in this world – them and us.*

'I'll do that,' Quinn said. 'Your regards.' He looked at his watch. It was almost ten.

'Has it snowed yet?'

'What?'

'Snow. Has it snowed yet? You're up in the hills, the back of beyond. Snow . . . you know.'

Quinn remembered the icy rain of a few days earlier. 'Six

feet deep in places. The hilltops are covered. Blinding when the sun shines on it. You should come up and see it. We've got icicles, log fires, mulled wine, the lot.'

'I'm on my way,' Lucas said, and clicked off his phone.

21

The following morning, before dawn, he left the motel and drove back to Pollard's new church. The construction site surrounding the original building was deserted, and in places the barrier panels had been pulled aside to allow heavy plant inside the perimeter.

Careful to park beyond the cameras at the site, Quinn made his way to the church avoiding the main streets, emerging at the rear of the building where he had been confronted by Pollard and Stearn ten days earlier.

There was no one there now. The guard cabin stood empty and dark beside the line of excavators. Arc lights still shone down on the site of the new building, reflected in the puddles and the water-filled foundations, but the old church itself stood mostly in darkness, a string of dim bulbs draped over its high entrance.

Quinn entered by a side door, surprised to find it unlocked. Inside, he found that the corridor leading into the body of the church was being used by the workmen to store the smaller pieces of their equipment.

He walked through this into the church itself, surprised again by his sudden emergence into so large and high a space. He saw immediately the outline of the original building and the rising walls of the new structure, the one appearing to grow through the other. He saw too where scaffolding and supports presaged the further extensive enlargement about to take place. The original building, he guessed, would have held two hundred people, its imminent reincarnation over ten times that number.

He waited in the darkness of the corridor for a moment, checking that the security guards had not come into the church for the night. The building inside was as cold as the air outside, and Quinn guessed that the work on the new foundations had caused the heating system to be put out of commission.

He stepped silently into the centre of the church, checking that its internal cameras were also inactive. The pale wooden pews stretched back and forwards from him, creating the illusion of waving lines. His breath clouded in the air ahead of him. He clicked his tongue for the simple pleasure of hearing the high, sharp echo. A finger tapped at the end of one of the pews created the same effect. A dropped Bible in that empty place would have sounded like a peal of thunder.

Crossing the central aisle, he approached the altar, a design of glass and aluminium high above the congregation. Pollard's pulpit rose even higher, and supported him on the wings of an eagle. A giant silver Bible lay ready to receive his own book. Cones and tape circled the pulpit, and signs warned that to go any further was unsafe. Quinn crossed this and walked beyond the choir stalls. An embroidered curtain concealed an entrance there, and he drew this aside and opened the door, pausing briefly to look back over the whole body of the church from his vantage point.

The door, as he'd hoped, led, through a small annexe, a registry and then a dressing room, to a further door, which in turn led to the basement of the church. This second door was locked, but its key hung on a rack beside it, and Quinn unlocked it and returned the key.

A steep flight of stairs led immediately downwards. There was a switch, but no light. A short distance ahead of him he saw blocks on the steps, and approaching them he saw that they were batteries. There were heavy cables attached to these, and by tracing one of these along the wall on which it had been hung, he came to the metal bowl of a temporary light. He switched this on and was immediately blinded by it, turning it away from him and then standing for a moment with his eyes closed.

When the dazzle finally cleared, he pointed the light ahead of him down the last of the steps and then dragged the slack in its cable towards him. He wondered why there wasn't a generator in the basement to provide the power.

He shone the light above him, revealing the plaster of the ceiling and the arched red brickwork of the walls. He was in the original vault, he guessed, and he saw that it ran unbroken the full length and width of the church.

Something in a corner reflected the beam of light and he peered through the darkness to see what this was.

What had reflected the light was a flexible metal hose, pushed through a hole high in the vault, probably at ground level outside. He calculated that he was looking towards the rear of the church, and that this was the means by which the concrete pourers were filling and reshaping the old foundations.

He followed the pipe downwards, guessing that it would end clear of the recently poured concrete. But as the beam descended and reached the open end of the tube, he saw that it hung inert in the space, and that beneath it, rather than the freshly poured concrete he had expected to see, there was an expanse of water. The hose – all the hoses, he realized, had not been for pouring concrete as Pollard had told him, but for drawing out the water in the vault. And if he'd been allowed to approach the noisy vehicles any closer ten days earlier, then he would have seen this for himself. The distant, faceless men of the Executive must have known precisely what was happening there. They might even, it only then occurred to him, have also known who *he* was standing at the distant barrier.

He traced the boundary of the wall and the ceiling and saw the other hoses dangling there, all of them driven crudely through the brickwork of the original church. He counted eight of these, following the line until the ball of light was aimed directly above him.

He then pointed this back to his feet, tracing several of the hoses into the dark water. Close to, this gave off a faintly sulphurous odour. Pieces of timber and empty cans clotted on the surface where the water met the steps. Slicks of oil and chemicals surrounded this and made shifting patterns in the strong light.

Quinn sat down and played the light back and forth over the surface. Hearing something ahead of him, he swung the light to watch a succession of bubbles rise and burst at the centre of the room, followed by a slight surge across the water. Planks knocked together close to his feet as the slow waves lapped against the steps.

He sat like that, searching the surface and listening to the noise the water made, for several minutes. When he switched off the lamp, he saw the dim natural light entering where the hoses had been knocked through the brickwork. He was surprised to see this and he wondered how long he had been in the church for daylight already to be showing.

And then he heard the sound of a distant engine, and he realized that the light was not natural, but was in fact the rising glare of the arc lights surrounding the construction site.

He lay his own lamp down and retraced his steps to the door, passing quickly through the registry and its ante-rooms back into the dark, cold body of the church.

Here, too, the lights outside were revealed at the stained-glass windows, casting their patterns over the pews and floor.

Quinn went back to the pulpit, and just as he was about to descend and leave by the same side door, the fluorescent lighting at the church's entrance flickered into life, causing him to duck instinctively into the well of the pulpit to avoid being seen. He looked at his watch; it was not yet six o'clock.

Other lights were switched on. Outside, a succession of cold generators were primed and coaxed into life. The church doors opened and a group of men came inside. They gathered at the head of the aisle for a moment, talking loudly among themselves before separating and leaving again.

Quinn raised himself from where he crouched and looked out over the silver Bible. The church was empty, though surrounded now by the noise of the men and their machinery outside. There were lights at every window, and each time the main doors were opened the glare of these filled the church.

Quinn left the pulpit and walked among the pews, sitting there and wondering how he might now leave the building without being seen. Each of the seats, he saw, bore a small plastic plaque announcing the person, business or agency that was sponsoring it.

In places, he could smell the same chemical notes in the air that he'd smelled in the vault below. Elsewhere, the acrid tang of the generator smoke had already penetrated the building.

A nearby door opened and closed and someone walked briskly into the church, his heels tapping on the wooden floor. A workman, perhaps, or one of the architects or managers who watched over them. Quinn waited, watching the figure out of the corner of his eye, perfectly still, his breathing silenced.

The solitary man walked to the front of the church, and only when he passed through the coloured light of one of the windows did Quinn finally recognize Pollard. It seemed unlikely that he hadn't already seen Quinn there, motionless and silent amid the shadows and the light.

But Pollard continued walking until he reached the steps leading up to his altar. And then he turned and looked out across the church. As he did this, several of the generators pumping out the flooded vault were switched on, and their noise – a rasping sound of choked pipes followed by a steady hum and then the splatter of drawn water – filled the building.

Pollard cursed loudly where he stood.

Quinn swung his legs from where he sat, and the instant he did this Pollard turned to him, shielded his eyes and shouted to ask who was there.

When Quinn didn't answer immediately, Pollard shouted again, even more angrily, telling whoever it was to stay exactly where they were.

Quinn expected that the man might come to confront him, but instead Pollard took out a phone and started calling someone.

Quinn stepped into the aisle and called out to identify himself.

Pollard stopped what he was doing.

'The book-keeper?' Pollard said disbelievingly. He continued to shield his eyes and search the church, calling for Quinn to come closer to him.

Quinn walked into a patch of coloured light, stopping ten feet from the altar.

'Whatever else you think you're doing, you're trespassing,' Pollard shouted down at him, but with considerably less hostility than before. 'How long have you been here?'

'Here, or in the basement?' Quinn said pointedly.

Pollard considered this. The drone of the sucking pipes continued to fill the space. 'It's called a crypt,' he said. There was now even a suggestion of amusement in his voice.

'A flooded crypt,' Quinn said. 'You're *reconfiguring* water?'

'I've got about as much chance of that as I have of walking across it,' Pollard said.

'Who did you think I was?' Quinn asked him.

Pollard shrugged, but the unspoken lie was unconvincing.

'Who were you expecting? Stearn?'

Pollard laughed. 'Why him?'

'To keep everyone except the suddenly-anxious Executive men away from your new foundations.'

Pollard laughed again. 'What, and you think the new church *isn't* still going to rise from them when they're properly emptied, dried out and filled in?'

'They'll never be dry,' Quinn said. 'The whole place is slowly filling up.' It was simultaneously a guess and a realization.

'So?' Pollard seemed genuinely unconcerned by the revelation, or by the man making it. 'You think this is just the physical foundations of a building we're talking about here? You think this is just earth, mud, bricks and mortar?'

'That's exactly what it looked like to me,' Quinn said.

Pollard shook his head, almost sympathetic now towards Quinn's lack of understanding or belief. 'You're an ignorant man, Mr Quinn,' he said. 'Intelligent, educated, conscientious and thorough, perhaps; even good at what you're here in the hope of achieving . . . but ignorant. Although I daresay you work solely at the paid bidding of others, rather than as a result of any more selfless motive.' Another of the man's evasive and confusing convolutions. 'But ignorant all the same. As ignorant as all those other poor, blind unbelievers wandering in the darkness out there looking for a light to lead them forwards.' And from the convoluted back to this over-rehearsed and unconvincing sermonizing.

'Or wandering in the flooded wilderness?' Quinn said. 'And by "unbelievers" I assume you mean all those worshippers of other faiths and other gods.' He paused. 'Or perhaps only those non-sponsors of this single shining beacon lighting the solitary way to Heaven.'

Pollard gripped the rail beside him, struggling to control his response to this. He closed his eyes and took several deep breaths. 'The foundations of any true church are the moral foundations of the society which has built up around that church, which worships in that church, and which supports it in whatever way is necessary.' And again from the shadows into the light of this practised rhetoric.

'Your sponsors,' Quinn said flatly. 'The foundations are still flooded and water is still coming from somewhere and looks set to carry on coming. Even you must see the irony of all this "foundations" talk.'

'The church has overcome considerably greater obstacles than a little water, Mr Quinn.'

'Not this one. What do you propose to do when it rises to the roof of your basement – sorry, crypt – and starts seeping up through these boards?' He stamped his foot on the floor.

'That will never happen. The crypt will be drained and filled and made solid. Greer himself has given me his personal guarantee of that.'

'Greer? I would have thought he had more—'

'You talk of a flooded wilderness, but that wilderness is not *here*, not *here*,' Pollard shouted. 'It's out there, out in the world you yourself inhabit, book-keeper.'

But it is here, Quinn wanted to shout back at him. *It's beneath your own feet and rising all the time. How much closer could it be?* But he said nothing.

'You seem strangely silent,' Pollard said, smiling.

'Whatever Greer's told you,' Quinn began, uncertain of what he wanted to say next, and seeing Pollard already shaking his head and laughing at him.

'Go on, Mr book-keeper, please finish whatever you were about to say. I daresay you disappoint even yourself with all these predictable remarks.'

Neither man spoke for a moment. Pollard released his grip on the rail and rose higher towards his pulpit.

Perhaps, Quinn thought, he intended to enter it and close its low gate; perhaps he wanted everything he now said to be a sermon, to be silently endured and unassailable.

But Pollard stopped short of entering the pulpit, instead looking fondly into it and imagining himself there.

'You've seen the model in Greer's foyer?' he said eventually.

Quinn nodded.

'It's nothing. The original proposal. Even at that scale, I doubt if the redevelopment in its entirety could be fitted into the ground floor of the Administrative building.'

'Is that why Greer is already behaving like a little king with the town as his domain?'

Pollard smiled. 'And not just the town, book-keeper – the future, too.'

'And what, he's convinced you that the church – that *you* – will also be at the centre of everything as that new future dawns?'

If Pollard heard the continued mockery in this, then he did nothing to refute it.

'Oh, this place will be attended,' he said. 'People will come. Mothers, fathers, children, all of them strangers in a strange land. All of them searching, all with their beliefs, all of them looking for a centre which for once might not delude and disappoint them and then evaporate from around and beneath them. All of them on a quest for . . .'

Quinn stopped listening to the man. It was part of his audit to examine the church accounts, and these were already prepared and waiting for him. Twenty years ago, these records had often been duplicated in handwritten ledgers and kept separately in the churches, chapels and cathedrals they represented. And because they were handwritten, and often by the very men of God whose incomes and expenses they had accounted for, they had always seemed to Quinn to be somehow more trustworthy and reliable, more dependable and credible – the four same sides of that single impenetrable square. He knew what a wasted exercise that same audit here was likely to prove.

When he next looked at Pollard, the man had stopped talking and was looking down at him, slightly breathless, clearly believing himself to have defeated Quinn by the might and persuasiveness of whatever he had just said.

'Is that who you were expecting to see here – Greer?' Quinn said, and he saw by Pollard's response to this that he had been right. 'In the middle of the night? When there was no one else around to see the pair of you or what lay beneath the floor you walked on?'

Pollard continued smiling at all of this. 'The middle of the night? Unseen? Open your eyes, Mr Quinn, your ears. No one to see us? It seems to me that you've been too long amid the deceits, evasions and subterfuges of others. This isn't night-time, there's no darkness, not here. You *know* where the darkness lies. This *is* the dawn, book-keeper, a new dawn, *the* new dawn. Not night-time, not darkness.' He paused and pretended to think. 'Or perhaps you, and you alone, are unable to see, let alone to properly embrace, that new dawn.'

Again Quinn stopped listening to the man, and instead he imagined the water coming up through the joists and the boards and the varnished parquetry of the church floor, and then through the soles of his shoes and his socks to soak into the flesh and bones of his feet.

22

No one stopped Quinn as he left the church and then crossed the building site back to his car. The mesh fence had been re-erected around the pumps and the tankers. The same guard sat in his kiosk and watched as he walked through the mud and the water to the empty street.

Back at his car, he tapped in the driver code and pressed the ignition. Nothing happened. He repeated the procedure with the same results. He waited for the control panel to signal the fault to him, but nothing came. A row of symbols was illuminated and then went dark. He waited before pressing the ignition a third time. Three failed starts and he would have to apply for a new code. He slapped his palms on the wheel and cursed. One of the first things John Lucas had taught him was how to bypass the allegedly tamper-proof ignition coding. He tried to remember how to do this, but couldn't.

The first of the day's light appeared on the horizon, delayed by the hills. He knew there were places in the Dales and the Lakes, and elsewhere presumably, which received no direct sunlight for days on end in the middle of winter because of their aspect and the proximity of their surrounding hills. He wondered if these patterns of short-lived shadow would be reflected in their own coming development schemes.

He waited a further few minutes, and just as he was about to leave the car and walk the short distance into the town centre, the line of dashboard symbols came unexpectedly back to life and the car's radio started playing. The eight o'clock time signal sounded and he watched as the clock reset itself to this.

A news broadcast started: notice of the rescheduled road network; notice of the consultation process whereby the more recently inundated zones were being redesignated in accordance with emergency procedure; more African governments closing their borders; the further collapse of housing markets around the Mediterranean as the rising costs of residency visas and healthcare again jeopardized property values; a family in Lincolnshire found dead after committing suicide by poisoning three weeks earlier; another Thamesmouth refinery lost to the water; parliament sitting for forty-eight hours; new rationing limits; increases in the tax on bottled water: small ironies, few mercies. All forty football results from the previous evening.

Quinn waited for the weather report to begin and then switched off the radio. The other lights remained on, their simple presence giving him hope that whatever malfunction had occurred had now somehow corrected itself. Perhaps it had been something to do with the transmission of the time signal. It frequently mystified Quinn how deeply these veins of illogicality and unreason – these new superstitions – still ran in him.

The row of lights flickered for a moment and then the ignition symbol flashed at him.

He pressed the button and the engine started. He pressed the accelerator and heard the engine strain. When he took his foot off, the counters hovered at their start points. He switched on his lights, and immediately every one of the warning symbols went dark, even their outlines lost in the glare of the screen.

It had been his intention after visiting the church to return to the Administrative accounts and bring his work there up to date. And then to schedule a further meeting with Greer now that plans for the place had changed so dramatically. He also wanted to find out what, if anything, Greer might already know of Webb's proposed visit to the town. He still doubted that this would happen.

He finally left the unlit road beside the church and drove the short distance into the town centre. He stopped at a signal beside the newspaper offices. A short queue of employees waited outside. He saw the man called Taylor he had spoken to a week earlier. On impulse, Quinn pulled to one side and walked back to the building.

At the entrance, the day's security codes had not yet been set and he was able to walk in unchallenged. Several of those already there turned to watch him as he crossed the room, but no one spoke to him or attempted to stop him.

He arrived at the glass wall of Fisher's office. This time, Fisher was at his desk, reading the front pages of a pile of papers while simultaneously scanning the screens in front of him.

Quinn went in and closed the door.

Fisher didn't look up at him. 'Put it down there,' he said, waving a hand at a second desk.

Quinn drew up a chair and sat facing the man.

'I said – ' Fisher began, finally looking up.

'You broke our appointment,' Quinn said. He watched closely and saw that the man knew who he was.

'And? I broke our appointment and what?' He remembered something and smiled. 'Oh, I remember – I broke our appointment and so you went off and talked to the local lunatic instead. I say "talked", but, depending on the time of day, you either listened to him ranting on without being able to get a word in edgeways or you sat looking at him, trying desperately not to let any of his stink rub off on you. Which was it?'

Quinn refused to answer.

'What?' Fisher went on. 'First you believed everything he told you, but now you're having second thoughts? Don't tell me – he showed you his photos of the flood. Big deal. Hundred-year-old pictures.'

Fifty-eight-year-old pictures, Quinn thought, but said nothing.

'And what if *I* showed you a picture of this place under a thousand feet of ice? What if I got you a mock-up of that? Because that was just as true. It doesn't mean anything. And it certainly doesn't mean that the ice is coming back.' He paused and searched among the newspapers on his desk. 'In fact I can show you exactly how unlikely that is. I can probably even tell you how many polar bears there are left and which cities they're most likely to be living in. Once it was pandas, now it's polar bears.' He pulled out a sheet of paper and waved it at Quinn. 'Seventeen deaths attributed to bears in the past month.' He read the smaller print. 'Two hundred and twenty culled within a forty-kilometre radius. What does that say to you? What it says to me is "problem solved".'

Quinn wondered about these diversions, about how far they were intended to take them from Winston and his tales and prophecies of the flood.

Eventually, Fisher stopped talking and waving the paper.

'OK,' he said, a forced note of weariness in his voice. 'Say what you've come here to say. Tell me which of his terrible predictions the poor old sod repeated to you.'

'The foundations of your new church are flooded,' Quinn said, catching Fisher off-guard for a moment.

'No – the foundations of the *old* church are flooded. The foundations of the *new* church will be as dry and as solid as . . . as . . .' He could think of no comparison.

'As the exhumation or burning sites?' Quinn suggested, remembering where Fisher had been when he'd last tried to see him.

Fisher considered his response.

'I thought it was why you went up there,' Quinn said. 'To let them know how dependent they were on you for whichever way the story was about to blow.'

Fisher smiled. 'Your girlfriend, you mean?' He waited for Quinn's response.

'Think what you like,' Quinn said, immediately wishing he hadn't. The libel laws had been dismantled and redrafted twenty years ago by a committee of new lords and newspaper barons. *Barons*, Quinn thought. *Barons, moguls, czars, commissars.* He looked at Fisher and almost laughed. 'So what's the story now?' he said.

'At the pits?' Fisher feigned indifference. 'Everything's under control. Some seepage. Nothing unexpected. Why, what did you think? What's your girlfriend telling you? Not very wise or discreet of her, don't you think. Not very – ' he pretended to think, 'professional.'

'*She*'s not said anything,' Quinn said, unable to conceal the lie.

'Of course she hasn't,' Fisher said quickly. 'That's why she wasn't called back to the capital for a bollocking. That's why she wasn't very nearly replaced and almost didn't come back.'

It was something Anna had already denied, and Quinn struggled to understand the wider implications of all Fisher had just revealed to him.

'You don't – ' he began to say.

'I don't what? I don't know any of this for certain? You should look at yourself, Mr Quinn. You're sitting there calling *me* a liar, and all *you* want to do is to rub an embittered old alcoholic's groundless theories in my face.'

The crypt was still six feet deep in water; the burial pits were still seeping uncontrollably; the hillside and road to the south were still saturated with run-off.

'Why did you fire him?' Quinn said.

'Winston? Who said he was fired? He was dismissed for a list of misdemeanours and failings as long as your arm. *Wilful* failings, I might add.'

Misdemeanours and failings. Everything followed its patient and perfectly reasonable course.

'I gave him every opportunity to keep himself onside. He liked to think he was a proper journalist, a cut above the rest of us. He'd worked in the capital and Manchester before washing up here. He liked to think he was too good for what I was asking him to do.'

'All this advertorial non-news?'

Fisher smiled and then gestured towards the framed certificates behind him. 'Most profitable local journal for the past seven consecutive years. Not two years or three years, Mr Quinn. Seven. Consecutive. That means one after another. One after another, and no one else getting anywhere close.'

'Presumably as all your so-called competitors went out of business.'

'In this office, we like to think of them as going under.' He laughed loudly at the old joke.

Men and women in the outer room paused to look in at the two of them. There were more of them now, most of them standing at the mounted screens and taking notes.

'News-gathering,' Fisher said.

'Copying old news.'

'It's not old here. You meet Winston's daughter yet?'

The question surprised Quinn and he nodded.

'She's the only reason he's still here. Probably the only reason he's still even alive. She lost her husband – a soldier – India. Something of a local hero. At least, that was always our headline here each time he came home on leave. Ten years older than her. She was only seventeen or eighteen when they married. Get this – his grandfather died in Iraq, his father in Pakistan, and he drew his own short straw in India. I suppose she should thank Christ she didn't have a kid. What would be down for him, eh? China?' He laughed again.

'Are you serious?' Quinn said. He hadn't even known the girl had been married, let alone widowed.

'Who would have believed that *that* particular wind was going to go on blowing for the best part of a century, eh? We still run features when somebody local cops it – though you'd be surprised what passes for "local" these days – numbers rather than names. We lost a bit of focus when they stopped repatriating the bodies. It's still a seller, but more and more we have to consider the changing nature of public opinion on these things. Keep it under your hat, but the families of serving men are about to have their home fuel allowances cut. Twenty years ago, there would have been an outcry; not now.'

'Meaning people don't want to be constantly reminded of what's still being done in their name?'

Fisher laughed at the old argument. 'If you understand that much, then you can surely see the need for everything to now appear to be progressing smoothly here.'

'Meaning you see no need whatsoever to sound even a faint note of caution?'

'About what? Flooded cellars? The expression "time immemorial" springs to mind. Besides, "faint notes of caution" never counted for much in this line of work. Perhaps you should have another cosy chat with your girlfriend. Or, if you've got better things to be doing with your precious stolen moments together, then you should at least be aware of what her own superiors will have said to her. I take it from your response earlier that your pillow-talk – at least on her side – hasn't been as open or as frank as *you* might have liked. You think everybody's going to want to go and live in Scotland? You think *that* particular deal's going to be done and dusted in anything less than ten years? You think the Scottish Government doesn't see how quickly everything's turning to shit down in the South, the Midlands, the East Coast, the Severn corridor? You think they're going to do everything as quickly and as expeditiously as possible to help us out? You think the rising water levels down there make their own high, dry, solid land *less* attractive, *less* valuable, *less* of a bargaining point?' He shook his head. 'You've had your nose stuck in your books – *our* books – for too long, Mr Quinn. You should climb a hill every now and again, look around you, look down.'

Quinn only half-heard most of this.

A phone on Fisher's desk rang and he silenced it.

'What *did* you come here for?' he asked.

Whatever Quinn said would have sounded contrived, lacking conviction.

'To see what kind of man I was?' Fisher said. 'To confirm another of your prejudices? Just to be certain before you joined Winston's crusade? What crusade? No one else listens to him. Prophet of doom, that's what he is. There are only so many you can listen to. Oh, he's got doom, all right – or at least the girl has – doom everywhere you look. But it's all in the past. Where it belongs. And think about it, Mr Quinn – if Winston could bring himself to put *her* future prospects ahead of his own failed fantasies for once, then perhaps both their lives might be improved. Because Christ alone knows how they could get any worse. And even if only *her* life could be made to look a bit brighter, it'd be something.' Fisher laid his palms on the desk. 'Look, I don't know what you thought all this might achieve – telling me what I already know, trying to convince me of something that convinces no one, but I doubt if even you have the courage of your convictions where Winston and all his scaremongering are concerned.' There was now something almost conciliatory in Fisher's tone.

'No,' Quinn said absently, as much and as little as he was able to concede.

Fisher's phone rang again and this time he answered it, identifying himself and then listening without speaking, glancing at Quinn and then spinning in his seat to turn away from him, as though by this simple expedient he might conceal even better what Quinn was already unable to overhear.

When the one-sided conversation was over, Fisher spun back to face him.

Quinn watched him for a moment. 'Bad news?'

'I think that would be for me to decide.' He searched over Quinn's shoulder for someone in the room beyond.

'I'll leave you to it,' Quinn said.

Fisher rose from his seat. 'Perhaps there'll be some kind of get-together to announce the new plans. Celebrate. Something inaugural.'

'Perhaps,' Quinn said, knowing that any celebration would take place long after he had gone from the place, and certainly long after all these doubts and contradictions had been in one way or another fully erased.

23

The same dark smoke rose into the sky ahead of him. A single massive blaze burning over a two-hectare site, its flames higher than the curve of the road's embankment and its smoke impenetrably black and filled with floating embers; and half a dozen smaller fires burning around this, their flames low and lost in the lie of the land, and their own columns of smoke rising into the wind in thinner, paler lines.

Quinn slowed at his approach to the pits, but then accelerated and continued driving when he saw the new and substantial barrier that had been erected there, complete with its own kiosk and guards, several of whom stood at the centre of the slip road and watched him drive on. Before, there had only ever been one of Anna's employees, and perhaps a line of tape, but now there was this. And if there was already one of Stearn's kiosks, then soon there would be cameras and lights.

A mile further and Quinn arrived at the entrance to the lost farm where he had spoken to Owen. The man was there now, standing beside his truck outside the fence. Previously, the land had been empty, level to the hills. Now, only twelve days after Quinn's first visit, it was filled with other vehicles, open carriers and earth-moving machinery, and the previously flat fields had been sculpted into steep ridges and enclosures. It surprised Quinn to see how much had changed in so short a time.

He pulled off the road and drew up alongside Owen's truck. The man watched him approach for a moment and then turned his attention back to whatever was happening inside the perimeter fence.

A succession of other vehicles followed Quinn to the entrance and then continued inside, their wide tyres throwing up water and dirt, which Quinn felt as it hit him and sprayed his car. Owen's truck, he saw, was already coated with the same thin mud.

He went to the man and stood beside him.

'It's finally started,' Owen said simply.

'Are they laying foundations?'

'Nothing quite so grand. It's a dump, another landfill.' The colourful hoardings still rose on either side of the men.

'A dump for what?'

'Rubbish, mostly,' Owen said. He pointed to their right, where a flock of gulls and crows already circled above one of the recently excavated mounds. 'They're turning the farm into a dump. It's not going to have houses on it after all. They're not even going to try and get the land back into any kind of production.'

That, Quinn knew, was never likely to have happened – another of Owen's irretrievably lost hopes.

'Rubbish from where?' Quinn asked him.

'Someone said they were shipping it in from outside. A lot of hardcore, old building materials from sites in the town.' He spoke absently, a man still not completely believing what he was seeing.

The fighting, shrieking birds meant there must also have been something edible being tipped there.

'They used to be like that behind the plough,' Owen said. 'Like spray behind a boat. Thousands of them after the worms in the turned earth. Either that, or they'd follow the drills for a chance of the seed. That's what my father always used to say – "One for the land, one for the wet, ten for the birds."' He shook his head. 'Fifteen years since that land was last turned. Look at the size of that machinery. It'll be like concrete by the time they've finished.'

'Are you still living at the house?' Quinn asked him. The building still stood in the distance, obscured now by the coming and going of the dumpers and diggers.

'You make it sound as though it was already abandoned and derelict,' Owen said.

Which, to Quinn's mind, it was, awaiting only its final gentle push before disappearing as completely as the fields.

'I just wondered if – ' Quinn began.

'I'm still there. Just. And my eviction notice still stands. Two weeks into the New Year. Not that the word "eviction" actually appears anywhere. In fact you'd have to read it ten times over just to understand that I'm being thrown out.'

And for the first time, Owen turned to properly face him, and Quinn saw the cuts and bruises on his face. Owen held his arm awkwardly across his stomach, as though it were already in a sling.

Quinn looked at all this without speaking, and Owen stood for a moment with his eyes closed, removing himself from the inspection.

'What happened?' Quinn said eventually, already guessing most of what the man was about to tell him.

'You can imagine,' Owen said. 'Me – *I* happened. They'd been telling me for months that they were coming. Everything in writing beforehand, duplicate, triplicate, letters I'm supposed to have been sent and then acknowledged. Then notices posted on my door. Every opportunity to prepare myself – only myself to blame.' He waved his hand over the busy scene before them. 'How do you prepare yourself for something like this? I've a picture of that land in my grandfather's day when half the fields – fields: that's a joke – were down to an orchard. Apples, pears, everything. Soft fruit. Even my father could turn three hundred pigs over on that land. Remember pigs?' He rubbed a hand over his face, flinching at the pain this caused him.

'Have you been to the hospital?' Quinn asked him.

'For what? Someone else to gawp and to notch me up another level on the stupidity scale? I've got a first-aid kit in the house. A few cracked ribs, that's the worst of it. Besides, I think I let my insurance lapse.' He laughed coldly at the remark.

'Who did it?'

'Me. I did it to myself. I even went high enough up that scale to threaten to barricade myself in.'

'And that brought Stearn and his men in?'

'Among others. Stearn's lot were there all the time.'

'But none of the National Police Force?'

'It hurts when I laugh, so the less said about them in this place the better, eh?'

'You still have the right to—'

'"Friendly persuasion", that's all this is. "Reasonable force", "justifiable restraint". Take your pick.'

'Why did you confront them if you knew what was likely to happen?'

'Because I'm stupid? Because all I could see was those fruit trees? I could give you fifty answers to that particular question and not a single one of them would make the slightest bit of sense to any reasonable man.'

'Was Stearn himself up here?'

'What do you think? Why get wet and cold when you can sit in a nice warm office and just whisper in their ears while watching it all on a screen like a soap opera? What did I think I was going to achieve? I watched them. They can dig out one of these pits and surround it with a ten-metre wall in a day. They're digging forty of them. Forty. What you can see there, that's six. Six in six days. Another thirty-four to go. They'll still be digging them after I've gone.'

'And the house?'

'The house will be flattened in less than an hour, scooped up and then tipped into one of them. Next question.'

Quinn left him and walked fifty metres along the fence to gain a clearer view of what was happening. Everything seemed disorganized, vehicles of all sorts coming and going at random. But, as elsewhere in the town, he knew there was some overall plan and purpose to all this frantic activity, and he guessed that seen from the distant hills, the pits and their surroundings would appear as regular and as precisely arranged as the carefully spaced trees of that lost orchard.

Dumpers climbed the steep, bare banks of the enclosures,

flattening their surface and leaving the pattern of their tyres on the slopes. They looked to Quinn as though they were climbing too steeply and might overturn, but he knew that that too would have been carefully calculated. He saw earth being scooped and mounded, the tops of cabs and hoppers where the vehicles already worked below the old surface of the fields.

A gust of wind brought the cacophony of the birds to him and he watched as they continued to gather, to rise and fall as though on other winds, their flurries of noise and activity as each new load of waste was tipped. He saw the rollers quickly flattening this waste, running over its moving surface as everything settled, like strata, solidifying, compacted, already turning to a new kind of soil.

And in addition to the noise and the movement, there was a smell, at once sweet and sickly, not unlike vomit at times, but with countless other aromas added. Quinn imagined he smelled coffee, and then roast meat, fuel, then disinfectant. He breathed deeply and felt himself gag, a sudden taste catching in his throat. He coughed and then spat this from his mouth. The farm would be surrounded by all this – this noise and commotion and stink – both day and night until Owen finally left it.

He watched as a lorry tipped its load of blue and yellow drums into one of the holes, where they were immediately covered with soil, and where that soil was equally swiftly flattened and levelled. Another dozen lorries loaded with more drums waited to continue the work. It was all part of the same carefully orchestrated process. A repeated procedure, making and remaking itself as the holes were dug, filled, covered, dug and filled again. A world in turmoil, and nothing as it seemed, only the same dark, slick soil creating the illusion of solidity.

Geography and history churned to mud, levelled and lost and ready to be made anew.

He walked back to Owen.

'Thought you was going to be sick. You get used to it.'

Even when the wind blew hard and directly over, around and through the house?

'I suppose so,' Quinn said. It was as much of the man's defeat as he was able to share.

'This helps.' Owen took a small bottle from his pocket and offered it to Quinn, who took it and drank from it. Owen did the same.

Then, without warning, Owen reached out and held Quinn's arm, not roughly or with any malicious intent, but still firmly, causing Quinn to tense and to try and draw away from him.

'Help me,' Owen said, his voice drying between the two simple words.

'How?' Quinn said, pulling again in an effort to free himself.

'I don't know how,' Owen said. 'I just want *somebody* to help me. Something. Anything.' He seemed mesmerized by his uncertain pleading, surprised that the words had come from his own mouth.

'I don't know what I can do,' Quinn told him.

And just as suddenly as Owen had grabbed and held him, he released his grip and drew back his arm, looking at his hand and his outstretched fingers as though he had no idea how they had come to be held like that.

For his part, Quinn resisted the urge to rub the sensation from his arm. He imagined the five fading marks on his skin.

Eventually, Quinn said, 'Would it help if I spoke to—'

'No,' Owen said immediately, and then he signalled his apology to Quinn. 'I didn't mean to hurt you.'

'You didn't,' Quinn said.

Owen looked even more closely at his hand, clenching it into a fist before opening it again and relaxing. He reached out, as though he himself was about to rub Quinn's arm, but then thought better of the gesture and withdrew. He stepped back from Quinn, towards his truck. 'I ought to get back,' he said. 'The farm.' It hurt him even to say it, to hear the toll of unavoidable condemnation the word now sounded.

Quinn struggled to think of something to say to the man. Something reassuring. But there was nothing. They were all now wanderers in the same strange, lost land. To some it was strange and lost because they had never been there before, and to others it was even stranger and more completely lost to them because it was where they had spent all their lives, and because they were part of that land and had been formed, directed and nurtured by it.

Owen waited at his truck, its door open, turning awkwardly to use his good arm, and causing himself even more pain as he pulled himself up into his seat.

Nothing Quinn could now say would make the slightest difference to him, his misguided sympathy only another finger jabbed into his chest. And so he said nothing.

Finally behind the wheel, Owen drove around Quinn in a wide half circle, leaving the snakeskin lines of his own tyres imprinted in the soft earth and then drawn in the colour of that earth over the dark, wet surface of the road.

24

'Is there anywhere to go?' Anna said.

At first Quinn didn't understand her.

'Here. From here. Nearby.' She swung her arms at the walls.

'Us, you mean?' he said, still guessing.

'It was just a thought.'

It was why the place had been accredited: its isolated location, away from all the so-called diversions of the place, away from the eyes of others. She, he realized, had been there almost three months.

'You think the man responsible for awarding the Government franchise to this place ever visited it?' she said.

'Just keyed in the requirements and let it pick itself,' Quinn said. Like countless identical others all around the country.

They were in Anna's room. She sat on the bed, the detritus of her day's work scattered around her. Quinn stood at the window and looked out. Unlike his own room, this one was at the rear of the motel, facing away from the ring road and its lights, and towards the distant hills, again reduced to outlines in the falling light.

They left the building by the staircase and a side entrance, avoiding the public rooms on the ground floor. Quinn paused in the darkness to look in at the men and women there, but Anna urged him on, unwilling to be seen or stopped. They left the car park and entered the rougher ground in that direction. They both carried torches and shone these ahead of them. Anna was the first to find a path through the grass and she traced it with her beam.

They arrived at a slab of concrete laid over a culvert. The land beyond was even darker, and considerably more overgrown as it started to rise.

They walked together, mostly single-file, along the narrow track for half an hour, pausing frequently to catch their breath and to look back at the spreading view of the illuminated town beneath them.

A further ten minutes' walking brought them to a broader path following the slope along a contour. The remains of a stone wall lay alongside this, a few foundation blocks still standing one upon the other, but the rest scattered and lost in the grass and the darkness. They followed it for a few minutes until they arrived at a slab of rock which protruded from the wall and formed a natural seat wide enough for several people.

Anna sat down, clearing the surface of soil with her gloved hand. 'Cold,' she said, shifting on the seat until it warmed beneath her and she was able to settle.

Quinn sat beside her.

'The wall was probably built along here because the stone was there first,' he said.

She said nothing in reply to this, closing her eyes and turning her face into the breeze which rose up the hillside from the town. For the first time that winter, the temperature in that part of the country had been forecast to fall below freezing and to remain there for the following four or five nights before warming again. Fifty miles further south, and along the lower land to both the east and the west, the nights would remain those same few degrees above freezing.

Beneath them in the distance, and beyond the illuminated circle of the ring road – visible almost in its entirety from that height – they could make out the shape of the town, its core of merged and stronger lights, its tendrils of white and yellow roads and the blocks of outer darkness. In places, this darkness seemed almost complete and Quinn pointed this out to Anna.

'They've been having problems with the power supply,' she said. 'We were warned to take extra fuel for our generators. Some of the sub-stations are being updated.'

Quinn tried to imagine how much more power the place would need once its expansion was under way, and how this might now be generated or imported. The nearest power station was forty miles away.

He gazed down at the brightly drawn outline of the motel, reduced to its interlocking rectangles and lines of light. The whole building appeared to be illuminated, already looking as though it were frozen over, ice forming and glinting where the lights struck reflective surfaces.

The cold from the stone seeped into Quinn's legs and back. Anna moved closer to him, pressing into his side, and he put his arm around her.

'We'll freeze to death up here,' she said. 'We'll die and in a few days' time they'll come looking and find us here like a pair of statues, a monument to unprepared folly.' She seemed almost pleased by the idea, something they might now consider.

'And then we'd thaw and rot and disappear completely,' Quinn said, and that, too, she seemed to appreciate.

They turned off their torches and sat in the darkness. It was a cloudless night, hence the falling temperature, and every constellation and scatter of stars was revealed above them. Anna leaned back on the boulder and traced outlines with her gloved hand, and Quinn confirmed what she pointed out to him. He remembered doing the same on that first night. He could hear running water somewhere behind them, and then more to one side. Another hill of small, unnamed streams and rills; yet more unseen and untended water rising, running, spreading and soaking away.

When Anna finally sat upright, he told her about his wasted day, of his three encounters. But she remained unconcerned about what he believed these had revealed to him, least interested of all in the flooded church. It was only when Quinn mentioned as an afterthought the history of Winston's son-in-law that she turned to him with any genuine interest.

She asked him to repeat every detail of the short, third-hand history, and Quinn did this, cautiously waiting for her own revelation.

When he'd finished, she said, 'My brother's in Pakistan.' She smiled as she said it, turning to look to the east and into the five thousand miles of impenetrable but brightening darkness which separated her from him. 'We're twins. He's a laser-guidance-systems expert.' She defused the title by her tone of voice. 'He started off by measuring the distances to some of those stars up there. He could tell you to the hour and minute how long it would take us – or probably one of his own missiles – to reach them. He used to say that it didn't matter how badly things turned out down here because he always had somewhere else to go and start anew.'

'Taking you with him?'

She smiled again at whatever fond memory this evoked.

Quinn waited for her to go on.

'And now he – ' She dismissed whatever she had been about to say with a wave. 'And now he plots coordinates to millimetres. Plots coordinates and then presses buttons and doesn't even hear the rockets take off, fly through the air or land a hundred miles away. He sometimes gets to see the reconnaissance photos beamed down to him from whatever satellite is tracking the rockets, but that's all. Negative images, or infrared, pocked with little black holes. They fire the things through 360 degrees. Some of them are launched from where he actually is, but most of them he calls up long distance and they stay just numbers on a screen. Apparently, it doesn't really matter where any of the weaponry is any more, only where it's going.' She paused. 'He claims he could do it all from a bar stool anywhere in the world now that all the air-space treaties have been ratified.'

Quinn heard her affection for the man in everything she said.

'Has he been there long?' he asked her.

'Two years. Three more to go. After that he can either retire or push for a position advising the Chinese now that they're getting interested in the rest of the world again.'

Thirty years had passed since China had closed its extended borders. If her brother was being considered for a posting there now, then he must possess considerable expertise in his field.

'What's his name?' he asked her.

'James,' she said. She looked away from him as she said this, and Quinn turned too, in the opposite direction, feeling the draught of colder wind against his face.

'I hope he gets home safely,' he said eventually, guessing she would say little more about him, that she would now guard even more closely what remained of him.

She pointed to the distant glow of the exhumation pyres, visible to them even at that distance. Men still tended the fires through the night, damping and banking as the last of the day's carcases were delivered to them, keeping the blazes going in readiness for the following day's work.

'Will you catch up?' she asked him unexpectedly, her face still turned away.

'Catch up?'

'Today. Your wasted day. The day you should have spent scratching away at your ledgers and lists of figures.'

He smiled at the gentle mockery.

'I'm scratching away at nothing. Irregularities and discrepancies that have already been reduced to the size of ants on a thousand-hectare plain that's soon going to be bulldozed to an even more perfect flatness. Whatever I uncover, whatever I recommend, it's still going to be a perfect and fully accounted-for site handed over to the developers.'

Neither of them spoke for a moment.

'Will Webb really come?' she asked him.

Quinn shrugged, knowing after his earlier doubts that Webb's arrival was now likely, especially if he was able to surround himself with all those prominent Executive members into whose elevated company he would by then have risen.

'Do you think he sent you here deliberately to get you out of the way while he ascended to his throne?' she asked him.

It was something Quinn had already considered, and his honest conclusion was that to have believed this – that Webb might have somehow considered him a threat to his own promotion – would have been to credit himself with considerably more power or influence than he actually possessed or exercised. Five years ago perhaps, but not now.

'I was only ever the weakest link in the chain,' he told her. 'If anything went badly wrong, I was always the one intended to be snapped in half.' He realized how melodramatic and self-pitying this sounded. And how easily deniable now that the Development Agency's plans for the place had changed so dramatically.

'Perhaps Webb thought the locals, the outraged villagers, might take against you and come looking for you in a mob with burning torches,' she suggested.

'Who knows? They still might.'

She shook her head. 'Not now. They need you to give everything your seal of approval.'

'As worthless as it may prove to be?'

'Not to Greer and his mates at the trough,' she said. She rubbed the cold from her arms. 'They're already collecting records of all the burial sites up in Scotland.'

'Ten years in advance of anything happening?'

'New directives. Time for people to forget and for the grass to grow again. In all likelihood, the incomers will know nothing whatsoever about the new site histories. They certainly aren't going to allow the mistakes they've – we've – I've – made here to be repeated there. Besides, the Scottish sites are smaller, more dispersed, better contained. They kept better records.'

'Because they knew all this might soon be coming?'

'I doubt it. It was fifty years ago. Probably just because they had fewer cattle to cull.' She stopped talking and looked back down the dark hillside.

A few cars moved along the ring road. The breeze brought the sound of a siren from somewhere in the town centre.

Quinn's face was starting to feel numb. When he breathed deeply, his throat ached and he tasted again what he had tasted at the landfill site standing beside Owen. He was about to suggest returning to the motel when Anna pushed her hand into his and said, 'My husband intends taking my son – Christopher; he's eight – to America with him.' She tightened her grip on Quinn's fingers.

Quinn waited before responding, letting her go on.

'He's already made the application. He's an important man now. Important to the Americans.'

'And you think that because they want him for their breeding programme, they'll make it easier for him to take your son with him?' He tried to sound incredulous.

'He told me it was what he intended doing when it became clear that he and I were never going to get back together.' She relaxed her grip on his hand. 'Besides . . .'

Quinn waited again, and then said, 'You think your son might have a better life there, with your husband?'

She nodded once, quickly, unable to speak, to make her belief any more concrete.

'He's a child,' she said. 'He'll adapt. It's what children do. What do you think the future holds for him here? Do you honestly think a ninety-year-old war is going to come to an end before he's old enough to go off and do whatever it is they might tell him to go off and do there? My husband's American lawyers have already started making noises about him and Christopher being awarded Privileged Alien status.'

'I didn't realize it had gone that far,' Quinn said.

'Me neither,' she said. 'I only learned about it when I went home. I should have told you before; about Christopher at least.' She held his gaze and he kissed her.

When he drew back from her he kept his face inches from hers and said, 'My daughter, Evie, was six when she died alongside her mother.'

She continued looking hard at him.

'So now we both know,' she said.

Quinn nodded, unable to speak. He felt the tears form in his eyes and saw the same in hers. He let his own fall and felt the sudden warmth on his cheeks, followed by the chill of her fingers as she wiped them away.

He did the same for her, and they sat like that for several minutes longer, sharing and containing their separate griefs so suddenly and unexpectedly revealed.

25

Greer came to where Quinn was working in the basement of the Record Office. He stood at the open doorway, looking in at Quinn and the few others in the brightly lit, windowless room. Quinn sat at the far end of one of the long tables; beside him a mound of ledgers lay on the table like a block of stone. Most of the others there sat scrolling their screens and tapping at their keyboards, filling the low room with their scratchy, arrhythmic insect noise.

The supervisor sat in her office, looking out at them all, occasionally walking among them and peering over their shoulders, watching what they were doing for a few seconds before moving on. She spent little time beside Quinn, merely satisfying herself that the records piled on the table tallied with the list she had earlier been given. Quinn had never taken to the woman. He imagined she reported on his appearances, the files he examined and the duration of his stay in the office. She seemed to Quinn in all this pointless yet authoritative wandering to be like a librarian without a library.

The woman was the first to spot Greer in the doorway, and she immediately went to him, standing and talking to him, neither of them lowering their voices, as was more usual in the room. After a minute, she turned, pointed to Quinn and returned to her office.

Greer came to him, nodding to the others as he passed. As in the Administration building, his heels tapped on the hard floor.

He sat beside Quinn. 'I was told I'd find you here.' He spoke in a loud whisper.

'I'm here most days,' Quinn said, exposing the lie about Greer not having known precisely where he would be. He finished running his finger down the page he was scrutinizing.

'Though not so much lately, eh?' Greer said. His cold smile lasted less than a second, but was emphatic enough for all it was intended to suggest to Quinn.

'What can I do for you?'

'For me? You?' Greer seemed genuinely surprised by the remark and held a hand to his chest.

Everything's a drama, Quinn thought. *Entrances and Exits.* Only twenty days after first having met the man, and already here was the *new* Greer, the man he would become, mantled in the impregnable and all-encompassing power he had so suddenly and unexpectedly acquired, and which he now paraded in front of others just as his ancestors – or even Greer himself – had once paraded in their embroidered robes and sashes and chains.

A woman sitting opposite Quinn picked up her papers and moved further away.

'Sorry,' Greer mouthed at her. 'Sorry.' He put his hand on Quinn's ledgers. 'What are these?' He turned the volumes to face him. 'Two-ten, two-fifteen? They were still making handwritten copies? Why?'

'Typed,' Quinn corrected him. 'Impulse, I suppose.' And because – like the church records – these handwritten and typed copies still suggested a greater degree of authority and reliability – even then, even fifty years after the vast majority of the population had stopped writing anything at all, even their own signatures.

Greer seemed mesmerized by the columns of figures. 'We must have all this on our secure drives.'

'You do,' Quinn said. 'It's just easier to read this way.' Easier on his eyes.'

'But why are you looking so far back?' Greer said. 'What are you possibly going to learn about anything by looking this far back – years before either of us was even born?'

'You'd be surprised,' Quinn told him, the throwaway remark sounding considerably more threatening than he'd intended.

'Oh?' Greer said, suddenly alert to all these other meanings.

'Cultures of corruption have deep roots,' Quinn said, and this time he sounded as portentous as he'd intended. Portentous and ridiculous.

'Go on,' Greer said, a mixed note of disbelief and amusement in his voice. 'Are you talking about me, about the Development Corporation, about today, all this?' Camouflage and protection.

Quinn waited before answering him, knowing they were

being diverted even further from Greer's true reason for being there.

'All I'm saying is that it's sometimes interesting to go looking in the substrata of these things, beneath the surface.'

'To what practical end? You're not going to put right anything that went wrong sixty, seventy, eighty years ago. No one's going to be brought to justice now for whatever might or might not have happened then.'

'Perhaps not,' Quinn said. *Brought to justice.* Another of those archaic phrases which still rang true, and which still possessed the power to unsettle and threaten.

'Two-twenty-three was the start of the serious flooding, earlier,' Greer said before Quinn could go on. 'Like I said – ancient history.'

'Antediluvian,' Quinn said.

'Whatever.' Greer put his hand back on the ledgers. 'Is all this because of Winston's photos? Or because of what you think you saw at the church? Because if it is—'

'It's part of my brief,' Quinn said, stopping him. 'I have the authority to go as far back as I feel necessary.'

'And you feel it necessary now?'

Quinn gave a dismissive shrug. 'Probably not.' He wondered how much more he might say – how many more of these vague and unanswerable accusations he might make before Greer mentioned Webb and the prospect of his imminent appearance in the place.

'I mean *now*,' Greer said. 'Now, today, with everything that's happened, about to happen. I don't mean when you arrived. I mean now.' On the ledgers, his hand closed into a fist, and he raised this slightly, as though about to slam it down on the books and all they might contain.

'I don't think—' Quinn began.

'And what *I* think, Mr Quinn, is that we stand at the cusp of history, you and I. At, on? Anyhow, the cusp of history. Whatever you think you've found here, whatever it is you're insisting on digging up, the world is moving on. I advise you to move with it.'

The sudden ferocity with which Greer made this small speech surprised Quinn and he waited without speaking to see what he might reveal next.

After a minute, Greer said, 'My apologies.' He mouthed the same to the others in the room. Then he took an envelope from his pocket and laid it in front of Quinn on the block of ledgers.

Everything else, Quinn realized, all these discursive remarks, had been preliminaries to this.

Quinn opened the envelope and took out its single sheet – as potent in its whiteness and crisp folds as his ancient ledgers. He recognized it immediately as a print-out of the briefing delivered daily by the Government to all its relevant bodies and local representatives.

'I've marked the important bit,' Greer said smugly.

A yellow band ran through a line of print halfway down the sheet.

'Or perhaps you've already been informed in your own Daily.'

Quinn's own briefings via the Audit department had contained nothing new for the past week.

'If you've found time to check today, that is,' Greer added. 'I understand you have a great many demands on your time.' He meant Anna.

The highlighted line confirmed the appointment of Webb to the Executive.

'Alexander's promotion,' Greer said, unable to remain silent.

In all the years Quinn had known him, none of Webb's colleagues had ever referred to him as Alexander. He doubted if Greer had ever even heard of the man before this audit, let alone met him.

'It seems our futures – you might even say our destinies – are more tightly bound together than either you or I might ever have imagined,' Greer said.

'I haven't really given it any thought,' Quinn said, the remark doing nothing to deflate the swelling balloon of Greer's own self-importance.

'Oh, but surely even you can see how this – Alexander's appointment – changes everything.'

'I can see that it might move things here on to a different level,' Quinn said.

'Oh, it does a lot more than that, Mr Quinn.'

All these 'Oh's, Quinn thought, *like sudden claps for silence or attention.*

'I imagine Alexander will be contacting you personally,' Greer said, probing. 'Concerning the arrangements for his visit? His first in his new capacity. Perhaps his briefings to you are more in that direction.'

'Everything I receive directly is strictly confidential,' Quinn said.

Greer smiled at this. 'Oh, absolutely, absolutely. Then Alexander *has* already spoken to you about his appointment?'

'I knew about it several days ago,' Quinn said.

'From Alexander himself?'

Quinn slid his chair away from the table, making a loud grating noisc. As he did this, Greer glanced up at the ball of cameras at the centre of the room.

'Was there anything else?' Quinn asked him.

Greer hesitated before answering him, and when he spoke his voice was low. 'Pollard told me you were trespassing. At the church.'

'I doubt he'll be pressing charges,' Quinn said.

'He won't. I've already spoken to him about it. Transparency, that's the issue here. Transparency and . . . and . . .' He waved a hand as though expecting Quinn to finish what he was saying.

'I don't know,' Quinn said. 'Transparency and what? Are you here to tell me that the crypt *isn't* full of rising groundwater?'

'And vision,' Greer said. 'Transparency and vision.'

Back at the agency, among his dwindling peers, the word was a joke. Like 'passion' and 'commitment'. John Lucas rattled a jar at anyone using the words. A euro for each one. The two of them made lists of the words, all of them crumbling to the same degraded mulch of lost meaning, obfuscation and disguise.

'Your *vision*?' he said to Greer. He knew what merciless pleasure John Lucas would have derived from the man.

'Mine, yours, Webb's, everyone's.'

'Stearn's and Pollard's?'

'Of course theirs, of course.'

'But not Winston's,' Quinn said. 'Not Owen's.'

'Who?'

'The farmer. On the ring road. The new landfill site.'

'Oh, him,' Greer said wearily. 'Another lost cause. Another wasted life. Someone clinging to the past as though it was going to come back and fulfil all its old promises. Most of those promises never existed, Mr Quinn. Not for Winston. And certainly not for this Owen character. Delusions, not promises. Built of desperation and despair. Nothing solid, nothing real. Desperation, despair, fear, shame, grief and anything else you can think of. And if you tell me you can't see that, then I *know* you're lying to me.'

While Quinn considered his response to this, he heard John Lucas whispering in his ear, *He's read the small print.* Another of their codes. Meaning Greer only felt himself able to provoke Quinn like this because he already understood everything that was about to happen, and because his own role in those events was both clear to him and assured. Another of those tipped balances never swinging true again.

'"Shame"?' Quinn said.

'Shame that neither of them – Winston or the farmer – did whatever it was they should have done long ago to put things right, to stop things happening. Shame that they didn't stand up or shout loud enough at the proper time. Winston? He's a joke. What do you think he's done for the past twenty years except drink himself into a stupor and abandon everyone he might once have ever cared for? Him *and* his wretched daughter. And don't read a sermon to me about *her* loss. She was only married for three months. A marriage made in heaven? Don't make me laugh. All the man was good for was her widow's pension. And how long do you think *that*'s going to go on being paid to her?' Greer stopped abruptly, aware of having said too much. He watched Quinn for a moment. 'I sympathize, I really do, believe me, but these are small, inconsequential, individual cases. Men like yourself and me, we have to look to the bigger picture. I apologize if I sounded harsh, if I—'

'And all your allusions to Anna Laing and myself?' Quinn said, interrupting him.

'I made no such – what? – allusions?'

'Oh?'

'What you do in your own time is, of course, entirely up to you. I hope you don't think I'm the kind of man to—'

'So you and Stearn haven't sat side by side and watched footage of the two of us together? In the motel car park, perhaps, the day she returned? Elsewhere in the motel? At the exhumation site?'

Greer paused before answering. 'If I've seen the pair of you together, then it's only been during the usual course of events. You must understand, I see a great deal, one way or another.'

'And especially if Stearn sees fit to bring it to your attention?'

'I think you'll find that that's a vital and integral part of Mr Stearn's work here as the chief of our Security Services.'

'I'm sure I will.'

Greer clasped his hands, exasperated. 'I really didn't come here to argue with you, Mr Quinn. I merely hoped to pass on my congratulations, via you, to Alexander.'

'I'll tell him I spoke to you,' Quinn said, unwilling to indulge the man any further.

'Will you speak to him tonight?'

'Very likely.' It had been eighteen days since Quinn and Webb had last spoken. And everything of Webb's true intentions had been kept from him then. Even now he'd had no direct or personal confirmation of Webb's promotion.

Greer rose a moment later, looking around him at their silent audience. He held out his hand to Quinn and Quinn took it, allowing Greer to shake it vigorously before releasing it and pulling on his gloves. Something else for the cameras; a cordial, informal chance encounter; a signal to Stearn, perhaps.

Alone again, Quinn turned back to the ledgers and journals. But whereas before their contents had intrigued him and drawn him into their possible secrets, now their pages seemed as empty and meaningless to him as Greer had insisted they were.

He waited where he sat for a further hour, reading and not reading, and then he signalled to the supervisor that he was ready to leave.

As he climbed out of the basement and into the reception area above, the strange thought struck him that he might now, without either loss or comment, never again return to the room or the building and his unfinished work there.

26

Arriving at his car, Quinn saw Rebecca Winston standing nearby, turning back and forth as though she were searching for someone.

A pall of smoke blew across the open space, and at first Quinn imagined this to be a fog, or perhaps a mist rising off the nearby river. But when he faced into it and felt it in his eyes and then tasted it, he knew it was smoke from a fire, perhaps from one of the building sites which surrounded them. After a moment, this cleared and through it Quinn saw the girl coming towards him.

'Were you looking for me?' he asked her. He wanted to avoid her – her and her father – not to have to confront either of them with what Greer had just revealed to him.

'He's gone,' she said, continuing to search around her as she reached him.

'Winston? Gone where?' He wondered where, beyond their dilapidated home and its few surrounding streets, the man might go. 'He'll be in one of the bars,' he suggested. He wanted to give her the impression that he was busy, in a hurry, and so he continued walking to his car, pressing the fob as he approached and seeing that there was no corresponding flash of light.

As he passed her, the girl reached out and held his arm, stopping him and forcing him to turn back to her.

'He was ranting and raving all night about what was happening to us,' she said, as though this might explain and excuse her own actions now.

It was the man's favourite pastime, Quinn thought, but to say this to her was beyond him.

'And you thought he might have come looking for me?' he said. 'Because I listened to him once?'

She released her hold on him and Quinn shook his sleeve straight.

'He's convinced himself that whatever he might have to say ought to be included in one of your reports.'

'It won't be,' Quinn said abruptly. 'I mean, it's beyond my remit. Perhaps he should approach the developers, or Greer directly.' He knew what a hopeless prospect this was.

More smoke blew across the car park and the girl started to cough. Quinn pointed her to his car, pressing the fob again, relieved to see the flash of light when he was almost at the door.

They both got in and Quinn adjusted the air conditioning to keep the smoke out.

'Where's it from?' he asked her, turning on his wipers to clear the dark film from the glass, leaving an oily residue, which he then tried unsuccessfully to wash clear.

'From the cattle pits,' she said. 'The wind's turned.'

It surprised him to hear this, knowing they were at least three miles from the site.

'Perhaps that's where your father's gone,' he said.

'To the pits? Why?'

Quinn was uncertain why he'd suggested it. 'Other Government officials? Perhaps someone there might have more cause to take him seriously?'

'Because you don't?' she said.

He couldn't begin to explain to her how far beyond her father's reach the future of the place had now moved, how insignificant both he and his warnings had become. Where once he might have been an irritant, something to be watched with amusement and then growing impatience and disdain, now he was not even that.

He made several more guesses where Winston might be, until she told him to stop.

'Like you said, he's probably in one of the bars.'

Quinn said nothing, his silence now more emphatic than any of his excuses or evasions.

After that, the girl's anger subsided.

'Fisher told me about your husband,' Quinn said, and he saw by her reaction to this that the loss had not been a great or a lasting one.

'My father sees only what he wants to see,' she said eventually.

Meaning he had stopped looking at her and *her* needs for the future.

She sensed his understanding of this and smiled at him.

'You need a new cell for the key,' she said. 'Any weaker and it'll affect your code-acceptance procedure.'

'It already has,' Quinn said.

She shook her head and turned to leave.

'What will you do?' Quinn asked her.

'Carry on looking. I've already looked in most of the bars. I suppose if I—'

She was interrupted by a sudden rapping on the window beside her, causing her to cry out and turn away from the glass. Whoever was outside rapped again.

Quinn lowered the window and saw Stearn standing there, crouched forward, his hands on his knees. He wore a paper mask covering his mouth and nose, and he pulled this down to speak to them. He did nothing to hide his surprise at seeing the girl sitting beside Quinn.

'What do you want?' Quinn asked him.

Stearn said nothing for a moment, perhaps calculating what Quinn and Winston's daughter were doing together in the car so soon after Quinn's encounter with Greer.

'This is—' Quinn started to say.

'He knows who I am,' Rebecca said. She turned to face Stearn, who pulled up his paper mask as though in response to this.

'We're warning people about the smoke, its toxicity. People with breathing problems. It's an amber hazard rating.'

'What, you personally?' Quinn said. 'Is this another of your man-of-the-people acts?'

Stearn was unprepared for the remark and he glanced back and forth between Quinn and the girl for a moment.

'I saw your car,' he said. 'I knew you'd left the Record Office.'

'And that I'd seen Greer there?'

'Hardly a secret.'

Smoke came into the car through the open window and Quinn felt the smuts on the back of his hand.

'I'll go,' Rebecca said to him.

'Not on my account, I hope,' Stearn said.

Quinn imagined the grin beneath his mask.

'Her father's gone missing,' he said.

'"Missing"?' Stearn said. 'Again? And what – that's preferable to him being present?'

Rebecca pushed her door open, forcing Stearn away from the car.

'A joke,' Stearn said. 'A joke.'

Quinn reached out to her. 'Will you let me know when he turns up?'

'*If* he turns up,' Stearn said.

Rebecca took down Quinn's number, but he knew it was only a gesture. She would encounter Winston in the next few hours, and the last thing either of them would then want to do would be to inform him of the details of that encounter – another dim, unwelcome light shone into their shared darkness.

As she left the car, Stearn held the door for her, and just as Quinn expected him to slam it shut, the man took her place beside him, pulling down his mask and clearing his throat.

'It'll end soon,' he said.

'The smoke?'

'The wind. None of this would have happened if they'd finished digging and burning when they said they were going to finish.' He wiped his lips with his fingers, studying the faint residue this left.

Quinn remained silent, unwilling to inadvertently reveal anything Anna might have told him in confidence about the prolonged exhumations.

Ahead of them, several of Stearn's men went from car to car, posting notices to their on-board hazard systems.

'We're warning – informing – them all to stop parking here,' Stearn said. 'The site's going to be closed and sealed off in five days' time. Something everybody here had better get used to. The whole place is going to be one giant building site for a long time to come. A bit of toxic smoke is going to be the least of everyone's problems once all that finally gets under way.' He turned to Quinn. 'Good meeting with Greer?'

'Is that what it was – a meeting?'

Stearn smiled again. 'It'll have been logged by Greer. Very good at record-keeping is Greer. Everything meticulously recorded and kept ready to be offered up for inspection. Never know when that sort of thing is going to come in useful.'

Quinn wondered what the man was telling him. He pressed the ignition, hiding his relief when the unreliable engine started.

'Was that another veiled warning?' he asked Stearn.

'Why should I need to warn you? Warn you of what? Of all Greer's other records and recordings? Of my own? All, incidentally, legitimately gathered and stored, all authorized. Is that what you mean? Besides, I thought you might have learned by now – I don't do anything *veiled*.'

Unwilling to listen to the man any longer, Quinn drove a short distance and braked sharply, throwing Stearn forward and forcing him to brace himself with both hands.

'I think you hear perfectly well what I'm saying,' Stearn said when he'd relaxed. He opened the door. Two of his men stood close outside, and Quinn recognized the man who had confronted him at the roadblock on the saturated hillside.

'Apart from which,' Stearn went on, 'I imagine you'll soon have enough on your plate without organizing search parties for every stray and deadbeat this place is about to throw up.' He laughed at the remark and then climbed from the car.

Leaving the town centre, the smoke thinned, and by the time Quinn reached the ring road the sky was again clear.

He continued to the motel, surprised to see so many of Anna's vehicles already there so early in the day. Men and women, some still in their protective outfits, congregated outside; others stood together in the foyer.

Quinn went in and looked for Anna, seeing her eventually in the closed bar, at a table with several of her senior managers. They were examining maps, blueprints perhaps, all of them leaning forward over a low table to scrutinize details. He knew better than to interrupt her. She wore her own protective outfit, folded down to the waist and fastened there with its bulky utility belt. If she saw him watching from the doorway, then she gave no indication of this.

Quinn went to his room and showered.

Later, as he was about to respond to his own belated notification of Webb's promotion – timed, he saw, two hours after Greer had relayed the news to him – there was a knock at his door and Anna called out to him.

He let her in, and as the door closed behind her she held him and pressed herself hard against him, her hands scrabbling at his back as though she were struggling to keep hold of him. He folded his arms around her and cupped her head into his chest. They stood like this for several minutes. At first, he thought she might be crying, but then realized that the noise she was making was the sound of her breathing, her nose and mouth pressed close to him.

After several minutes, she slowly disengaged herself, pausing a few inches from him and breathing deeply. Her hands moved from his back to his arms and she held these just as tightly.

'I saw you in the doorway,' she said. 'I thought you'd be gone all day.'

'You've smoked everyone out of the town centre.'

She laughed at the remark.

'Why are you all back so early? What's happened? Another setback?'

She sat on his bed and then let herself fall back, raising her arms and then clasping her hands beneath her head.

'As if everything else wasn't already slowing us up,' she said. 'Up? Down? We've just had word that there was human bone amid one of the animal samples we sent to our lab.'

'You didn't spot it yourself?'

'The various bones were no longer than six inches long. They turned up in a ten-ton sample of waste.' She closed her eyes.

'Has it forced you to stop work?'

'Pointlessly,' she said. 'The sample was sent eighteen days ago. No one's even certain which part of the site it came from, what depth, which burial it represents. What we're hoping now is that it was taken inadvertently from somewhere beyond our originally designated perimeter.'

The remark surprised Quinn. 'Why? Because that would invalidate it and everyone could then just ignore it?' And only then – perhaps prompted by his earlier encounter with Rebecca – did he remember Winston's drunken remark about the exhumation teams having little true idea of what they were likely to discover the deeper they dug into the contaminated land. He stopped himself from telling her this.

Anna pushed herself up on to her elbows and looked at him. 'You really think they're going to let a little thing like old human bone delay things? After everything else that's already happened?' She signalled her apology for the remark. 'Our own best guess is that the sample was fifty years old. The second burial phase.' She let herself fall back again. 'According to the lab, there were pieces of bone belonging to at least seven different people. Fragments mostly; one piece of jaw. The whole sample was totally organic: earth, bone and rotted flesh. It's a wonder anything was spotted at all. None of us out in the field really believed that the tests were actually carried out, just that the samples were sent as part of procedure and that the green lights kept on flashing.'

'Are you any closer to identifying where the sample was taken?' He remembered the maps in the bar. Anything else would have sounded too critical, condemnatory perhaps.

But she heard this in his voice anyway.

'Are we any closer to assuaging our own consciences, you mean?'

'It wasn't what I said.'

'No. But it was what you meant.' There was neither anger nor disappointment in the remark.

Quinn sat beside her on the bed, resting his hand on her leg.

'Stearn was at the site,' she said. 'Apparently – though God knows why – he was informed of the findings at the same time I was. I suppose it's a police matter.'

'Did he cast any light on what might have happened?' Quinn wondered what part this might have played in either Stearn's or Greer's supposedly casual encounters with him earlier.

'Before his time, he said. That was the first thing he made clear to me. Long before.'

Just as Greer had made the same point to him, Quinn, his

hand on the ledgers as though it had been resting on a Bible as Greer swore an oath.

'All he could tell me,' she went on, 'was that after all the early culls there had been a massive movement of workers, migrants mostly. When the cows and then the sheep were killed, they came and did most of the dirty work. Presumably watching their own livelihoods going up in the same smoke. Thousands came and thousands went. Apparently, there was always some animosity between the various groups. Stearn's most likely explanation – and by which I assume he meant the most convenient explanation as far as he was concerned – was that one of these factions took advantage of all the unrest and uncertainty to settle an old score. The bone analysis might give us a better idea of the ethnic origins. We've also got some plastic tags from the animals to help us with the timings.'

'But seven bodies . . .' he said.

'Don't,' she said. 'I know.'

'Will you be delayed for long whatever the outcome?'

She sighed. 'Only until we identify the sample site and we're able to keep clear of it. I can't think it will be a real problem once the date of fifty years is made to stick.'

'Another piece of history conveniently out of reach,' Quinn said.

'For which I, for once, am not to blame.' She struck his arm and he apologized for the remark.

She turned on her side, facing him, their bodies and faces close.

'I heard about Webb,' she said.

'He's waiting for my very own slap on his back as we speak,' Quinn told her, indicating the messages still blinking on his screen.

'What will you say?'

'That he's a gutless, time-serving, lickspittle, shiny little bastard and that the other gutless, time-serving, shiny little bastards who want him as one of their own deserve everything they get.' He heard John Lucas's voice again.

'So – "Congratulations. Every best wish for your continuing success in the future."'

'Probably. And I'll probably even be able to say it to his face soon.'

She laughed.

'What?'

'"Lickspittle"?'

'It's—'

'I know what it is. I'm just amazed that you're prepared to reach back five hundred years for an insult.' She pressed herself hard against him and kissed him.

27

The following morning they drove together to the road where Quinn had twice met Wade. Earlier, there had been a local news item about the road's long-term closure – something Wade had predicted at their last encounter. Having found the road unexpectedly flooded, the report had intrigued Quinn. Anna accompanied him because of her own enforced absence from the exhumation site. She had hoped to hear more about the samples she'd sent, but so far there had been nothing. She checked frequently for messages as Quinn drove.

He told her about Wade and his connection to Winston, but she remained distracted, concerned more about the likelihood of being further delayed and of becoming embroiled in the buried history of the place.

They turned up the hillside, and after only a few hundred

metres they encountered a fuel tanker blocking both carriageways. A group of men stood around the cab; others sat on upturned canisters along the side of the road.

Quinn pulled over. The men beside the tanker saw him and someone shouted.

'Why don't we just turn back?' Anna said, and Quinn heard the frustration in her voice.

Before he could respond to her, he saw Wade detach himself from the men and come towards them.

Quinn climbed out alone to meet him.

'They've closed it completely this time,' Wade said. 'You'll have to turn back here.' He shielded his eyes to look at Anna in the car. 'We heard they found some bodies.'

'Old remains,' Quinn said. He indicated the tanker. 'Is all this on Stearn's say so?'

Wade smiled. 'Higher authority this time.' He jabbed a finger upwards.

'Greer?' Quinn said and they both laughed.

'Higher even than him – at least for the present,' Wade said.

'More water?'

'More water. Followed in the middle of the night by half the hillside coming down and taking a good stretch of the road with it.' Wade gestured around the bend beyond the tanker.

From where they stood, there was nothing to see, and Quinn searched higher up the slope for some sign of what had happened. He started walking along the road and Wade followed him. At first, he imagined Anna might leave the car and join them, but she remained where she sat, not even watching him.

Quinn and Wade reached the tanker and then walked

around it, the other men falling silent at their approach and then resuming their conversations as they passed by.

'They're angry,' Wade said when they were out of earshot. 'We spent two months digging out those channels and culverts. And now this.'

'And no warning whatsoever from the engineers?'

'All *they*'re interested in these days is all the work that's going to start down there.' He gestured towards the town, which at that moment was illuminated by a succession of beams of vivid, shifting sunlight through the cloud, looking momentarily to Quinn like a painting. And just as quickly as the effect was achieved, so it was lost as another passing cloud flattened and darkened everything.

They continued uphill and further round the curve of the road until they arrived at a point where the whole of the landslip was visible to them. It was an impressive sight – as impressive in its simplicity as in the display of force it revealed. The whole of that part of the hillside appeared to have been scooped out and pushed several hundred metres down the steep slope, leaving a naked scar of rock and mud at least a hundred metres wide and three times that long. The road lay completely buried beneath this to a depth of ten metres.

'A few thousand tons, they reckon,' Wade said. The calculation was probably his own.

Everything that had once been on the surface – boulders, vegetation and the dense mat of grasses – had been turned to sludge and lost. Water still poured from the edge of the slip and gathered in a tan-coloured pool at its lower edge.

'It's still running,' Quinn said.

'Of course it is. The water's undercut everything, lubricated it all to slide down.'

'Can you clear it?'

Wade shrugged. 'I doubt it. Besides . . .'

Quinn waited, seeing how unstable all this loose material still remained. 'Besides, they might not want it cleared?'

'There are other roads,' Wade said. 'And talk now of linking them with the motorway. It's an old story. And after that a new railway and even an airport.' His own lack of conviction was evident in everything he said. 'Would *you* waste time and money reopening this when all *that*'s coming?'

Quinn shook his head. 'It's still the main road to the south,' he said.

'And when did that last count for anything?' Wade said. He rubbed his face and then stretched his arms and yawned. 'There was never much traffic up here, not recently. Even you thought you'd taken a wrong turning into the back of beyond along it.'

Quinn smiled at the truth of this.

Wade continued walking ahead of him, kicking at the stones and earth which filled the road. There was a bulge in the mound above him, mud that had stopped flowing because its own lubricating water had drained away. If it moved again, without warning, then it would bury Wade where he stood.

'You ought to be careful,' Quinn called to him.

Wade pointed up the hillside. 'That? It'll come when it's ready, whether I'm here or not.'

It seemed an uncharacteristically fatalistic remark for the man to make.

After standing alone for a few minutes, he returned to Quinn, making calculations on his fingers as he came.

'What are you doing?' Quinn asked him.

'Nothing,' Wade said quickly.

But he was lying and Quinn saw this. 'What is it?'

'That's where we were supposedly digging out the drains,'

Wade said, pointing.

Quinn looked, but could see nothing beneath the slipped land.

'Higher up. This side and that side.'

Still Quinn could see nothing. 'Meaning what? That you might actually have done more harm than good by the work?'

'Something like that.' But Wade was suggesting considerably more, and Quinn quickly understood him.

'You think this was the *intended* outcome? Are you serious? Surely not. Who would want it? To what end? And what if it had happened when you and your men had still been working up here?'

But Wade would not be shaken in his belief. 'There were engineers here an hour after it happened. Stearn's guard reported it to Stearn, who obviously told Greer. You've seen how they work. Greer told my supervisor that he'd been so concerned by what had happened that he'd been up here himself while it was still dark. *We* were all told to hold off this morning until it became fully light.'

Quinn looked again at the ravaged hillside and the lost road.

'In addition to which . . .' Wade said, but then fell silent.

'What?'

'It's just hearsay.'

'What?'

'Someone told one of my men he'd heard bangs up here, just before it was supposed to have happened.' He seemed less certain of himself now.

'You mean explosions? Someone deliberately triggering the slip? You said a moment ago that you believed your digging had done it.'

'I know. And I think our drainage work helped it happen, that it set boundaries, that whoever wanted to be able to close the road wanted it to be done here, at its most inaccessible, and where it would be the most costly to put right. Look at it – there's been no real maintenance up here for miles in either direction for the past thirty years.'

'Who heard the explosions?' Quinn said. 'Someone who might stand up in a court and say the same?'

'What court? How is a thing like this ever going to come to court?'

'Have you reported these allegations to anyone?'

Wade bowed his head, and in that simple, revealing gesture Quinn finally understood the true and precise nature of the man's defeat. *Following in Winston's footsteps*, he thought, but said nothing.

Wade scooped the mud from his feet.

'I appreciate you telling *me*,' Quinn said eventually, as though this might be some small consolation to the man for all his wasted labour.

'But there's nothing you can do, either?'

Ever since his arrival, Quinn had been credited with authority, power and influence he had never possessed, and he was growing tired of being forced into making these denials, and of the disbelief, disappointment and suspicion they created.

Wade walked back past him without speaking.

Quinn imagined the aggrieved incredulity both Greer and Stearn would display were they to be confronted with the man's angry, unfounded allegations. And whatever evidence Wade might imagine himself to possess was surely now buried beneath all those thousands of tons of unsettled soil and the act of God that had scooped out the hillside and destroyed the road.

He followed Wade back to the tanker, where again the conversation fell silent at their approach.

Back at his car, Quinn told Anna what had happened, and then repeated Wade's suspicions.

'Do you believe him?' she said, unconvinced, and then, 'I suppose it makes as much or as little sense as any other explanation.'

'Have *you* heard anything?' he asked her, meaning her lab results.

She turned her phone to him. 'No signal.' It was another silent plea to him for them to return to the motel, to reconnect this other severed line.

28

She left Quinn's room at six the following morning, appearing in the lobby an hour later to announce to her workforce that she had finally received a message telling her to postpone work at both the exhumation and burn sites for a further twenty-four hours.

The news was met with disappointment by all concerned. It was impossible, however, to simply abandon the smouldering fires, and Anna asked for volunteers to attend the site until the blaze could once again be built up and do its work properly. She allocated a four-hour shift of this work to herself, but was persuaded by others that she need not attend, that of them all she was the one who might now benefit the most from this enforced break. She finally acquiesced to this, telling her managers that she would let them know the moment she heard anything new.

Quinn waited in the empty bar as she announced all this. Afterwards, as the others dispersed around her, she came to him.

'I need to get out of here,' she said. She confided in him that she had been told she would hear nothing new until six that evening at the earliest.

Quinn suggested another short journey away from the town, expecting her to reject this, but this time she agreed and followed him to his car.

'Won't someone be monitoring your trackers, your fuel consumption?' she asked him as she climbed inside.

Quinn dismissed her concern. 'There's always someone, somewhere, watching something with someone else watching over their shoulder in case there's something they've missed.' Another old, unfunny joke.

Anna said nothing in reply.

They left the motel and drove in a direction midway between the exhumation site and the blocked road to the south. North-east, Quinn supposed. Smoke still rose on the horizon, but now only in slender threads, widely spaced and dispersed by the wind before these gathered into the usual cloud.

Circling the ring road, Quinn came to the garage where he had first arrived in the town. He pulled up close to the kiosk and saw Rebecca Winston sitting there. He explained to Anna about his failing cell and took his fob in to the girl.

'He finally turned up,' she said to him, meaning her father, embarrassed by the simple revelation.

'Where had he been?'

'First to harass Greer's secretary, and then to mouth off all his church stuff to Pollard. Afterwards, he got caught by the wind and was blown into one or other of his usual haunts for the rest of the day.' She searched the cards behind her for a replacement cell.

Outside, Quinn saw Anna looking in at them and he raised his hand to her.

'How long were you looking for him?'

'All day.'

'At least he was safe.'

'Is that what you'd call it?'

He didn't know what else to say to her.

Eventually, she found the correct cell and fitted it into his fob. She tested it by pointing it at the car, watching as the lights flashed.

Quinn gave her his credit card.

'Why did he go to Greer?' he asked her.

'So he could act like a monster and tower over Greer's new, expanded model?' She raised her arms, her hands spread into claws.

'And the church?'

'There was some kind of ceremony taking place, a very select invited audience. He probably just felt he had a right to be there.'

Perhaps the foundations and the crypt had finally been pumped dry and the new church – the New Church – was already starting to rise with Pollard standing squarely in his pulpit and already dispensing his calculated benedictions.

Quinn continued to watch Anna as Rebecca spoke to him. She rested her hands on the dash and then brought them back to her face. She looked out at him, but gave no other indication of actually seeing him there.

'I have to go,' he said to the girl.

Rebecca looked out at Anna. 'Is she crying?' she said.

Quinn shrugged and took back his card.

'Thanks,' she said.

'What for?' He paused on his way out and looked back at her. 'You do know that your father isn't going to achieve anything, don't you?'

She bowed her head briefly. 'He called Greer "King Canute". "King fucking Canute", to be precise.'

Quinn almost laughed at the comparison and wondered what she herself might have understood by it. It seemed to him that, rather than Greer, Winston himself was the new Canute, the coming flood of people and change his unstoppable tide.

'I asked him what he meant,' she said. 'But he was too drunk to explain.'

'It's often spelled "C-n-u-t",' Quinn told her.

She laughed. 'I bet he knew that, too.'

And again Quinn heard the affection in her laughter, her buried pride in the remark.

'Tell him I said hello,' Quinn said.

She motioned to Anna, who had now lowered her hands and was looking back out at the pair of them. 'The word in the town is that they're about to stop the burning, that they should never have started the work in the first place. Too much trouble. In fact – ' She was interrupted by the appearance of the youth who managed the garage, and who immediately called to her. He asked her why the car on the forecourt wasn't pulled up closer to the pumps there. And then he saw Quinn and fell silent, looking at him suspiciously as he came to the kiosk.

'Trying to buy fuel off-card again, is he?'

Quinn held up his fob.

'He was telling me about King Cnut,' Rebecca said.

'Who? Never heard of him. King of where?'

'A big man. He reminds me a lot of you.'

Stranded by his ignorance, the youth diverted from them and walked without breaking his stride through a door marked 'Personnel'.

'That's us,' Rebecca said to Quinn. 'Me and him. Personnel. He'll have gone in there to punch the wall. I'll tell my father you were here.'

Quinn left the building and walked back to Anna, testing the fob as he went. He'd been convinced by John Lucas that the agency never replaced any of its fleet's cells, knowing that the expense would always be borne by cautious or anxious drivers.

Back beside Anna, he explained to her who the girl was. But she'd no real interest in Winston, just as she'd had no interest in the man's step-brother the previous day. To her, they were only two more figures in the shadows. Two more men increasingly lost in their own detached and faltering orbits.

They left the garage and drove further along the ring road, leaving it at the first intersection and heading into open, empty country away from the town.

After only a few minutes, nothing of either the road or the town was visible to them, and they skirted the rim of another vast depression surrounded by yet more low hills.

'All this will be covered,' she told him. 'A grid of roads and apartments, nothing else.' She drew on the glass with her finger where the roads might run and intersect.

It seemed impossible to Quinn that so vast a space could ever be filled, and he wondered how she knew about it.

'As far as the eye can see,' she said. 'And then further. The valley beyond this one and then the one beyond that.' Another of those dark, deceptively hopeful fairy-tale endings.

They rose to an escarpment, where the surface of the little-used road was pocked with unfilled holes, and where grass grew along its centre.

'We came up here when we first arrived,' Anna said. 'Surveying for outlying sites.'

'Are there any?'

'Officially or unofficially?'

'Meaning you're not coming this far out to clean them up?'

'What was the original question?'

Quinn stopped talking, concentrating on manoeuvring over an abandoned and rusting grid set into the road, feeling it sag beneath his wheels.

'There's an intersection off to the right,' she said. She thought for a moment. 'To the east.' She pointed where the invisible road ran.

A flock of birds rose ahead of them – crows or rooks; ravens perhaps; neither of them could be certain. Most of the birds flew only a short distance to the side – more blown than flying – and then fell back into the grass and disappeared. A few hopped back and forth at the edge of the road, unwilling to take flight, almost as though expressing their affront at being disturbed in so isolated a place.

Reaching the intersection, Anna directed them to the right, and they crossed another five miles of the same open, undulating land. It seemed even further beyond belief that all this too was to be built on and consumed.

They drove for half an hour, passing a few abandoned, unworkable farms on the empty and overgrown roads, occasionally hearing the amplified noise of another engine as someone passed them by out of sight.

Rising to the brow of a hill, driving in low gears as the road steepened, as it turned in a zigzag, and then as its surface was strewn with stones, they came eventually to the summit, where they were both blinded by the low sun ahead of them.

Quinn stopped and looked out at the road descending into the valley beyond, steep at first, and with the same number of twists and turns, and then levelling out and running along the empty bottom-land until it was lost to sight in the expanse of green.

They got out of the car and stood together in the strong wind. Anna held her hands to her ears and Quinn put his arm around her shoulders. He felt her steadying herself against the wind.

In the far distance, almost on the horizon, moving cars caught the sun and flashed their presence to them.

'I feel like an explorer,' Anna said to him, shouting above the noise of the wind.

'Perhaps that's what we are,' he said. It was easy for him to believe that there were places in the surrounding expanse where no one had gone before them, where no one else had ever walked or stood and imagined the same. But even as he tried to convince himself of this, he knew it was a delusion, a conceit, something he would never be able to believe with any true conviction. And realizing this, he also understood that Anna felt the same. And he understood too that neither of them would now say anything to break this brief, shared reverie.

Eventually, Anna said, 'Would you come back to live here? Here, I mean – this exact spot?'

Quinn considered what she was asking him. 'If it stayed like this,' he said. And if he could keep out of the rain and the wind and the snow and the cold; if he could provision himself, provide his own power and amenities; if he could fill his days in such a bleak and sour and desolate place without becoming the same; if he could convince himself that he could continue to draw something sustaining from it for the years and decades ahead and not only for the few minutes they had already spent looking at it all and seeing all there was to see. And only if the past could be kept in its proper place and this near-impossible future assured. And only if she were there with him, and she too wanted all these other things.

'Me, too,' she said, interrupting and echoing this sudden rush of thought.

But even as she said it, again making herself complicit in this shared conceit, Quinn knew that it was nothing more than another of those old dreams, and one that had long been lost to both of them.

Then Anna pointed to the shell of an abandoned farm, as though this might be their new home. And simply by looking at it there amid so much emptiness, Quinn knew that the place had never done any more than struggle for its own survival – even when the land had been good and filled with animals; even when the economic equations had still made sense; and even when no one else had had any intention of coming within sight of the place to challenge its lonely dominion.

The shadows of high clouds crossed the open land like the lost herds that might once have grazed there, and the two of them stood in silence and watched them.

Eventually, after fifteen minutes, the cold became too much for Anna, and she pulled herself from Quinn's loose embrace and went back to the car, following a curving line as she was blown off course by the rising wind.

He joined her a moment later, and she sat beside him, rubbing her face and hands to restore their feeling.

Quinn switched on the engine and turned up the heater and the car grew quickly warm.

There was more cloud now, gathering from the north, and slowly the land grew darker, losing its definition, flattened and rounded where previously it had revealed its ridges and gullies in the winter sun. It was how the place must look for most of the year, and they both understood this.

Quinn pulled back on to the narrow road and held the car on its brakes as it moved downhill. The view from their vantage point was quickly lost to them, and after only a few seconds even the abandoned farm had disappeared from sight.

Part IV

29

Upon their return, Anna was immediately approached by one of her managers, who signalled to her, and who, Quinn noticed, held back from approaching her any more closely when he saw that the two of them were together.

Quinn told her he'd see her later, but she left him without answering, anxious to discover the cause of the man's barely disguised urgency.

In his room, the blank screen beeped at him and flashed its own Urgent Communication signal. He switched it on and opened his secure link, identifying himself and then confirming how long had passed between the message being sent and acknowledged. It was from Webb. Who else? Two hours and forty minutes. The coded mail history showed that Webb had repeated the message twice during that time. The second time had been only fifteen minutes earlier. Quinn switched on his palm-top and saw the same encrypted messages there. He replied using his phone.

'At last,' Webb said, and then, 'Finally.' As usual he did nothing to disguise or temper his exasperation.

Quinn told him where he'd been, but Webb immediately interrupted him and told him his explanation was of no consequence. These were his exact words, and Quinn felt them like the blow they were intended to be. He apologized again, starting another explanation of the poor reception in the valley above the town. This time Webb waited without speaking. Eventually, Quinn fell silent. A firebreak silence, after which Webb said that he would soon be able to see for himself all that Quinn was talking about. He confirmed that he was part of a delegation coming to the town. His first public engagement since his appointment. Quinn heard the suppressed note of excitement in his voice. Perhaps not excitement, exactly, but something close to it, the testing of a new muscle. Then Webb thanked him for his earlier message of congratulations, and thus prompted, Quinn repeated it.

The delegation – Webb made it sound as though he might even be its leader – would be arriving in seven days' time and staying there for two. Various ceremonies were being arranged – various 'opportunities' – but Quinn need not concern himself with any of these. He would be required – invited – to attend, of course, alongside Webb – a brief pause for Quinn to consider the temporary status thus conferred upon him by this proximity – and if he liked, Quinn might also arrange one or two additional side-visits – Webb made these sound almost illicit – which more closely embodied or encapsulated their own more specific area of interest. He might have been promoted, Webb said, but he was still an auditor at heart. He waited for Quinn to laugh at the remark.

Quinn closed his eyes as he listened to all this.

'Anyhow, give it some thought,' Webb said, the casual imperative. 'I'll leave everything in your more than capable hands.'

Webb then listed the men who would accompany him. A dozen politicians would be present, along with at least one Senior Minister from a prime department. No confirmation as yet. Several juniors, too, hopefully, and perhaps even some of Quinn's own colleagues, if they could be spared. Upon hearing this, Quinn started listening more closely, hoping that John Lucas might be included. But he wasn't, and Quinn knew better than to ask Webb why, or even to suggest his inclusion.

'I'll look forward to it,' Quinn said, interrupting Webb, who fell silent again and then said, 'Right. Well,' and 'Yes,' as though by this simple expedient he might simultaneously reassert his own distant authority and let Quinn know that he, Webb, understood exactly what he had intended by the interruption.

Webb then told him to delete the coded message and reminders from his record file. Those local officials, financiers and Government organizers who needed to know about the visit and its subsequent announcements would learn of it through their own channels.

The remark put Quinn on his guard, and he asked Webb to be more specific. But again Webb seemed affronted and told Quinn that he'd already said more than he'd intended. He then said that he hoped Quinn hadn't become *too* involved in Anna Laing's own 'embarrassing' problems. As so often with Webb, the question framed its only answer.

'"Involved"?' Quinn said. 'As far as I know, they're just having some difficulty—'

'I know exactly what kind of *difficulties* she's having. All *I*'m saying is – keep your distance. You're doing a good job up there, a great job, and I fully anticipate all the audit schedules to be confirmed according to our original timetabling.'

'I hear what you're saying,' Quinn told him.

Webb waited a few seconds. 'Of course you do. You're a steady pair of hands, always have been. Everyone here has every faith in you.'

'Faith'? I do your bidding, that's all. Faith in what?

Webb let out his breath. 'I hope I'm making my meaning clear.'

'Of course,' Quinn said. He held up his arms in a gesture of surrender.

'Good,' Webb said quickly. Another small diversion completed. 'Besides, I imagine you'll all have enough on your hands with the weather alert.'

'The forecasts are usually—'

'An alert. Issued two hours ago. While you were' – Webb cleared his throat – 'incommunicado. Significant Event bronze, possibly silver. By the look of things, you're going to get wet. Very.' He laughed at the remark.

Quinn scanned his screen until he came to the alert. Heavy and persistent rainfall and strong winds. Still a bronze. Denoting what? He checked further. Ten to fifteen centimetres of continuous rain in a twelve-hour period. Continuous but non-prolonged. He tried to imagine what it meant.

'Have you found it?' Webb asked him. 'Look at the map. There are some excellent predictors already showing.'

Quinn brought up the map and keyed in the town's name, creating a flashing point in the midst of a ball of moving colours. The timescale ran from late evening until noon the following day. The rain surge moved from north to south, breaking and weakening and becoming less predictable as it went – reds turning to yellows, yellows to blues, and the blues fragmenting and scattering like raindrops the further south they blew. A hundred miles further and all that was left to the system was a dying wind veering to the east and out to sea.

Quinn looked closer. It was the third bronze alert the place had received in the previous six months. Two of these had briefly turned silver. A high likelihood of the coming rain also being upgraded, possibly even prior to its arrival, and especially if the accompanying winds slowed in pushing the system south. He watched the alternative predictions and saw the ball of rain spin in place over the town for thirty-six hours. There was a 20 per cent chance of this. Again, he wondered what all this meant, how these predictions manifested themselves on the ground beyond the obvious.

Webb would be looking at the same mesmerizing graphics. Whatever the outcome of the storm – and few called them that any longer – it would all be over long before he arrived and the red carpets were rolled out.

'I take it you see what I'm seeing,' Webb said.

'The rain,' Quinn said.

'And that's all it is. Rain. Not a flood. Rain. My word is that you can go with the primary prediction, but that the rain might last longer as it eases.'

'How much longer?'

'Just longer. I shouldn't really be telling you even that much. This is executive-level disclosure only.' A great favour, then. A favour for a favoured employee, colleague.

'No. Sorry,' Quinn said.

Webb lowered his voice again. 'Think an extra twelve

hours,' he said. 'The second alternative – the surge moving swiftly south and then east isn't really on the cards. It's just the official announcement for public whatever. They want to keep it bronze for as long as possible. Fewer come-backs if it turns into something worse.' There was no real logic to any of this, but Quinn remained silent.

So it would be raining for up to a day and a half, starting in six hours' time, after dark.

'I can't imagine it will cause *you* any real problems,' Webb said.

'None whatsoever,' Quinn said.

'Good man. That's what I thought. Everything you've sent has been filed, forwarded and confirmed at this end. The stats people are working on it now, polishing things up.'

'Good,' Quinn said absently, still watching the spinning ball of approaching rain.

'Oh, it's much better than "good",' Webb said. 'When all this gets under way we'll be working to a whole new set of flagship standards. We're already taking on board a new system of performance monitoring. They'll break the mould with this one.'

Again, Quinn thought.

'They're already calling it a Pilgrim Project.'

'"Pilgrim"?' Quinn said. The ball of changing colours ran down his screen, edge to edge, every twelve seconds, pulsing, forming and breaking, bouncing almost, like the ball it appeared to be, top to bottom, top to bottom.

'You know – like the pilgrims,' Webb said. 'Pilgrim fathers. The founding fathers. Looking for a new home. The Pilgrim Project.' He laughed. 'I imagine they'll want something a little more Scottish for everything afterwards. New Caledonia, something like that.'

How about The Clearances?

There were already a dozen New Caledonias in the atlas – and none of them so far superimposed on the *Old* Caledonia – but Quinn resisted pointing this out. 'Sounds good,' he said.

'It does,' Webb said. 'Stirring, even.'

'You should suggest it to whoever names these things,' Quinn said.

'Perhaps—' And only then did Webb grow suspicious, uncertain of Quinn's true intent.

'What?' Quinn said.

'No, you're right – perhaps I *will* suggest it. Right. Anyhow, glad I finally caught you. Beginning to think you'd gone native or something. You do realize it's still procedure to check for missed messages every hour – '

'On the hour,' Quinn said.

'Not necessarily. Anyhow, like I said, no harm done this time. Good to catch up with you, to hear everything's on track. Give some thought to those little local events. I'll get clearance for everything at this end, let Greer know what's likely to happen, some kind of timetable.'

'Of course,' Quinn said. No further mention of Anna or the avoidable contagion of her own insurmountable difficulties.

'I have to go,' Webb said. 'You know me – always taking too much on, right?'

'I look forward to seeing you,' Quinn said.

'Likewise. Now go and batten down the hatches or whatever it is they do up there.' The line went dead to the sound of Webb's laughter.

A moment later, the screen flashed with a reminder about deleting news of the forthcoming delegation, and Quinn did this.

Afterwards, he lay on his bed and fell asleep, waking

with a start several hours later. He felt cold, and when he sat upright his head spun and he waited for a moment to regain his equilibrium before standing. The room's heating was on, already causing condensation to form low on his window.

He looked out over the illuminated car park and the road beyond. It had grown dark while he'd slept, but there was no indication yet of either the approaching wind or rain. He watched the high tops of the bare trees moving slightly and tried to remember what he'd been taught as a child about the old visual system of calculating wind speeds – breezes, winds, gales, storms, hurricanes, typhoons. He couldn't remember the exact order, or if he'd missed any: shaking leaves, blown smoke, whipped branches, waves turning white, branches broken, trees and chimneys toppled, damage to buildings. It was all still there, but in no true or reassuring order – the jumbled notes of another lost song.

He considered calling Anna, but then thought better of this when he remembered the urgency of the man who had greeted her. He checked for further missed messages, but there were none.

He switched on the local news channel and watched the weather forecaster tell him again of the approaching storm. That was what she called it, smiling as she spoke, turning from side to side on her map, revealing and concealing, adding further small and unnecessary dramas to the one she was describing. Quinn wondered if her authorized use of the word 'storm' now suggested more than continuous heavy rainfall and wind, and imagined that it did.

30

He didn't see Anna again until much later that same evening. He went to the bar and then outside, returning to his room when he failed to spot her among the others there. The screens above the bar and in the foyer were filled with repeated warnings of the approaching bad weather. By eight that evening, the earlier bronze alert had been upgraded to silver. Staff secured grilles and shutters; the motel's own service vehicles were drawn into a line along the slope of the slip road; emergency lighting was tested and portable pumps were filled with fuel and wheeled to their designated positions.

Quinn moved his own car to the elevated land at the rear of the motel, walking back against the strengthening wind. A group of waiters and porters were stacking casks and crates in an outbuilding, securing its metal doors before running back inside.

Directly outside his window, the exterior lighting was switched off, replaced a few minutes later by the even whiter glare of security lights running the full length of the building.

He watched the continuous news and saw the reports being broadcast from those places the storm had already reached. He listened to a meteorologist talking about the severity of the storm being a direct consequence of the lost Pacific currents and the continually changing weather patterns worldwide.

It was a story Quinn had been hearing all his life.

At ten, it started raining, lightly at first, but then with a quickening intensity until it blew in sheets against the large windows, individual drops lost in the near-horizontal flurries. Puddles formed quickly under the lights, and these merged into broader sheets of water. The slip road drained from the peripheral carriageway, a two-lane river channelled into drains and soak-aways which quickly filled and overflowed, adding to the standing water which rose in measured inches against the wheels of all the cars.

At eleven, the silver alert was raised to gold. It sounded almost like an achievement. The power in Quinn's room went off and then returned. The screen readjusted and then reasserted itself, the words 'Temporary Power Loss' flashing across its full width for several seconds afterwards. An alarm sounded in another part of the building, and Quinn waited for the screen to warn him of a fire. Nothing came.

A moment later there was a knock at his door and he opened it to see Anna there. He beckoned her inside, but she hesitated where she stood for a moment. Quinn held the door, knowing that if he released it then it would close slowly in her face and that she would do nothing to prevent this.

Eventually, having decided, she went past him into the room, sitting on the edge of his bed and watching the storm reports. Quinn muted the sound and waited for her to speak, to tell him what had been so urgent earlier in the day. He saw already how far they had come from their morning drive in the deserted, sunlit hills.

Anna concentrated on the screen. When another spinning ball of rain was shown, she touched the point at its outer edge where they were now waiting.

'It'll flood your sites,' Quinn said.

'Is that the good news or the bad news?'

He told her what Webb had told him about the likelihood of the storm being more prolonged than initially predicted. The ball on the screen appeared now to be spinning in place as the hours ticked by alongside it.

'Greer's applied for a Closure Order,' she said.

Uncertain what this was, or what precisely it meant for her and her work, Quinn said, 'To stop everything?'

'Technically, it'll mean the work is finished. The so-called crime scene has been downgraded. The remit now – or in twelve hours if Greer gets his way, and which is looking increasingly likely – is to move to Preparatory Two, getting the ground ready for basic infrastructure work.' She spoke every word in the same flat, resigned tone.

'Meaning no more exhumation or burning?'

'I imagine the water will see an end to all that.' She gestured at the screen. A reporter with a microphone was leaning at an angle into the wind and trying to talk. 'Why do they always do that? We know it's raining; we know the wind's blowing.

Why doesn't he find somewhere sheltered to stand and tell *us* what to expect?'

'For the same reason they like to position themselves within the sound of gunfire,' Quinn said. 'Look, I'm sure you must—'

'Don't,' she said abruptly. 'I've spent all day listening to people telling me what's probably best for me.'

'Sorry,' Quinn said. He'd been about to say that she must have considered every way forward still available to her.

'It's out of my hands,' she said, turning to face him for the first time. 'The simple fact that Greer's made his request means he was probably prodded into it by someone higher up the food chain. It's the endgame. This is it – bangs-and-whimpers time.'

'Has the same thing happened to you before?'

'Once. Fifteen years ago. A site in Sussex. Poultry. The last of the avian viruses. They restocked for eight years in a row, and for eight years in a row the virus mutated and came back. We dug and burned for two pointless months before somebody finally saw sense and activated the order.'

'And is somebody finally seeing sense here?' he asked her cautiously.

'Either that, or they're looking at all those other hidden, unrecorded sites in that back-of-beyond building land and finally working out the cost and the consequences of checking and clearing it all thoroughly.'

'And have you warned them of the consequences of *not* doing it thoroughly?'

She shook her head at the question. 'I never won many popularity contests as it was,' she said. 'Forget it. Greer's been persuaded to press the button and he's pressed it. Greer's happy, everybody else here is happy, and all those others higher up the pole with their own wet mouths hanging open are happy.'

A stronger gust than usual blew against the window, surprising Quinn where he stood. He drew the curtain, shutting out the sight if not the sound of the driving rain.

'Besides,' Anna went on, 'you're right – this lot would have been the final straw whatever we'd turned up. I imagine the man who whispered in Greer's ear knew everything your Mr Webb already knew.' She watched him closely as she said this.

Had Webb himself done the whispering? Is that what she was suggesting to him? Had that been the whole point of Webb's earlier, almost accidental warning?

Unable to respond to this, Quinn took a bottle from the cabinet beside his bed and poured them both a drink.

'I ought to go down to the others,' Anna said, holding the glass close to her nose and breathing deeply. 'They were clearing things off the ground floor when I last looked.'

It was a common enough precaution those days, and Quinn said nothing, wondering if she was now merely looking for an excuse to leave him.

Water from a gutter high on the building overflowed and ran down the window, adding its own noise to the rising cacophony of the storm. Quinn drew back the curtain and watched it stream across the glass and then pour over the sill to the ground below. The cars in the car park were already sitting up to their hubs in water, and the river of the slip road now overflowed its high kerbs into the bordering shrubberies. As he watched, a succession of fire engines drove along the ring road, their sirens silent, only their flashing lights denoting any urgency. There would be a Priority Plan already in operation, with Greer,

Stearn and the others already gathered like a War Cabinet to direct the town's responses. The thought of this made Quinn smile, and he sipped his drink in a silent salute to the men.

He told Anna about Webb's proposed visit as part of the delegation.

'I know all about it,' she said. 'They want guided tours of the supposedly cleared land.'

'And you to give them?' It occurred to him only then that the Closure Order might mean her own imminent departure from the place.

'Who else?' she said.

On the screen, the man finally lost his footing and fell into the water, which covered him completely for a moment, leaving him struggling to regain his breath and his balance and to stand again, brushing the water from his arms and face before turning back to the camera and starting over.

'Some of my own people here think Greer and his waiting developers have been learning more about the dig and burn than we ourselves have been letting on,' Anna said unexpectedly, and Quinn understood immediately the seriousness of what she was suggesting.

She turned to look at him again, holding his gaze before lowering her eyes. It took Quinn a moment longer to further understand what she was saying.

'Me?' he said. 'You think *I*'ve been talking to Greer? Telling him what? Me? *Me?*'

'I told them they were being ridiculous,' she said, but he heard the note of uncertainty in her voice.

'Told who?'

'Those in my teams who suggested it.'

Quinn waited a moment and then held her and turned her

to face him before speaking. 'If anyone was going directly to Greer, then it wasn't me. Look at me.'

She looked.

'It wasn't me.'

'I believe you.'

Quinn continued to hold her until he was convinced of this. 'How long have they thought it?' he said.

She shrugged.

'How long?'

'Since I gave you a tour of the site. Since you and I . . .' The rest remained unspoken.

Quinn moved away from her, sitting between the bed and the screen.

'How long did *you* think it might be me?'

She shrugged again. 'Not long.'

'When did you *stop* believing it?'

She became angry at this continued insistence. '*Someone* must have been telling Greer – whoever – more than was in my own reports.'

Quinn was at a loss to know which was worse – the fact that she might have believed *him* to be deceiving her, or that her own superiors no longer had faith in the confidentiality of her reports to them. And if she believed the former – or even only half-believed it – then what else might she believe him capable of?

She held out her hand to him. 'I don't believe it of you,' she said quietly.

'Is that the same as saying you believe me?'

She rubbed her face and then took back her hand and held it over her eyes. 'It was only openly suggested to me today when we got back. *Something* happened to make Greer brave enough to apply for the Closure Order – even if he *was* prompted.'

'And that "something" couldn't simply have been your own superiors ensuring that all the allegedly "lost" or "hidden" unofficial burial sites remained exactly that – lost and hidden? You go away and the problem goes away with you.'

It seemed as likely to her as any other explanation, and she conceded this.

'Besides,' Quinn went on, reasoning as he spoke, 'Owen told me about the hidden sites, not you. If I *had* been passing on information behind your back, Greer would have been prodded into action much sooner.'

She accepted the logic of this, too.

'*This* is why it's happening now.' Quinn motioned to the window. 'This and the additionally inconvenient discovery of the human remains. The last thing Greer or his backers are going to tolerate now is yet another delay while that particular dirty little stain gets wiped clean.'

'Meaning the storm will flood the burial site and put out the fire and that's all the excuse they'll need?' She rose from the bed and went to the window. 'The pits will already be full,' she said. 'And I doubt if anyone here has the faintest idea where all that contaminated water is soon going to be flowing.'

And the fires would soon be out and the unburned carcases starting to float to the surface.

'We've spent the afternoon taking the heavy plant off the site,' she said. 'Some of it was already starting to get bogged down. They wanted us to go on pushing soil over the uncontained rubbish at Owen's farm, but there wasn't time. God knows what state that place will be in by now.'

Quinn imagined Owen alone in his farmhouse, the already blighted land around him changed yet again out of all recognition, and changing ever faster as the water continued to rise.

Neither of them spoke for several minutes, listening to the rain and the wind. It was only eleven. If Webb had been right, then the downpour might last for the whole of the night and the following day.

'It wasn't me,' Quinn said again, this time more to himself than to Anna.

'I know,' she said. 'Once the guessing and the finger-pointing started, there was no end to it.'

'I'm glad you believe me,' Quinn said. But they both knew this was no true reassurance, and that whatever it was, it had come too late.

He tried to imagine what else she might have been openly or silently accused of by her unhappy workforce.

'I don't know how I could begin to prove it to you,' he said.

'No.' Under other circumstances, she might have laughed.

'Besides, Greer would have known about the hidden sites – they all would – long before any plans were laid and the roulette-wheel ball dropped into their own tiny world.'

'Of course they would,' she said.

Outside, there was a loud, drawn-out creaking sound, followed by a crash, and they both went to the window. Anna raised the curtain.

'A tree,' she said, both of them peering out into the darkness at the fallen trunk and shattered branches which now lay across the car park, already half submerged in the rushing water.

31

When Quinn woke, Anna was gone. It was not yet light, and the rain was still falling heavily and still blowing hard against the window in the wind.

He rose and went to look outside, accidentally kicking over the half-full glass where Anna had left it.

He felt suddenly faint, and then started coughing, convulsively almost, dropping back on to the bed to steady himself. The room's heating was off – another failure in the storm – and he climbed back into the warmth of the bed.

When he next woke, it was light, and the rain running down the window cast its liquid pattern over the room's walls, giving them the appearance of melting and running to the floor. Quinn remained where he lay and watched this, listening to the relentless splatter and drip of the water. He felt unwell. His head and throat ached. He looked around him for any indication that Anna had even been there the previous night, that they had made love and then fallen asleep together, but there was nothing, only the empty glass and the fading stain on the floor. His fingers felt cramped, numb, and he flexed them weakly to revive them.

It was after nine, and he heard engines and shouting voices in the car park below.

He turned on the screen to watch further reports of what was happening all around him, feeling increasingly detached the more he saw. The rain-laden pressure system – now apparently a 'storm surge' – had slowed considerably in its passing and was now moving through its time sequence without change, a spinning disc centred directly on the town, flicking its tail slightly as it turned, but little more. The weather alert remained gold. A second system was also stuck somewhere to the west, over Ireland, and was expected to resume its own track eastwards later in the day.

The system already over the mainland, the experts now warned, would maintain its intensity because it had fixed itself at the dividing line between two air masses, one Arctic, one much warmer and wetter, and neither of these was now powerful enough to dislodge the other. Quinn heard a new note of concern and urgency in their voices, and they spoke of the wind and the rain, of their 'stubbornness' and their 'ferocity', as though they were determined and vindictive living things. The air from the north, these experts said, came in a limitless supply, and when the system did finally shift to the south-east, then the weather would change swiftly and dramatically.

A new map was shown to indicate where the Gulf Stream current had last made its effects known over the preceding decades. Soon not even the South-West would feel its tempering benefits. It was another thing come alive in their language – another malicious creature stalking a beleaguered island.

Quinn silenced the screen and lay back on his pillow.

He slept fitfully for a further hour and then woke suddenly. He pushed himself upright, already knowing that whatever remained of the day was lost to him. The voices below resumed shouting and he went to the window to look out.

The car park and surrounding land was already under a foot of water, moving in currents and eddies as the rain continued to fall and replenish it. Men pushed stalled cars and vans from one side of the space to the other, gaining inches that would also soon be lost. The fallen tree had already been sawn into lengths and dragged clear of the drowned roadway. Only the tops of the shrubs rose above the gathering lake, surrounded by a floating scum of soil and bark chips. Litter from toppled bins clotted around the cars like foam on a rocky shore.

Some of the men below wore waterproofs and waders, and Quinn guessed these were members of Anna's teams; others, the motel staff, worked in overalls, waterproof capes and wellingtons.

A lorry stood across the slip-road entrance, water streaming beneath it. A line of traffic stretched along the road beyond, and Quinn saw the trapped occupants of the cars sitting and looking out at everything, forced off the flooded road and waiting for the water to subside, listening to the same dramatic warnings and wondering how long they too would have to wait for the solid land beneath them to reassert itself. Some had already left their vehicles and had struggled through the water to the motel; others, having calculated their chances, and knowing – *knowing* – that the rain could not continue falling this heavily or this continuously for much longer, made their own hopeful calculations and took their chances where they sat.

As Quinn watched, a family came down the slope – two adults and two children – and all four of them lost their footing in the torrent through which they waded, forced down on their backs into the deeper water below. The children and their mother screamed. The husband and father was the first to regain his footing and he shouted for them to go to him. The water rose to his thighs; it would reach the chest of the smallest child.

Another noise distracted Quinn and he looked along the face of the building to see men and women descending a fire escape. He guessed that the ground-floor entrances had been sealed and that this was how people were now coming and going from the place. He recognized more of Anna's workers, and he searched for her among them, but saw little beyond their bulky, fluorescent waterproofs.

He felt better than earlier. His headache had gone, but his chest was still tight, and when he coughed both his throat and his temples ached.

He showered and shaved and left his room.

The lift had been switched off due to the flooding in the basement, and arriving at the first-floor landing, he saw that the lobby and other rooms below were already under several inches of water. A receptionist told him that everything was now being carried out on the first floor, where communal rooms had been opened for the motel's unexpected guests.

Quinn looked into these and saw the travellers gathered there, sitting around heaters and watching screens, talking on their phones, waiting to be told that everything was about to improve, and endlessly calling their children to them. A makeshift bar and cafeteria had been opened, and these too were crowded. A sense of shared endurance filled the place, what the broadcasters never tired of calling 'community spirit', when in truth it was far from that.

Beside Quinn, a man shouted angrily into his phone, telling someone that, no, he didn't know where he was, and no, he didn't know how long the fucking rain would last and when he would finally fucking arrive wherever it was he was expected to be. People close to him cast him angry glances, and seeing this the man shouted to ask them what they were looking at. A woman told him pointedly that there were young children in the room and that there were laws about the kind of language he was using. The man laughed at her. Two of the motel's security guards, Stearn's men, stood nearby and watched him, unwilling to intervene on behalf of this silent majority, but clearly intending the swearing man to be aware of them and what they might do.

It was then that Quinn saw Anna coming along the corridor in her waterproofs, carrying a case and leaving a trail of wet footprints behind her. She saw him where he stood and came to him.

'Everything's ground to a halt,' she said. 'Both the sites are inaccessible and the excavations are filled and overflowing.' It was no more or less than she had predicted the previous night.

'Is there nothing you can do?' He wanted to ask her when she had left him, how long she had stayed beside him, if she had slept and woken, or if she had merely waited for him to fall asleep before easing herself from the bed and silently leaving him.

'Sit and watch?' she said. 'I've left a team on the hillside above the exhumation site. The burn's finished. One of our fuel tanks has flooded. Twenty tons of accelerant in the water.

We drove past the dump. Everything's been washed out and the farm's under water to the tops of its doors and windows.'

'Is anyone doing anything?' He wondered if she'd left him of her own accord or if she'd been called away to attend to one or other of these emergencies.

'What do you suggest?' she said. She turned to look at the growing crowd around her.

She was joined by others in her team, and Quinn saw by the way they regarded him, and by the way they looked at her talking to him, that they still mistrusted him. He wanted to shout and tell them that whatever they believed, they were wrong.

'Don't,' Anna said quietly, guessing his failed intention. 'Two months' work down the drain. Literally. Or perhaps "down the drain" would be preferable to where it *has* actually gone.' She signalled for those men and women gathering around her to wait where they were. 'I have to go,' she said to Quinn, and then left him before he could speak.

He watched her walk to them, unable to call after her.

One of the motel's receptionists stood to one side of the corridor, and as Anna passed her, the woman raised her hand to Quinn and he went to her.

'You have visitors,' she said to him, her voice low. And caught unawares like this, Quinn's first thought was that Webb himself had turned up unannounced in advance of the delegation. But as suddenly as the thought occurred, Quinn realized how unlikely it was, and he equally quickly dismissed it.

'Who?' he asked the woman.

'Executive Greer and Mr Stearn,' she said.

Quinn guessed by the way she said it that the two men were nearby.

'In this?' Quinn said. 'What do they want?'

'They're through here,' the woman told him, indicating the closed door beside which she stood.

Quinn had been in the corridor for at least fifteen minutes, and so the two men must have been present and waiting for him all that time.

The woman opened the door and held it for him as Quinn went inside. All these small dramas.

Greer and Stearn and four other men were sitting in a circle at the centre of the room. It was a small conference room and the tables and chairs had been pushed aside and sofas put in their place. The men were laughing as Quinn entered. A tray of coffee and spirits stood on a low table.

Stearn was the first to stop laughing and he rose and came to Quinn, telling the woman still beside him to wait outside and to ensure that no one disturbed them. He pushed the door shut, catching her foot as she left. Then he put an arm around Quinn's shoulders and Quinn immediately shook himself free of the embrace.

'What?' Stearn said smiling. 'We welcome you into our inner . . . inner . . .'

'Sanctum,' Greer offered.

'Into our inner sanctum, and you still insist on being above it all?' Stearn raised the glass he held and Quinn caught the sharp aroma of the brandy it contained. It was a little after eleven.

'Oh, I see,' Stearn said, watching him closely. 'Had a long night? You and the ever-convenient Ms Laing making the most of your own enforced confinement?'

It sounded ridiculous and contrived and Quinn refused to be drawn by the remark.

'What's he talking about?' Greer called to him, sharing Stearn's laughter and raising his own glass to Quinn.

'Is this some kind of celebration?' Quinn asked Greer, deliberately bypassing Stearn.

'Of sorts,' Greer said. He beckoned Quinn closer to him.

'I would have thought you'd all be otherwise engaged this morning.'

Only Stearn shook his head at the remark.

'We are – were,' Greer said. 'For your information, most of us have been up all night, if you must know. Working hard. Coordinating.' He unfastened a second button on his shirt and pulled his tie an inch lower.

'*That* hard?' Quinn said.

Greer didn't understand him. 'For your information, Mr Quinn, we've just executed our first full-scale Gold Alert and everything has gone according to plan, to procedure.'

'The whole place will be under water by the end of today,' Quinn said. He wondered if the predictions of the rain's duration had taken any more leaps ahead of them since he'd last checked.

'Everything is according to plan and everything perfectly under control,' Greer said. 'Meaning we're on top of things, meaning we know what's happening, where this thing is going.'

Stearn came to join the others, refilling his glass and gesturing with the bottle at Greer, who hesitated and then accepted a refill.

'Is this the Emergency Committee?' Quinn said, looking at the others.

'No, this is me and Greer,' Stearn said. 'And these are some of *our* people. "Emergency Committee"? You make it all sound so . . .' He turned his back on Quinn and spoke only to the others.

None of these men, Quinn saw, held glasses, only coffee cups.

'What Mr Stearn is trying to tell you,' Greer said, 'is that we've all had a busy night making sure the alert was put into operation and that our priority responses were properly activated.'

'Meaning what, exactly?' Quinn said.

'Meaning there has been no loss of life and that the threat to property has been properly assessed and monitored.'

'But not prevented?'

'Prevented how? We used to refer to events like this as Acts of God, Mr Quinn. Surely you remember those?'

Quinn's resolve failed him in the face of these worthless arguments, and he sat down. 'So why are you here?' he said.

The simple question amused Stearn. 'Because this is our designated post-crisis debrief centre.'

'That explains everything,' Quinn said. 'And what are you *doing* here now that the crisis is *post* and the threat to property is being properly assessed and monitored?'

'What do you *think* we're doing?' Stearn said angrily. 'We're doing what everybody else is doing. We're climbing up out of the water and then we're all just sitting on our arses waiting for it to go away. What, you think it *won't* all just go away as fast as it came? That's how it worked last time.'

'It's forecast to—' Quinn started to say.

'It's forecast to stop raining some time later today.'

It was an unrealistic and hopeful estimate, and everyone in the room understood that.

'And when that happens, everything will—'

'Everything will be sound again,' Greer said.

'"Sound"?' Quinn said.

'Sound,' Greer repeated, looking to Stearn for support.

But even Stearn seemed surprised by the choice of word and he looked back and forth between Greer and Quinn as though trying to ascertain which of the two men now struck him as the most ridiculous. And then he smiled. 'Oh, and concerning all that other business at the cow pit,' he said.

'The human remains,' Quinn said.

'If you say so. Anyhow, the Ministry prosecutors have looked at everything and they agree with myself and the Regional Police Chief that there are no real grounds for a full-scale investigation to be launched. Too long ago. Too much water under the bridge. Too costly. Too many unconfirmables and inconsequentials for any—'

'"Inconsequentials"?' Quinn said.

'It's what I said. You know the language better than I do.'

Quinn doubted this. 'And the police – the *real* police – they're happy with that decision?'

Stearn smiled. 'Happy? Delirious, I'd say. Besides, when did you last hear of anyone going against what the Government prosecutors deemed the proper course to follow?'

'We did our best for them,' Greer said. 'Whoever they were. But like Stearn says, it was all too long ago. You know how these people operate, same then as now. Everything below the surface, nothing properly registered, nothing accredited, nothing ever permanent or secure or established about their lives.'

It was how they would all soon come to live.

Children ran shouting and laughing in the corridor outside.

'So the file's conveniently closed?' Quinn said.

'And sealed and buried,' Stearn said.

'Is that what you brought me in here to tell me?' Quinn asked him.

'Call it a common courtesy,' Greer said. 'In advance of Alexander Webb's own courtesy call.'

'And you honestly believe the visit will still go ahead after all this?' Quinn asked him. 'After all that?' He pointed to the window, and Greer alone turned to look. It was only a guess, but a good one. Who, knowing what was about to be attempted there, would come all that way to cut the ribbon, draw aside the curtain and wave their arm over that drowned and struggling world?

'Of course it'll happen,' Stearn told him. 'Unless *you*'ve turned anything up to suggest otherwise.'

Beside him, Greer put a hand to his mouth to prevent himself from laughing.

Then one of the men beside Stearn attracted his attention and announced that they ought to be leaving. He held out his watch to Stearn.

'Oh?' Greer said, surprised by the news.

'I'm expected elsewhere,' Stearn said. 'The flooding's triggered a lot of alarms. A lot of unattended calls. I need to go and mop a few brows, make a few reassuring noises, reassess a few premiums, that sort of thing. I take it I can promise *your* every assistance on behalf of the Executive?' He waited for Greer's answer.

'Naturally,' Greer said, angry at having been outmanoeuvred like this.

'Good,' Stearn said, and then signalled for the men around him to rise, which they did.

In an attempt to reassert his own authority, Greer said loudly to Quinn, 'I shall be talking to Alexander personally later.'

Quinn shrugged. 'He already knows what's happening here.'

'Happening?'

'The rain.'

'You worry too much about nothing, Mr Quinn.'

Stearn and the others left the room, leaving Quinn and Greer alone briefly. And then Greer rose and followed them, emptying his glass and saying nothing more to Quinn as he went.

32

The rain continued to fall steadily until noon, when it ceased as abruptly as it had started fifteen hours earlier. The forecasters said immediately that this was only a temporary break, and that the downpour would soon resume. Some said it was only an hour away; others disagreed and said nearer three. Most called it a 'respite', as though it were an opportunity to be seized.

In the motel, people went to the windows and looked out at the standing water. In places the surface was calm and reflective; elsewhere it flowed in torrents and rills, either disturbed or draining or flowing to its natural levels in advance of that balance again being disturbed.

In the makeshift bar and cafeteria, Quinn wondered if this break in the downpour was similar to the calm eye at the centre of a hurricane, a mid-point marker, another measure of endurance, a new beginning and another end already in sight.

Water still poured from the gutters and rose from the drains. Tidemarks were revealed on the walls and the sides of vehicles where the level slowly fell. A patch of clear blue sky showed through the cloud and people pointed this out to each other. A fleeting beam of the midday sun shone for a few seconds in this break, and opportunity was coloured briefly by hope. The rest of the sky remained dark, charcoal with low, sliding clouds of beaten pewter.

Some of those stranded there took the opportunity to return to their cars, either to retrieve their belongings or to drive to where the water was less deep, where what lay beneath remained at least visible or knowable.

Groups of men arrived with equipment to unblock drains and to sweep the water into flowing gullies. Quinn wondered why they bothered, knowing as they did that the rain was about to resume. He saw Wade and his men dropping hoses into the drains along the ring road, splashing through water which rose to their knees. The river flowing down the slip road continued unabated. Water rose in boiling mounds along the edge of the motel property where drains were being tested far beyond their capacity.

Quinn watched the men working, and others gathered beside him, speculating on what little the drainers might achieve, or how long the rain might now hold off.

Some – those whose journeys had been interrupted by the storm – speculated on their chances of getting away while the slender opportunity existed. They studied the forecasts and calculated that a journey of only thirty miles to the east would bring them back out into the dry, bright weather they had set off in. They spoke of this unflooded landscape as though it were a different country completely, a land of lost certainties from which they had been inadvertently and unhappily diverted.

One man asked Quinn how long he had been stuck in this dump, and Quinn said merely that it seemed like for ever.

The family he had yesterday watched floundering through the water came to the window and the husband announced to everyone nearby that they were going to attempt to leave. He said the dry spell would last longer than predicted, that he could see their abandoned car standing above the water, and that most of the ring road would already be clear, standing as it did on its raised embankment. Others encouraged him in this speculation, eager to believe him and to share his confidence.

The man's wife stood beside Quinn, her two young children clinging to her coat, frightened by the prospect of wading back through the water into which they had already fallen. She tried to reassure them, but succeeded only in frightening them further the more imminent she made their departure sound. Her husband told his small crowd that he refused to be beaten by the rain, and several of the men around him raised their drinks to him.

Turning from the window, Quinn saw Anna in the doorway, watching him. He expected her simply to leave, but instead she raised her hand to him and he went to her.

'I'm going to the sites. The all-terrains have no trouble getting through the water.'

'Why?' he asked her.

'I need to see for myself. Whatever might be about to happen now, I'm still responsible. Others have been there through all this. I've called them in. They're telling me that everything's worse than I can imagine.'

'I'll come with you,' Quinn said, hoping she wouldn't refuse him.

'We won't leave the vehicles, or probably even drive off the ring road. I just need to see, that's all, to be ready to answer questions and start to work out what to do next.'

It seemed unlikely to Quinn that there remained any 'next' left to consider; at least not where that place was concerned. Besides, all she had to do was to look out at the land surrounding the motel and at the water rushing down off the slopes to know what her own sites now looked like.

He met her a few minutes later at the first-floor fire exit. She gave him waterproofs and waders and they followed the shallower water to where her vehicles were parked. She climbed into the driver's seat of a cab which stood several feet clear of the water and Quinn pulled himself up beside her. There was a smell of sewage in the air, and this floated in slicks where the drains had backed up and overflowed.

Anna started the engine and they rose out of the car park on to the empty road. The lines of cars sat where they had been abandoned, those lowest to the ground already filled with water. A short distance from the motel they saw where several vehicles lay slewed on the embankment, either as the result of accidents or because they had been swept off the road by the surging water.

In places, salvage crews were already at work, clearing the road and ensuring that there was no one still sitting in the cars.

The driver in the motel had been right – the ring road itself was covered with only an inch or two of water, and this was draining fast from its cambered surface, flooding the land on either side and giving the road ahead the appearance of an ancient and monumental earthwork – something that might have been deliberately erected against the coming flood.

They followed this to the exhumation site, where Anna pulled to the side and sat looking out over the plain of water below. Only the outline of the site was now visible to them – the raised line of its containing walls, a track leading to the edge of the massive hole. A darker rectangle of water revealed the drowned excavations.

'Fifteen metres deep along the far edge,' Anna said, indicating the depth of the water in the more recent of the diggings. It seemed impossible to Quinn that so much water had collected there so quickly. Elsewhere, the unexcavated parts of the site were flooded only to a depth of a metre or so. He saw immediately the impossibility of ever draining so vast a hole or of work ever resuming there.

Anna left the vehicle and walked to where the gradient steepened beyond the crash barrier. She took out a camera and filmed the site.

Quinn joined her. Beneath him, the edge of the contained water was clotted with the remains of the carcases that had been excavated but not yet removed for burning. There was nothing recognizable as any part of a cow – no limbs or torsos, heads or white bones – just a jumbled mulch of dark material that had been sucked clear of the ground and then been washed back and forth until it had caught and settled and accumulated again. The smell of this rose to them where they stood. It was not as potent as the smell of the effluent surrounding the motel, but it was distinctive none the less.

'The whole site will have to be sealed,' Anna said, but without any true conviction that this might be achieved.

How? Quinn thought. *And to what end?*

She started pointing, drawing imaginary barriers across the flood.

The tops of several vehicles showed through the water where they had been abandoned at the edge of the workings, and she speculated on how quickly these might be retrieved and restored to action.

That, too, seemed an impossibility to Quinn. The ground beneath the machinery would become more and more saturated and they would sink even further into it under their own weight. And soon the rain would resume and the water level would rise again.

The land was flooded far beyond the perimeter of the site, to where the surrounding hills started to rise. They saw the white courses of new and revived streams pouring down these slopes.

Movement in the far distance attracted Quinn's attention, and he watched as a car came down the hillside along an invisible track, its headlights marking its progress until it was lost to view.

A light rain resumed falling.

'We ought to get back,' Quinn suggested.

Anna stood with her back to him for a few minutes longer, and when Quinn repeated what he'd said, she shouted, 'I heard you,' still not turning, still standing and looking out over the waste and loss of all her work there.

Quinn returned alone to the vehicle, climbing into the high seat and switching on the headlights.

Anna joined him a few minutes later.

'I don't know why I came,' she said. It was an apology of sorts.

'You needed to see it,' he told her. 'That's all. You weren't ever going to rescue or resume anything in the face of all this.'

'So – the world drowns and all *we* do is sit looking at it and waiting for everything to come right again?'

The remark contained too great a question, and so Quinn said nothing.

Eventually, after several more minutes of silence, they returned to the roadway, their heavy tyres digging into the loose ground as they went, spinning and slipping briefly before gaining traction higher up the slope.

They returned to the motel and were stopped at the slip road, where a new barrier had been erected in their absence, and where a line of twenty or so recently arrived cars now queued ahead of them. Two of Stearn's men stood at the barrier.

'What now?' Anna said, letting her head fall briefly to the wheel.

Quinn climbed down and walked past the cars to the barrier. He recognized the guards, and they him. He told them about Anna and pointed her out to them. Other vehicles had already joined the queue behind her.

'We're telling people to drive on while the good weather lasts,' one of the guards said. It was already raining more heavily and the water still ran over the road's smooth surface. 'Go back, tell her to pull out and to come up to the barrier. We'll let her in.'

'And the rest of them?' Quinn looked up at the darkening sky.

'No chance,' the man told him.

Several of the drivers at the front of the line sounded their horns, and this amused the guards.

'Where will they go?' Quinn said.

'There are designated collection points further on.' The man pointed along the line of the road.

'Indoors?'

'Designated collection points,' the man repeated angrily. 'Look, if she wants to come in . . .'

'Plus,' the other guard said, 'this place is running out of supplies. You let any more in and there won't be anything for anybody. No deliveries until tomorrow at the earliest.' He made it sound like a month away.

'That's right,' the first man said. 'In addition to which, Greer ordered the clean water supply to be shut off an hour ago. Contaminated. All part of the Gold Alert roll-out.'

Quinn walked back to Anna and told her what he'd just learned.

They drove past the line of cars to the barrier. When this was raised, the foremost of the motorists tried to follow her through, but were prevented by the guards, who lowered the barrier on to the bonnet of the leading car so the driver was forced to reverse, colliding with the car behind. A third car turned sharply to avoid a further collision and slid off the road on to the embankment.

Quinn and Anna continued down the slip road and into the deeper water of the car park.

Once back inside, Anna went immediately to talk to her waiting supervisors and Quinn went to the bar.

Men approached him and asked him about conditions on the ring road. He told them about the new barrier and everything else he'd seen. A woman told him that the family of four had left the motel soon after his own departure. Two hours had passed. In all likelihood, she said, they would now be safely beyond the reach of the rain. Quinn doubted this, but said nothing. If there was a barrier at the motel, then there would be others further along the road, and the so-called designated collection points would be considerably less comfortable than where they all now stood and waited and speculated, with or without clean running water.

Growing tired of the woman's blossoming speculation,

Quinn insulted her by telling her to believe what she wanted, and then he left her and climbed the stairs to his room. People sat in the stairwells and along the corridors, drawing in their legs and watching him without speaking as he made his way through them.

33

He slept fully clothed, and when he woke a few hours later, disturbed by the growing number of people in the corridor outside, and by the comings and goings of the overcrowded rooms on either side of him, Quinn felt ill again.

It had resumed raining heavily, as heavily as earlier in the day. The revised forecast was for this renewed downpour to last until the following dawn, after which the weather system would continue belatedly to the south, weakening as it went until it finally dried and its winds blew themselves out. Twelve more hours. The same cold weather was still predicted to follow in the wake of this, and 'Arctic' was still the preferred epithet, occasionally 'Polar'.

Quinn went to his door and opened it an inch, peering out at the people gathered along the full length of the corridor. His screen had flashed with messages from reception asking for single occupants to consider sharing their rooms and facilities with those now temporarily stranded at the motel. Quinn had dismissed the idea. His room still contained confidential files and papers. Besides, he felt worse than ever. People would watch him, note his symptoms and then refuse to share with him. He turned the screen off. The motel management thanked him for his patience and understanding in these times of hardship.

He drank what was left of his whisky and the liquid left its sour aftertaste in his mouth.

He tried to sleep again, resisting the urge to go out into the corridor and shout for silence.

The rain made its familiar noises on the window, blowing more from the north than the west now, striking the pane at a different angle, and again overflowing from gutters all along the building. The fallen tree had by then been sawn into short lengths and these were stacked in the rising water like giant bobbins, vivid in the darkness beneath the lights.

Shortly after finally falling asleep – or so he imagined – he was woken by someone banging loudly on his door and calling in to him. A man's voice – one he recognized vaguely, but couldn't place.

He waited where he lay for a moment, hoping that whoever was there would go away, that whatever demand was about to be made of him would be made of someone else. *Go away*, he mouthed. He wondered if any light showed beneath his door.

But the knocking persisted, more urgent and prolonged this time, and the man outside continued shouting, calling for Quinn by name and insisting that he knew he was in there.

Quinn went to the door, and the instant he unlocked it, the

man pushed it open and grabbed Quinn by the arm. Quinn recognized one of the guards from the slip-road barrier.

'You've got to come down. There's a man downstairs, a lunatic, armed, he's got a gun, a rifle, and he's threatening to do something. He says he knows *you*'re here, mentioned you by name, said he'd talk to you.' He shook Quinn, trying to pull him from his room.

Quinn freed himself of the man's grip and pushed him back, surprising him.

Along the corridor, others were waking where they slept on the floor and calling to silence the commotion. A baby started crying, and the disturbed, angry sleepers complained of this too.

'What?' the guard said. 'What? We called Stearn and he said that if this madman was prepared to talk to you, then to do it. Anything to calm him down. Didn't you hear me – I said he was armed.'

'I heard you,' Quinn said, struggling to understand exactly what was being asked of him.

Winston, he thought. *But why here, and why now – it's after eleven – twenty-four hours after the rain started? And armed?*

The guard reached out again to grab Quinn, but then held up his palms.

'OK, OK,' he said. 'No one's forcing you.'

'What do you expect me to do?' Quinn asked him.

'I already told you – talk to him. Keep him distracted until Stearn gets here – anything. I don't know. Just until we can disarm him, I suppose. I don't know. Christ, as if we didn't already have enough to cope with without this fucking lunatic turning up.' He glanced back along the corridor, where the watching crowd had grown largely silent in an effort to overhear what he was saying.

'Are there many people down there?' Quinn asked him.

'Hundreds. And he's swinging that gun around like it's – like it's a stick. And he sounds drunk or something. The point is, he said he'll talk to you. When I told Stearn, he said straightaway that I should fetch you and that you could at least talk to him and find out what he wanted. Who knows, perhaps that's all he wants to do – talk.'

'Is there anyone with him?' Quinn said.

'Such as?'

'A younger woman.'

'And who would she be?'

'It was just a thought,' Quinn said, guessing that Winston had come alone.

'Stearn is on his way. Not easy in all this.' He looked at his watch. 'Another half an hour, he reckons. He'll bring some back-up.'

'Meaning they'll be armed?'

'What do you think? You think he's going to let some lunatic go around in the middle of all this waving a gun at people? How's *that* going to look? How's it going to make *Stearn* look?' He shook his head, his eyes closed. 'Knowing Stearn, he'll give the bastard one chance – one – to put the thing down and hand himself over.'

Quinn considered the implications of all this with growing concern, and sensing this, the guard turned away from him and said, 'But if that's the way you want things to work out . . .'

'Wait,' Quinn told him. He owed Winston and his daughter this much at least.

The two of them left the doorway.

'I'd make sure that door's secure,' the guard said. 'Otherwise you'll come back and find the room filled.'

Quinn followed him through the parting onlookers to the top of the stairs, descending and turning a corner to look down into the room below. A crowd of people stood against one wall, and seeing the guard, several of them motioned to the far side of the room.

Quinn told the man to stay where he was while he went on alone. Several in the crowd tried to hold him back, urging the guard forward instead. Women did their best to calm crying children, but with little success.

Quinn arrived at the bottom of the stairs and turned into the room, momentarily blinded by the makeshift lighting which had been erected there. Temporary beds and cushions had been laid against every wall, and people lay on these fully clothed. Shielding his eyes, Quinn looked across the room.

Someone called to him, and instead of Winston, he heard Owen's voice, and was surprised by this after all he'd expected, and forced to quickly reconsider everything he imagined he was about to confront and attempt. At least with Winston there had been the possibility of Rebecca also being present.

'Owen?' he called out. 'Is that you?' He wondered if he had ever known the man's Christian name.

'You tell me,' Owen shouted back. 'Put your hands down.'

'I can't see you properly because of the lights,' Quinn said, lowering his voice, his throat still aching with everything he said.

Owen moved to one side. 'What about now?'

Quinn followed him. He saw the shotgun Owen held, pointing and swinging it around him.

'I don't know what you want, why you're here,' Quinn said.

'What I want? Why I'm here? Why I'm here? I'll tell you why I'm here.' But then he fell silent, as though suddenly uncertain or shocked by what he might have been about to reveal.

'Go on,' Quinn prompted him.

'I'll tell you why I'm here.' Owen seemed confused now, repeating himself merely to stake whatever measure of control he might still exercise over the situation. He'd been drinking and everyone could hear this in his voice. He was soaked from head to foot, his arms bare.

'How did you get here?' Quinn called to him, wondering why the guards hadn't stopped him at the barrier.

'How do you think? I walked. I walked through the water.' It was at least five miles to his farm turned rubbish dump.

'In this?' Quinn said.

'Why all these stupid questions? Yes, in this. What, you think no one can walk five miles any more? Not you, perhaps, not *any* of you, but to a man like me, five miles is nothing. Where's the guard who went running up to fetch you? Hiding somewhere? Waiting for Stearn to get here? Still trying to get through to him?'

'He's on the stairs,' Quinn said. 'He's not prepared to get himself killed for the minimum wage Stearn pays him.'

Someone in the watching crowd laughed at this.

'Killed?' Owen shouted, lowering and then raising his shotgun. 'Is *that* what he thinks I've come for? What's he told you to do – to keep me talking until Stearn gets here and does the job himself? Why not? Might as well. What else have I got left to lose? You seen the farm, my home, recently? Because—'

'I saw it yesterday,' Quinn said, his voice low. It was a lie; he was merely repeating what Anna had told him.

'Oh?' Owen said suspiciously.

'I saw that the ground floor was under water and that

everything that's been dumped there was starting to wash loose.'

'I had to practically swim to the road,' Owen said absently.

'I can imagine,' Quinn said. He took several more paces towards him.

Owen watched him approach but said nothing.

When Quinn stopped moving, Owen said, 'What, you think I should shout and tell you to stay where you are?'

'What do you want?' Quinn asked again. 'You were about to tell me. Why don't you put the gun down and tell me.'

He wondered how quickly Stearn might now arrive, and what he would do when he finally got there – if he would be content to wait outside and watch what was happening; or if he would intervene immediately in an attempt to take control of the situation. It also occurred to Quinn that the first any of them might know of Stearn's presence was when one of the armed men accompanying him shot Owen without warning from a vantage point on the raised road.

Quinn looked to the windows and tried to estimate where someone might position themselves to gain a clear line of fire into the room. And perhaps Owen himself had also considered this, because he remained at the far side of the room, close to the wall and away from the nearest window.

'You could turn that light out,' Quinn said, motioning to the glare beside Owen.

'And why would I want to do that? So I won't be able to see what you're doing?'

'So that no one outside can see you,' Quinn said.

Owen considered this and all it implied and then pulled the cable from the battery.

Quinn took several more steps towards him. 'You're here

because you're angry and because you could think of nowhere else to go,' he said.

Owen laughed at this. 'I'm *here* because most of the bars in the town are flooded and I had nowhere to carry on drinking. And because my truck got flooded and I had to leave it. You think I came here straight from the farm?'

'You still haven't told me *why* you're here,' Quinn repeated, wanting to keep Owen focussed now that he was starting to flounder in all these angry diversions.

And again Owen looked puzzled by the remark, either still uncertain of his answer, or lost for the words with which to express himself as forcibly as he wanted.

Quinn watched him closely, remaining silent as Owen struggled with his thoughts.

'They took everything off me,' Owen shouted eventually. 'Everything.'

'The farm was—'

'I know what the farm *was*. And I know what *they* made happen to it. Compulsory purchase? What's that except outright theft?'

'You've known for a long time that all this was about to happen.' It sounded more provocative and uncaring than Quinn had intended.

'And that makes everything all right, does it? That makes *me* the stupid, greedy bastard who ought to take the pittance they're offering me and get out of their way, does it? That makes me the same as them, does it?'

These last remarks confused Quinn. He had been about to say that he understood how Owen must be feeling, but he thought better of this now and remained silent.

'What, lost for words?' Owen shouted at him. 'Lost for words because you're in this with them, because you're as much a part of it all as any of them – Greer, Stearn, the developers, the Agriculture people? Because all this is in *your* interest as much as theirs? You don't know the first thing about me, people like me, not the first thing.'

Quinn took some reassurance in the speed with which Owen's anger again lost its focus and footing, repeating old grievances and exhausted, futile demands. Soon he would come to sound self-pitying, and whatever understanding or sympathy he might have commanded from that crowd of watching strangers would also be quickly squandered.

'Just put the gun down,' Quinn said to him.

Owen considered this and took several paces towards Quinn, causing those now suddenly close to him to back away. People scrabbled from their makeshift beds. The crying children had finally been taken away, but the noise they continued to make still came into the room, distorted and muted.

'If I put the gun down,' Owen said, grinning, 'how will I be able to shoot you with it when you finally get too close? Or when *I* finally see sense and work out just exactly *how* tight you and the others are in all of this.' He laughed, but the laughter was forced, and this, like the complaint which preceded it, reassured Quinn further.

'You aren't going to shoot me,' Quinn said confidently.

Owen immediately raised the shotgun and pointed it at him. 'You seem very sure of that,' he said.

Both men, or so it seemed to Quinn, understood that a point had been reached and then passed, and that what remained now was only this worthless posturing on both their parts.

Quinn waited.

'What?' Owen said. 'What? Don't tell me you're trying to convince yourself that what you just did was a brave thing, that you're a brave man.' He drew back both hammers on the gun. But that too seemed an empty gesture.

At the far end of the room, behind Quinn, several of the onlookers called out and Quinn heard the noise of people pushing themselves out of Owen's line of fire.

'Well?' Owen said to him.

'I honestly don't know what you want of me,' Quinn said. 'I don't even believe I'm the one you wanted to find standing here like this.'

Owen paused before answering him. 'If it had been any of the others, everything here would be long finished by now.'

Uncertain what he meant by this, Quinn remained silent for a moment, and then said, 'I'll come with you. When Stearn gets here. He isn't going to let you just throw the gun down and walk away from all of this. Not now. You know that. I'll come with you, make a statement, make sure everything's done properly. There are a lot of witnesses. If you just—'

'Walk away?' Owen said. 'Walk away and go where?'

'If you put the gun down I'll tell Stearn that I was the only one you threatened with it – none of these others – and then you can start to get things sorted out.'

Owen laughed again at the words. '"Sorted out"? Is that what's going to happen? Is everything going to get *sorted out*, auditor? Is that how things work in your little world? Do things get *sorted out*? Do *people* get sorted out – sorted out and then live happily ever after? Is that what *you*'re going to do now that you've convinced yourself that I have no intention whatsoever of using this thing? Now that you're such a brave man? Is that—' He stopped abruptly, and in the silence Quinn heard running footsteps along the corridor leading from the first-floor fire escape. He heard Stearn's voice calling for men to follow him.

'That's it, then,' Owen said.

'Put it down, quickly, and put your hands up,' Quinn told him, hoping Stearn couldn't hear him.

He walked back to where he could see up the staircase. Stearn stood at the bottom of the stairs, whispering to the guard who still waited there.

'It's Owen,' Quinn said loudly. 'He's airing his grievances again, that's all.'

'What, and you're still making excuses for him?' Stearn said.

The remark surprised Quinn. He was only there, confronting Owen like this, because Stearn had told the guard to fetch him.

'No – I'm still here doing *your* dirty work,' Quinn said.

Owen laughed at the remark and called for Stearn to show himself.

Stearn hesitated before coming down the final few stairs and turning to face Owen.

'*Is* he doing your dirty work?' Owen called to him.

Behind Stearn, several armed and armoured men pushed people up the stairs and out of the way.

Hearing this, Owen shouted, 'How many have you brought with you?'

'There are twenty of us,' Stearn told him flatly. 'So, all things considered, I'd say that just about equals your chances of walking away from all of this, farm boy. Twenty to one.'

But instead of the insult this was intended to be, Owen seemed to appreciate the name and he smiled at it, as though at some distant fond memory suddenly evoked.

'That's right,' Stearn said. 'Farm boy.'

And even as the words crossed the room to where Owen and Quinn still stood, and in the instant both men began to consider what Stearn might say next, Owen pushed the gun hard up into the flesh of his chin, pulled both triggers and filled the room with the explosion of his own decapitation, falling headless to his knees, balancing there for a few seconds and then toppling slowly backwards, bleeding in a pulsing spray from the great open wound of his neck, swaying slightly as his weight and length settled, and looking to everyone still watching like someone about to spring suddenly upright and confound them all with the miracle of his own bloody resurrection.

Quinn closed his eyes for a moment, his ears ringing with the explosion and its echo in the confined space, and the smell and taste of the powder filling his nose and mouth. He had raised both his hands, and stood poised like that, as though by this means alone – this shield of the thin flesh and brittle bones of his fingers and palms – he might protect himself. Beside him, he saw that Stearn had thrown himself sideways, where he had collided clumsily with the wall and then fallen on his face and chest to the floor.

34

Already summoned by Stearn, Greer arrived an hour later, and the two men went together into the now empty room in which Owen's decapitated body still lay. A screen had been erected to conceal the bloody mess, and everyone else in the overcrowded room had been forced out into the few remaining corridors and open spaces.

Along with Greer, Pollard arrived, and a dozen more of Stearn's guards. He positioned these around the room, effectively sealing it while he and Greer entered it to consider the way ahead.

Pollard insisted on entering with them, proclaiming loudly his intention of saying a prayer for the dead man. He went halfway to the screen and then stopped there, dropping to his knees on a convenient cushion. Holding his clasped hands above his head, he asked God to forgive Owen for what he'd done, to understand his despair, and to forgive him too for being unable to see and to grasp and to reap the bounty of God's great riches all around him, here, now, in the present, and in the months and years ahead.

Quinn watched all this from the stairs, ignoring Stearn's repeated demands to leave. He laughed aloud at the last of Pollard's imprecations, at the insincerity of the cheap prayer and at the misplaced and convoluted piety in which it was wreathed. Stearn and Greer were similarly embarrassed by the man's presence and the attention he drew to himself in that blood-splattered room, still tainted with the sharp odour of the gunshot and its consequences.

Greer's first question was to ask pointedly if anyone could be said to have provoked Owen into doing what he'd done. No one answered him. He then listed his own unhappy dealings with the man, making it clear to everyone still watching that he was not wholly surprised by what had happened, and that it might even be regarded as the predictable conclusion to a long and sorry journey.

Pollard's prayer finally ended amid a minute of subdued murmuring, and he rose awkwardly to his feet and came back to the two men. There were now tears in his eyes and running down his cheeks, and he wiped at these for a long time afterwards.

When Greer learned that Quinn had been negotiating with Owen during the final few minutes of the confrontation, that he had been trying to reason with the man prior to Stearn's arrival, he said that perhaps the failure to appease or convince Owen was his.

Quinn looked at Stearn as Greer suggested this and said,

'You believe that, too, Stearn? *Was* it me who pushed him over the edge?'

Stearn hesitated before answering. 'It was always going to end like this, one way or another, where Owen was concerned. Here or somewhere else, out in the open or locked away and unseen somewhere – wherever he dragged himself and his pitiful history. You can only lick those kinds of wounds for so long.'

'Is that the best you can do?' Quinn said. '"One way or another", "here or somewhere else".'

Pollard started to say what a waste Owen's suicide was and Greer told him to shut up.

Pollard looked at Greer for a moment and then wiped again at his shining cheeks. 'Am I the only one here feeling any true compassion, any true grief for this unhappy and cast-aside man?'

'Cast-aside *dead* man,' Quinn said. 'The unhappiness part is over. And if you want to thank God – even your God, Pollard – for anything, then you can thank him for that.' Even as he said it, it felt like an ill-considered remark to make.

But Pollard only smiled at it, and said, 'Whatever you say, Mr Quinn,' and then went on wiping his face.

'We'll need to have an investigation,' Greer said, turning to Stearn, who agreed with him, but only because he could do nothing else while the two of them were being so openly watched and judged.

'Perhaps that would be a job for the real police,' Quinn suggested, and he left them, pushing his way through the crowds now filling the staircase.

Greer shouted for him to go back to them, but Quinn kept on walking. He imagined Stearn holding Greer's arm and telling him to shut up. Perhaps it would be in *all* their interests if the police were now called in and this simple case was handed over to them. What more was there to say except to repeat what Stearn had already said about the single unhappy path Owen had been following since the farm had failed and his own forward momentum along with it?

Quinn also imagined the two men already starting to distance themselves from Pollard, anxious to avoid his own self-serving gloss on what had just happened. He felt almost reassured by the predictability of everything that would now take place, by the speed with which Owen would disappear and by the thoroughness with which everyone else would be exonerated. In a decade, perhaps less, all that would remain of the man would be the name of the vanished farm attached to the expanded dump which buried its long-lost orchard and fields.

Reaching the second floor, Quinn went to Anna, who told him she'd been waiting for him. She already knew what had happened.

'Look,' she said, indicating the window and the darkness outside. 'It's stopped raining.'

Quinn crossed the room and looked out. Water still coated the glass, and under the bright lights the drains still seethed. Uprooted shrubs floated in the deeper pools, drawn back and forth in unseen currents.

'In time for you to salvage anything and resume?' he asked her, already knowing the answer.

Anna said nothing.

'The forecast now is for much colder weather.'

'Why did he come here, do you think?' Anna said, meaning Owen. 'Why here? Why not just do what he intended doing all along at the farm? In his parents' bedroom, perhaps.'

It was a question Stearn and Greer would soon be asking.

'Because he intended killing others, someone else, before himself?' Quinn said, unconvinced.

'Someone like me?' she said. 'Someone like you?'

It was something neither of them could answer. The two of them would be lost, hidden, kept safe and reassured amid that crowd of blameless, exonerated others.

'Only *he* would have known the answer to that,' he said. He remembered his few conversations with the man, everything laced with futility and hopelessness.

He returned to her and she opened her arms to him, drawing him to her and then clasping him tight. Owen's death filled every room in the building.

They stood together like this for several minutes, until she eventually released him and took a step back from him.

'They want me to make a final evaluation of the sites and then to abandon them.' She motioned to the screen on which the message was displayed. Quinn saw by its wording that there was to be no consideration of any alternatives. It spoke of 'insurmountable eventualities' and 'higher priorities'.

'And we all know what they are,' Anna said, resigned to acceding to these demands and to playing out what little remained of her own role there.

She scrolled through further messages, pausing to reveal the one telling her to prepare all personnel and equipment now surplus to requirements in advance of their imminent redeployment.

'Anything about where *you* might be sent?' Quinn asked her. He wanted the simple question to reveal much more to her.

'They'll wait until they decide whether or not they need to consider what's happened here a success or a failure.'

'Surely they can't—'

'Don't,' she said. 'Nothing's going to make any difference now to what they do. Besides . . .'

'What?'

'I heard from my husband. His application to take Christopher to America with him is definitely being supported by the Breeding Programme Executive. They're going to fill what's left of the world with healthy and viable animals, and he's going to play a big part in that. No one's going to do anything to upset *that* particular plan.' Her anger quickly subsided. It was why she had held him so tightly – not the death of Owen or the uncertainty concerning her own future, but the loss of her son.

'I'm sorry,' Quinn said.

'The address of his new lawyer is in Washington. Apparently, everything that now happens will be based on a full and fair assessment of Christopher's best interests. "Full and fair". Their very words. How can I argue against that?'

'Does he want to go?' Quinn asked her.

She half turned from him. 'Probably,' she said after a minute. 'There will even be full and fair provision made for me to go over there and visit him. How often do you think that will be, given the new flight restrictions? Once a year? Once every two years, three? Until he forgets who I am?' She turned back to him. 'Sorry. Ignore me. Perhaps Owen should have given me some advance notice and I could have gone down to him. We could have made a double act.'

'You'd have needed your own shotgun,' Quinn said, and she smiled.

'I'm not that brave,' she said.

'It would have saved your husband's new employers a lot of lawyers' fees.'

'There is that,' she said.

Outside, a helicopter circled the land beyond the motel, its beam of light searching the black and sodden landscape for somewhere to land. Quinn saw that it was marked 'Police', and he knew that Greer and Stearn were already in complete control of the emptiness into which Owen was about to disappear. The same emptiness into which the men and women killed and thrown into one of Anna's pits fifty years earlier had disappeared and then been forgotten. Dirty secrets turning slowly back to dirt.

'Unless it's the opposite,' Anna said.

Quinn didn't understand her.

'Of bravery,' she said. 'Owen. Perhaps the brave thing to do would be to embrace everything that's happening, to do what people like Stearn and Greer and Pollard keep telling us to do. Is this it, do you think – the brave new world everybody tried for so long to avoid thinking about?'

The helicopter passed back and forth across the motel, its light still searching, until it flew over the building and finally settled on the road beyond the line of abandoned cars.

'It may well be,' Quinn said, wondering what might be considered truly brave or new, necessary or even desirable about any of it.

35

The following morning, an air of numb relief pervaded the motel. The storm and its attendant dramas had arrived, been endured and survived, and everything had passed. Stalled and diverted lives must now be resumed; curtains drawn; messages checked; reassurances sought and given; journeys rescheduled. Everything that had stopped must now be re-started; the illusion of unbroken continuity must be made to persist. There was no other course. Doubt and weakness had been tested and burnished and turned magically into strength and conviction.

Numb relief and – after Owen – a kind of unfocussed gratitude. People convinced themselves they had looked into the abyss and that they had then retreated from its precipitous edge and unknowable depths. Or if not retreated, exactly, then with the easing of the rain they believed that the abyss was no longer at their feet, but was again somewhere distantly ahead of them, somewhere in the future, weightless, another uncertain reprieve, out of sight, where it belonged.

The first people Quinn encountered on descending the stairs were Winston and his daughter. They were standing at the door to the room in which Owen had killed himself, prevented from entering by four of Stearn's men and two uniformed police officers.

Upon seeing Quinn, Rebecca held her father's arm and pulled him back to her.

Quinn heard the man's voice before seeing the two of them, and his first instinct was to remain hidden from them and to wait for them either to leave or be thrown out of the motel.

There were already people working on the floor below, salvaging furniture and skimming the last of the silt and detritus from the floor. This was now intermittently both liquid and solid, and moved across the floor in slow, settling waves, shapeless and then formed into its own miniature landscapes. Quinn watched this for a moment until he realized that Winston and Rebecca were now much closer to him, and that both were watching him, waiting to speak.

'They won't let us in,' Rebecca said, indicating the guards.

'Why do you want to go in?'

She nodded at her father. '*I* don't.'

Another of Winston's futile complaints, another of the fading ripples which controlled his own angry and powerless existence, pushing him back and forth, and soon perhaps beyond every last vestige of reason.

Winston left the girl, returned to the locked door and pulled at it.

'The body's long gone,' one of the guards called to Quinn.

'Police, hospital, all that. Tell him, will you? Any more of his threats and accusations and we'll have to notch things up a gear.'

The others considered this amusing and they laughed.

Eventually, Winston returned to his daughter.

'They're telling the truth,' Quinn said. 'How did you find out?'

Rebecca took a rolled newspaper from her bag and held up its front page to him.

'Already?' Quinn said, surprised to see Owen's younger, smiling face looking out at him. *Sad Outcome of Personal Tragedy.*

'I knew him,' Winston said. 'We grew up here together. I knew his father when he had the farm.'

'Did you have any idea that Owen was going to do this?'

'He threatened to do a lot of things. And his name was Sam – Samuel.' He glanced to his daughter for her support, but the girl refused to give this. As before, she seemed a little embarrassed by her father's behaviour.

'Go to the hospital,' Quinn suggested. 'Perhaps they'll let you see him there.'

'There's no other family left.'

Quinn tried to remember what Owen had told him about his wife in Spain.

'*We*'re not family . . . Dad,' Rebecca said, the appended name marking the extent of her own gentle insistence.

'No, I suppose not,' Winston said. To Quinn, he said, 'Is it true that he . . . that his . . .' He held a hand to his neck.

Quinn nodded.

'The report says trained negotiators tried to persuade him to put down the gun, that he was threatening too many innocent people.'

'I was there,' Quinn said. 'I spoke to him. No one wanted this to happen.' He considered carefully everything he was avoiding saying.

'Except him,' Winston said. He turned and looked at the locked door. 'Show him the other,' he said eventually to Rebecca.

Rebecca searched the paper and showed Quinn the photograph of Greer, Stearn, Pollard and half a dozen others standing in their suits, yellow hats and fluorescent jackets beside the pristine and undamaged model in the foyer of the Administrative building. The base on which the model stood now rose only inches above two feet of water. *Hope for the Future.*

'The Administrative Centre flooded?' Quinn said, surprised.

Winston smiled and shook his head. 'Ground floor's dry as a bone. They spent hours moving the model to a basement room that *had* flooded just so they could all pose for their picture. Greer called them all personally in the middle of the night and Stearn sent cars to collect them.'

'Not *last* night, surely?' Quinn said.

'It's true,' Rebecca told him. 'They paid Wade and half a dozen others double-time to set it all up. Ask Wade if you don't believe me.' She rolled up the paper and pushed it back into her bag.

Beyond them, Quinn saw Anna and several others come down the stairs and continue to the ground floor, their conversation unbroken. She saw him and signalled to him, identifying Winston and his daughter and then casting Quinn a puzzled look as she disappeared from view.

'This'll change nothing,' Winston said, distracting Quinn.

'How did you get here?' Quinn asked him.

'What does *that* matter?' Winston said angrily.

'I borrowed a car from the garage,' Rebecca said. 'The fuel tanks are all flooded and contaminated. They're already saying it won't reopen.'

Quinn wanted to say something hopeful to her, to encourage her with speculation of all the coming opportunities, as yet unseen beyond the high wall of her father's intransigence. But he thought better of this in front of Winston, and so he said nothing. Besides, the girl would soon leave, detach herself completely and then drift until she was able to re-create herself anew somewhere else. He knew without asking her that it was something she was already considering.

And almost as though to confirm these unspoken thoughts, Winston said, 'We've been flooded. Up to our knees. Everything. No heating, no electrics whatsoever. Whole street, sixty houses.'

'I don't think there's much room left here,' Quinn said.

Winston shook his head.

'What, you think we've come looking for charity?' Rebecca said.

It wasn't what Quinn had been suggesting, but coming from the girl and not Winston, the angry rebuttal struck him all the more forcibly. He wanted to counter the remark and explain himself, but he knew that whatever he said would also be misconstrued by her. He wanted to ask her where the pair of them might go now their home was lost to them.

'I'm sorry for the loss of your friend,' he said to Winston.

'I knew him,' Winston said. 'That's all. I suppose it still counts for something.'

'He couldn't—'

'They pushed him,' Winston said. 'They pushed him and

pushed him and pushed him. All the way from being a boy on that farm to the back of that room with all those strangers looking on, and half of *them* secretly excited at the prospect of him doing what he said he was going to do.'

Quinn tried to remember if during all the time he'd been talking to Owen the man had once made his true intentions clear. But most of what he remembered was confused, filtered through his fear and then relief. All he could clearly remember was Stearn's final jibe at Owen and the way Stearn had then half fallen, half thrown himself against the wall out of the imagined cone of the shotgun blast.

'I know,' he said eventually to Winston. 'And I'm sorry for that, too.' He wondered why Winston refused to see the mirror image of himself in the dead man, refused to hear the perfect echo of his own repeated complaints.

Rebecca tugged her father's arm and Winston allowed himself to be led away by her. It was still beyond Quinn to ask her where they might go, and he guessed that emergency provision had been made for those already affected by the flood.

It had been his intention to drive as far as possible around the town to assess for himself what damage had been inflicted by the storm. But he decided against this – already knowing what he would find there – and amid the clutter and the noisy farewells of all those now departing, he returned to his room.

The corridors and staircases were empty again, and an hour later, after most of the newcomers had gone, the usual midday silence and calm fell back over the place. Muted music returned to the public rooms, and the elevators resumed rising and falling, their humming and the pinging of their doors adding to the background noise.

A potent odour filled the air, sweetened with freshener in places and sharpened with disinfectant in others. Doors and windows were opened, but to little effect other than to let the approaching cold air into the building.

In his room, Quinn was alerted to a message he had just missed. John Lucas had tried to contact him. He returned the call immediately.

'It's off,' Lucas said simply, after asking Quinn if he was alone.

'What's off?'

'Webb's grand visit. Gather up the palm leaves, silence the trumpets and put the donkey back out to graze.'

'Why?'

'"Overtaken by events". You're there; you tell me.'

'The publicity surrounding Owen?'

'Who's he? I'm talking about the flooding. They now consider it wiser to wait until spring. You know – spring: hedgerows full of flowers, pale-blue skies, rainbows, fluffy little clouds and fluffy little lambs gambolling everywhere. Spring. Is that what fluffy little lambs do – did – once?'

'It makes sense, I suppose,' Quinn said.

'Of course it does. It makes perfect sense. Especially to Webb and all his new friends.' He paused. 'Is it really as bad as Webb seems to think it is? We've seen pictures, nothing much. We saw the picture of Greer and his model.'

'It was a stunt,' Quinn said.

'I thought as much. Then tell him it backfired. It scared Webb, seeing them all like that. It won't affect the overall plans for the place, of course, but they still want to wait for one of those warm, sunny days to make their own orchestrated appearance on the scene. Perhaps you could arrange for a couple of dozen of the local maidens to dig out their traditional costumes and perform some sort of dance.' He stopped talking, aware of having said too much. '*Are* you suffering?' he said eventually. 'And who's Owen?'

'A man who died.'

'Sorry to hear it. There were no fatalities reported. Everything here's gone off for the PR people to start polishing up.'

'I can imagine,' Quinn said.

'As far as they're concerned – and at Webb's urging, of course – you were there, you survived it all, you're a survivor. A good word from me and he'll probably even upgrade you to "hero".' Another of their tired jokes.

'It rained,' Quinn said. 'That's all.'

'I suppose so. Sadly – ' He stopped again.

'Sadly, what?'

'All this delay and the slapping on of new coats of gloss means that you – you, specifically – won't get your smiling, man-of-the-people face in any of the photos. Yellow hat, champagne flute, local beauty hanging on your arm. One of the men who Made All This Possible.' Finally picking up on Quinn's own lack of enthusiasm, John Lucas said, 'Did you know this Owen?'

'Not very well,' Quinn said. *But well enough.*

'And one way or another his death was tied in with everything else?'

'One way or another,' Quinn said; another page turned, book closed.

'Sorry,' Lucas said. 'I just thought I'd give you advance warning of Webb's own call.'

'It's what he'll expect you to do,' Quinn said.

Lucas conceded this. It was the end of their conversation, and they said their farewells.

Everything changed and yet nothing changed. Plans were laid and everyone played their part.

On the bed, Quinn's mobile rang and he picked it up and looked at it, waiting ten seconds before answering.

'Webb,' he said. 'Alexander.'

He looked out of his window to where men continued to scrape and brush the liquid mud from the car park. A mound had been made of all the washed-out soil and uprooted vegetation, a near-conical island in a dirty, shallow sea, the sliced trunk of the fallen tree like stepping stones through the water, still vivid where the clean white wood rose above the surface.

36

The cold weather arrived later that same day, freezing in a skin over the standing water and casting a hard frost across the waterlogged country beyond.

The temperature fell and then rose slightly, and then fell again at the early onset of night.

Men continued working on the ring road to unblock its drains. Gritters arrived to sow their chemical grit, and the sparse traffic resumed flowing, single-file mostly, drivers following the dark tracks of the cars ahead, as though these alone were some guarantee of undisturbed motion. A fine grey spray rose behind the cars, creating sheens of powdery light in the freezing air.

Quinn saw Wade and his men working on the slip road. He watched them walk knee-deep through the water at its lower end, probing for sunken gullies with metal rods, reverse dowsers, probing water for air.

Above the men, the few remaining cars were finally towed away from the motel entrance.

The ground floor of the building was swept clear of the bulk of its mud and debris, but no attempt was made to return the reception and its staff to their usual places. Delivery lorries appeared. Fans, driers and heaters were distributed and switched on, creating hot-spots and currents of chilled air. The same sour odour filled the corridors and rooms.

Earlier, Quinn had asked Webb about his own imminent recall, but Webb had become evasive, telling him to wait where he was until plans were finalized. It was as specific as Webb was prepared to be, and Quinn had known not to persist.

After this, he had slept for several hours, making up for the sleeplessness of the previous night. There had been no further calls or messages from Webb; nothing more from John Lucas, either. Quinn knew that he'd offended and disappointed his friend, and he wondered what to say to him when they next spoke; apologies would only compound and exaggerate the rift.

Later, upon waking and looking outside, he saw Anna sitting alone on the low wall beyond the vehicles. He watched her for several minutes and then went down to her.

She was wrapped in her work clothes, unfastened at the front, and with a face mask and breathing apparatus on the ground beside her.

'Sitting in the dark?' he said to her, alerting her of his approach out of that darkness.

'I heard you coming,' she told him. She brushed the hair from her eyes with her fingers.

'Busy day at the office?'

'Something like that.' She blew a plume of clouded air above them.

Quinn felt the shallow mash of ice beneath his feet, the muddy surface growing slippery.

'What did Jeremiah want?' she said, meaning Winston.

'To find out what happened to Owen.'

'Not to gloat now that all his prophecies of doom were about to come true?'

Quinn let the remark pass.

'And what about that wretched girl trailing round in his wake? What's she supposed to be?' Her despondency now surrounded her as completely as the cold night air. Her thoughts lay elsewhere, and Winston and his daughter were the last and least of her concerns.

Quinn remarked on the emptiness of the car park and she told him that most of her own vehicles had been recalled.

'Where to?' he asked her, again hoping for an indication of when she herself might now be leaving.

'To depots,' she said.

'You don't sound very—'

'I don't sound very what? Concerned? Surprised? What? What don't I sound very?' She closed her eyes and let out her breath, sagging where she sat. 'Sorry,' she said. 'Try undermined. Very undermined. Can you be *very* undermined?'

'If you wanted to be,' Quinn said. It was another apology of sorts.

'I suppose I could be argued down to "disappointed" if "undermined" sounded too embarrassing or excessive.' She put her arm through his and drew him closer to her until they sat pressed side to side in the cold air. Her feet swung a few inches clear of the icy ground.

'It's going to get much colder,' she said.

'Arctic winds.'

'Cold, but clean and invigorating – a sharp, cleansing blade instead of all this . . . this . . .' She waved her hand. 'Instead of all this damp, sodden, pointless mess.'

After this, they sat without speaking for several minutes.

Lights were switched on high on the motel wall, casting their glare in hard-edged discs all around them, and illuminating the steam which rose from vents lower down. Icicles were already starting to form along the gutters and lintels in the freezing air.

'I can't feel my face,' Anna said eventually, and Quinn suggested they went inside.

At first, she seemed reluctant to do this.

'What?' he asked her.

'There are reports in some of the forecasts of roads being blocked by the coming snowfalls,' she said, almost as though continuing another conversation.

Quinn considered this unlikely, but said nothing.

A coach arrived at the bottom of the slip road, sending waves through the water. Wade and his men gathered to climb on to it, their work there finished, all urgency gone, even though in some places the water was no less deep than when they'd arrived.

The police helicopter could still occasionally be heard and seen over the road, circling the darkened centre of the town as though spinning on the anchor cable of its beam.

Eventually, Anna climbed down from where she sat and waited for Quinn to join her. They walked together back to the motel, avoiding the deeper pools and following the lines of washed-up detritus along the paved edges of the building.

Anna went first to her own room, and then an hour later she arrived at Quinn's carrying a bottle.

They sat together and watched the forecasts, listening to the ever-worsening predictions, to temperatures which continued to fall – 'plummet' was now the preferred word – and to snowfall amounts which likewise grew heavier and more disruptive as the night progressed.

When the drink was finished, they turned off the reports and undressed each other.

Hours later, in the middle of that winter night, Quinn woke to find the bed beside him empty. He looked around him, and in the dim light he saw Anna standing naked at the window, the curtain draped loosely over her head and shoulders like a shawl.

He spoke to her, and she turned to him and held the curtain away from her, revealing her face and, in the darkness beyond, the steadily falling snow, each large and drifting flake vivid and separate in the glare of the lights, and each flake seeming to leave behind it some faint and scribbled trace of its own slow descent. Anna's skin was cast in the same unnatural glow.

So, this is how it ends, Quinn thought, surprised that he felt neither anguish nor even any true sense of disappointment at the sudden and unexpected understanding, merely a kind of painless regret that passed as quickly as the realization itself. He felt the sudden beating of his heart and the solid pulse of blood in his temples and his wrists.

'Look,' Anna said to him. 'It's snowing.' There was wonder in her voice, and awe.

Robert Edric was born in 1956. His novels include *Winter Garden* (1985 James Tait Black Prize winner), *A New Ice Age* (1986 runner-up for the *Guardian* Fiction Prize), *A Lunar Eclipse*, *The Earth Made of Glass*, *Elysium*, *In Desolate Heaven*, *The Sword Cabinet*, *The Book of the Heathen* (shortlisted for the 2001 WH Smith Literary Award), *Peacetime* (longlisted for the Booker Prize 2002), *Gathering the Water* (longlisted for the Booker Prize 2006), *The Kingdom of Ashes* and *In Zodiac Light*.